Murda was the Case 2

Lock Down Publications and

Ca$h Presents

Murda was the Case 2

A Novel by *Elijah R. Freeman*

Lock Down Publications
Po Box 944
Stockbridge, Ga 30281

Visit our website
www.lockdownpublications.com

First Edition September 2022
Printed in the United States of America

Lock Down Publications
Like our page on Facebook: Lock Down Publications
@
www.facebook.com/lockdownpublications.ldp

Book interior design by: **Shawn Walker**
Edited by: **Nuel Uyi**

Stay Connected with Us!

Text **LOCKDOWN** to 22828 to stay up-to-date with new releases, sneak peaks, contests and more…
Thank you.

Submission Guideline.

Submit the first three chapters of your completed manuscript to ldpsubmissions@gmail.com, subject line: Your book's title. The manuscript must be in a .doc file and sent as an attachment. The document should be in Times New Roman, double-spaced and in size 12 font. Also, provide your synopsis and full contact information. If sending multiple submissions, they must each be in a separate email.

Have a story but no way to send it electronically? You can still submit to LDP/Ca$h Presents. Send in the first three chapters, written or typed, of your completed manuscript to:

LDP: Submissions Dept
Po Box 944
Stockbridge, Ga 30281

DO NOT send original manuscript. Must be a duplicate.

Provide your synopsis and a cover letter containing your full contact information.

Thanks for considering LDP and Ca$h Presents.

Prologue

Ken rested in the soft, white linen-covered hospital bed with Nae's well-being on his mind. His recovery was slow, but certain. The doctors proclaimed his status a miracle. His body was showing great resilience, his mind rambunctious. Ken sunk lower in grief each time he thought of the prior events. He couldn't believe his hospitalization caused him to miss Chingy's funeral. That was his best friend and top dog. He almost threw up as that night replayed in his mind. He'd watched Chingy's head explode.

Tez came to visit several times and had done a good job of keeping Ken updated, especially on the death of Diamond and the shooting of Nae. He'd soon found out which hospital Nae was in. At first, Ken was irate about his woman's body being the home for two of Smoke's bullets, but at the same time he knew Nae would've notified the law about her sister's death. Tez stressed his concern to Ken that Nae could've possibly seen his or Smoke's face, and that if she survived she was a liability.

Ken ordered the two on a trip to Jamaica for a couple of months, just in case she did see them. Even with the risks involved, he hoped she pulled through. Why? He loved her dearly. He couldn't stand the thought of ordering the hit to kill his lady, let alone actually doing it. But ultimately, if Nae knew who was responsible for the deaths, Ken would be left with no choice. Even with Diamond being deceased, it still hurt Ken to know that J-Bo and Flip had to sit in prison for the next decade. *Ten years is better than life without parole any day*, he thought, cheering himself up.

***

"Ms. Waters, can you describe the gunman?" asked the detective, pen and pad ready. He was a tall, thin Caucasian man with fading brown hair, dressed in slacks.

She shook her head. "It happened so fast." She began weeping as she thought of her sister and Garrett.

"She needs more rest, detective," said the doctor.

The detective nodded, placed his card on the table and left.

"Ms. Waters, you're going to recover beautifully," the Asian male doctor said.

A frail smile covered her face, followed by a deep breath.

"I have good news for you, ma'am," he smiled.

She was confused.

"You're pregnant!"

He then left to attend to other patients. Nae was overwhelmed with joy.

"Oh, Ken. Please make it through this," she said out loud, reaching for the bedside phone.

Chapter One

Nine Years Later—

J-Bo sat on his bunk, sweat dripping from his face. His t-shirt was drenched, and he smelled like old socks. He'd just completed his daily workout routine: five hundred push-ups, two hundred pull-ups, five hundred sit-ups, and two hundred squats. It was his primary workout three days a week for the past five years. He was definitely in shape; his entire body was cut, and he felt better than ever.

"J-Bo!" Bo-G yelled from the bottom range.

"Yo?" J-Bo called breathlessly, stepping out of his cell and looking down from the top.

"You got the message?"

"What message?" J-Bo asked.

"Go check," he said, headed back to his cell.

J-Bo returned to his cell and retrieved his cell phone from the hiding spot cut into the vent. He powered it on and found a chain text from Bull, sent to all the GDs at Smith State Prison. It read: *Flip just touched, make sure he good!*

J-Bo's slowing heart raced again. Excited, smiling ear to ear, he dialed Bull's number.

J-Bo and Flip had been together for their first year in prison. They made it through Jackson Diagnostics, and were eventually shipped to Autry State Prison, a medium security facility in Pelham Georgia. But J-Bo, having joined the Gangsta Disciples' organization, was caught in the middle of a deadly knife fight against the Muslims. His security level was raised to *Close*, and he was transferred to Smith State Prison as a result. The cousins have been pushing for a reunion ever since.

Flip never joined any gang, nor had he any interest in doing so. J-Bo, on the other hand, had followed in his deceased older brother's footsteps. The *G* was in his heart.

Smith State Prison was notoriously violent. Known for more deaths than any other prison in the state of Georgia, neither staff nor officers were safe. With that, J-Bo had given word to the brothers of his organization to look out for Flip if he was to set foot on the compound.

"Hello?" Bull answered.

"Where shawty at?" J-Bo asked.

"He in G building," Bull said. "BG got the message, so he good."

"Shawty?" J-Bo couldn't help but question. "You sure it's my cousin?"

"Yea, folk. I talked to him. Listen, I got my hoe on the other line."

"A'ight." J-Bo hung up and searched his contacts for BG's number.

***

"Fresh meat!" several voices called, but Dre's voice was the most prominent of those making the call. Contrary to the belief that the loudest one was the weakest of the bunch, Dre was a shooter on the streets and a shooter in the chain-gang. Dre, along with his GD brothers—Lil Will, BG—and several members from the Crip and Blood gang were gathered around the window and the front door, looking for those they recognized or those that were affiliated with either gang.

G-2's outer door was popped, and the CERT Team directed the newcomers into the sally port. The anticipating circle of inmates tightened as the inner door was popped.

"Get back!" Deebo yelled. Dressed in all black, he was the first CERT Team officer through the door. His true name was McPharlan, and he was the CERT Team Lieutenant. It was his strong resemblance to Friday's character that got him the nickname. Not only did he look like Deebo, he acted like the character as well, shaking down inmates and taking their phones, knives, and whatever other contraband they were slipping with. The fact he would pull up alone and from out of nowhere added to the persona. He wasn't alone now, however; two other CERT Team members were present.

"Get the fuck back!" Deebo yelled as his fellow officers pushed through the door. CERT was an acronym that stood for Correctional Emergency Response Team. They were more actively aggressive than other prison officers. Their numbers ranged from five to fifteen men per team, dressed in all black, carrying slapsticks, tasers and large cans of OC spray. Big and muscular, they were called upon for tactical purposes. However, their job was universal, and they were also tasked with housing new inmates when they arrived on Tuesdays and Thursdays, as was the case now.

Deebo called for the inmates to quiet down, and they did; it wasn't often that back talk was given to CERT, and no one took light their commands. There were those who did, but it was something the individual would usually regret. CERT was known for cuffing and severely beating inmates—to death in some cases.

The CERT Team called the names of the new comers, told them what cell they were assigned to, and left immediately after. The gang members uttered their calls, the affiliated newcomers hollered back and were officially greeted by their own and assisted with carrying their property to their new living quarters. The civilians were left to fend for themselves, and as the crowd dispersed, escorted by their affiliated members, two newcomers remained. With Will at his side, BG pushed up on one of the two.

"What up, Folk? I'm BG. You J-Bo people?" He knew already, having seen a picture of Flip about six months ago. To add to it, Bull, the intake barber and orderly, had sent word that Flip had arrived and would be assigned to his dorm. However, there was nothing like confirmation.

Flip nodded. Bull had already told him he would be greeted by the Gangstas. The lingo was clear. "Yea."

"What room?" BG asked.

"Uh, two-forty-six," Flip answered.

BG pointed at Flip's property and shot a quick glance at Will. “Take his shit up dea,” he said, then gestured at Flip. “Follow me.”

With forty-eight cells housing ninety-six men on a top and bottom range, the dorm was literally a warehouse. There were six benches and just as many tables. Mounted on each of two vertical beams at the center of the dorm were 32-inch TVs. Fans with dusty grates hung high on each beam.

“You smoke?” BG asked as they entered his room.

“Yea.” Flip pointed at the foot of BG's bed. It was chain-gang etiquette to ask for permission to sit on someone's bed.

“Yeah,” BG said. “You family. Go ahead.” From inside his mat, he pulled an ounce of Mango Kush which, at Smith State Prison, could easily sell for a thousand dollars, but this was his personal stash.

“No disrespect.” Flip wanted to set the record straight. “But I ain’t tryna get down with y’all or nun like that.” Over the years, he'd seen the horrible situations gang-banging brought to a person's life.

BG laughed as he rolled some of the loud in a torn segment of Blue Steele, the wrapping from a roll of tissue paper. “Ain’t tryna recruit, fam.”

BG was a six-foot tall, two hundred eighty-pound man with dark skin. At thirty-five years old, he was a high ranking Gangsta Disciple, having been G.D for twenty-two years and counting.

The joint in one hand, BG reached with his free hand to pull a cell phone from his pocket, looking at the screen. “Hea go J-Bo right hea.”

Flip smiled.

“What’s good, fam?” BG answered with his New York accent. He smiled then passed Flip the phone.

Flip's smiled widened. “What’s up, cuz?”

“What's good, fam?” J-Bo replied. “You straight over there?”

“Ain’t been in this m’ufucker five minutes, shawty. BG just rolled a fat ass stick we ‘bout to smoke. I’m gone unpack my shit and get my ass in the shower after that. What up with you, though?”

J-Bo brought Flip up to speed with what he had going on, and schooled him to the compound's movement. It wasn't as if the two hadn't conversed in years, but it was the closest they had been, and the underlying tone was apparent. The joint was long gone, and they were nearly an hour into the call when J-Bo put Flip on game regarding the talk he was going to have with the counselor.

"Just be cool," J-Bo said. "Much love, shawty." He broke the connection and extended the phone to Frank, his fifty-year-old cell mate.

Frank was a slim, brown-skinned fella, but in good shape for his age. He was convicted of child molestation, and was sentenced to life in prison. However, after serving twenty years, he was set to make parole next year.

"I gotta hit the shower and shoot out," J-Bo said. "You want to hold the phone down until I get back?" They had been roommates for several years; he knew the man could be trusted to handle the business.

Frank accepted the phone. "I need to make a few calls anyway."

J-Bo took what he needed for the shower and left the cell. Afterwards, he was going to have a talk with the counselor about getting his cousin moved in the dorm with him. The administration was against housing family members in the same unit. But if there had been no exception to the rule before, there would be one now; J-Bo was that guy.

***

"Sake Pase bel?" Tez put on his best Haitian accent, asking Djouveline *what's happening* as she came to the backyard of their home. Tez was relaxed in his tanning chair next to their two hundred square feet swimming pool, bare from the waist up in swimming trunks. Djouveline was one hundred percent Haitian. Petite, her skin tone was caramel, her smile was gorgeous, and she sported flip-flops and a blue bathing suit that revealed a gorgeous body to match her smile.

"Hey, you!" she exclaimed, running her index finger along his naked collar bone.

Tez met her gaze. “How much do you love me, Djouveline?” He was the only person to refer to her as Djouveline; she was called DJ by everyone else.

“A lot,” she said, settling into his lap. “But if I were to ask you that same question, the response wouldn't be the same. Her English was good, but the accent was strong.

“Pou Kisa?” Tez asked, which translated to *Why*.

“Because if you did, you would leave the other shit alone and live here with us,” she whined.

Tez enjoyed being in Haiti, but he wasn’t ready to make it his permanent home. They had a beautiful daughter, Gia. He loved her more than words could express, and DJ had no qualms about using that to her advantage whenever the opportunity presented itself.

“Listen, mami.” Tez kissed DJ’s soft lips. “You know I can’t just leave now. When the time is right, I got you, shawty.”

DJ didn’t fully understand the word *shawty*, but she loved when he said it to her. She had to conceal her smile in order to appear serious. “It’s not fair that Gia can’t see her papa whenever she wants to.”

Tez took a deep breath. And there it was.

“Cry dey,” which translated to *look*. DJ pointed to their three-story home. It was like a house from MTV Cribs. “We have a beautiful house, a beautiful family, and money. Why can’t you just stay now and never go back, eh?”

Tez laughed. “We gone talk about this later.” He looked at his watch. “How long before Gia gets out of school?”

DJ grabbed his wrist and looked at the watch. “Two hours,” she said and smiled as she felt his erection flex under her backside.

“You so sexy, Djouveline,” he said.

She closed the distance between them, touching her lips to his. Their tongues explored each other’s mouths, and DJ's soft moans were tantalizing to hear, driving him mad with lust. Tez squeezed her little butt cheeks, slid the bikini to the side and slowly massaged her clitoris with his index finger as their tongues continued to attack each other.

"Ummm!" DJ moaned when she felt his finger on her prized possession.

He gently unsnapped her top and began licking and sucking on her hardened nipples. DJ loved the sight of her chocolate man treating her nipples like an ice cream cone. Without warning, Tez flipped her over on her back and kissed from her lips to her waistline.

"Martez, eat it, Martez!" DJ moaned out in anticipation.

She tilted her head back and let her eyes roll with pleasure as Tez's tongue crept closer to her clit. He teased her purposely. He liked when she begged for it. As soon as his tongue almost touched her clit, he shifted to the left and began sucking her inner thigh.

"Um," she moaned. It all felt great, but she wanted her pussy ate. "Please, daddy," she begged.

"What?" Tez stroked her clit one time with his tongue, then looked her in the eyes. That drove her crazy.

"Eat it, baby, please!" she yelled in ecstasy.

Tez then began sucking on her clitoris like he'd never do it again.

"Oh, my Go—" DJ tried to say, but her body began to shake due to the orgasm she was having. She tried to scoot backwards and push Tez's head away, but he had her lower back in a lock that made it practically impossible for her to move.

"Wait, wait, Martez," she said out of breath. It felt too good. She needed a break, but it was just the beginning. Tez used two fingers, his index and middle, to slide inside DJ's hot, moist cave

"Djouveline, this pussy taste so good," he told her as she moved her body with the strokes of his fingers.

"Oh shit," she moaned.

Tez's manhood was almost busting through the polo shorts he sported. He stood up and pulled it out.

Damn! He looks so good naked, DJ thought. He laid on top of her in the sixty-nine position and slid his dick in her mouth. She began sucking him off, and he fucked her with his tongue. Her moans were muffled because his dick was in and out of her throat. Tez began licking her butthole, and she pulled his penis out of her mouth and moaned, "Oh, Martez."

He smiled. "Shut the fuck up and suck my dick!"

She took him in her mouth again, and he continued eating her ass like a tasty cupcake. After a few moments of their oral pleasures, Tez got up and spread her legs wide. He got on top of her in the missionary position and began slow stroking.

"Martez, I—I love you," she moaned as Tez's dick touched every spot past the threshold to her treasure.

"I luhh you too, girl," he whispered.

DJ squeezed his butt cheeks when she felt the next orgasm coming. They climaxed together the second time around, and he released deep inside her, unconcerned about getting her with child, as she was on the pill.

The two had met nearly ten years ago when he and his friend—Smoke—took a trip to Jamaica. She'd been there visiting a friend. With trips back and forth to Haiti, it took Tez months to get DJ to open her legs. Having made it official, they never lost contact. And six years ago, after finding out she was pregnant with Gia, he returned to Haiti to purchase a three hundred-thousand-dollar home and a couple of cars for DJ. Gia was his heart, and on several occasions he had brought her to the States to see her grandmother and his friends.

***

"Mr. Griffith, you have an urgent call on line two," Susie's voice blared through the intercom.

Ken was at his desk, on the other side of which was his good friend—Higa, a fat, fifty-year-old, gray-haired Mexican. They were concluding the details of a large marijuana shipment.

"Have them leave a message," Ken replied.

Susie felt he needed to address the call, but he was the shot caller, and she did as she was told.

"My apologies," Ken said to the older man. "Please continue."

"When all the *dinero* is counted," Higa said, "I'll send my nephew to meet you with the drop."

Higa was a notorious drug lord that only dealt with the high spenders.

Ken smiled. The two had been dealing for nearly a decade, and he felt there should be more trust in their relationship. "You honestly feel as if you have to personally show your face every time?"

"Since eighteen, I've been doing this." Higa paused, considering his words. "If I can't teach you a lot, always remember to trust no one." His emphasis on *no one* was strong. "I don't even trust my own wife."

"A'ight," Ken said. "It's all there. Call me when you get back to Texas."

Higa stood up, crossed the floor, then paused with a hand on the doorknob. "Kenneth." He turned back to face Ken. "Fifty thousand pounds could have me put away for a long time." He searched Ken's face for any sign of betrayal, finding a bit of nervousness instead.

Ken threw up a hand to a halt the man's next line, indicating that kids, friends, wives and family would all be left without a head in the event that Higa was targeted by the law on behalf of their exchange. "I understand, Higa." He wanted to get an attitude, but he knew it was safer not to. Although Ken had a nice group of killers, his chances of beating Higa's gunmen at war was slim. Higa was the highest-ranking Zeta alive. His men were all over the globe, but they were prevalent in the states such as California, Texas and Colorado. The Zetas were a large Mexican cartel that didn't miss a beat. They knew everything about the people they dealt with, and were eager to kill even if they thought they smelled a rat.

"Very well." Higa nodded and opened the door to Ken's office, where his armed bodyguard, Pablo, stood waiting.

"Bien?" Pablo asked.

"Si," Higa responded as they exited.

With Higa's trust issues, his security was always close. Higa had access to every drug known to man, but he chose to deal with marijuana alone, knowing he would get less time if caught. Besides, the claim would never make it to trial.

Chapter Two

J-Bo entered his cell to find Frank with his head down on the table, weeping audibly. “Yo, Frank. You a’ight?”

Frank nodded without lifting his head.

“It don't sound like it, shawty.”

“It's just—” He struggled to get the words out. “It's just another year that my daughter's been gone.”

J-Bo had heard about the man's daughter being executed ass naked in doggy style position, but he didn’t know the specifics surrounding her death. Frank told him that she was free picked, but J-Bo wasn’t going for it; he knew for a fact she hadn't been killed that way for no reason. Sounded like an execution or a scorned lover.

“I wish I could find the mufuckas that did it,” Frank barked with tears flowing down his face.

J-Bo retrieved his phone from its harbor and laid back on his bunk. *Some things are better said with silent words*, he thought.

***

“You gotta be strong, Nae. You know Diamond would hate to see you like this.” Asia was trying her best to comfort her friend. They were in one of the salon's back rooms which served as Nae’s office. Nae was normally strong, hardly disturbed by anything. At least it appeared that way on the surface. But today was the day she broke down every year.

“They should have killed me instead,” Nae cried. Asia stood over Nae, sliding a hand gently along her back.

“Don’t talk like that, Nae. You know God allows everything to happen for a reason.”

Nae nodded, knowing her friend was right. She just missed her little sister so much. Nearly a decade now, and not a day went by that she didn't think of Diamond. The years that passed hadn’t made her loss any easier to deal with. The pain she felt for her sister with each passing year brought her to the realization that when you lose someone you truly love, you grieve forever. You do not *get over* the loss of a loved one; you simply learn to live with it. You heal and rebuild yourself around the loss you suffered. You may be whole again, but you will never be the same. Nor *should* you be the same or want to.

After she and Ken recovered, he offered to move her to Florida, away from the madness and all the bad memories that were in Atlanta. Nae refused, wanting to live in Cobb County, close to where Diamond had lived her life. Ken agreed but he didn't like the idea; didn't like the fact Nae cried every time they drove past the apartments on Thornton Road where Diamond was executed. He felt bad at times but reminded himself that he had given Diamond a fair chance to live. In fact, he felt she had gotten exactly what she deserved for crossing him the way she did. It was only his regard for Nae and her feelings for Diamond that mattered to him. They had now been married seven and a half years.

"I know," Nae whispered, wiping tears from her eyes. She stood and hugged Asia. "Thank you for being here for me, Asia."

At Diamond's funeral, Asia had promised to be there for Nae through thick and thin for life. And when Nae's shop was moved and rebuilt on Austell Road, Asia was there to help.

Asia grabbed a tissue from the pack on Nae's desk and wiped her face again. "I told you I got you." She took Nae's hand and pulled encouragingly. "Now let's go get some of this money, girl,"

Nae rose from the chair, and together they left the office for the huge, twelve-chair salon, all of which were occupied. The floor was waxed and shining, buffed weekly as a result of the continuous traffic. The equipment there was top-of-the-line, and every workstation mirror was trimmed in thick gold to match the sign outside. Nae was a millionaire, and the shop reflected her status.

God, just give me the strength, Nae thought as she returned to her station to finish with Stephanie's hair.

***

Smoke was shaking his head. "Shawty, I'm so tired of seeing this typa shit." He was in the living room of his condo, seated on the leather couch with Peanut beside him. Together they watched the news as Fox 5 told the world of another young black teen shot and killed by police.

"How the fuck dese crackas keep getting away wit' this shit?" Smoke barked.

"They white," Peanut said.

"For the past couple years, over fifty innocent, young black men done been killed by white officers. 'Oh, I thought it was a gun, your honor'. They always get away with that line, and the majority of the victims were unarmed." Smoke fell silent as he listened to the details.

"*Sixteen-year-old Wade Williams was gunned down by North Atlanta Police last night, after leaving a friend's house and walking to the store. Police were called on the scene for a domestic disturbance. Witnesses say Mr. Williams was ranting when police arrived. He was told to drop the black object he was carrying. Mr. William's refused, raised his hand and police opened fire. Mr. Williams was shot eight times and was pronounced dead on the scene. The object he carried was later identified as a black cell phone, and he had been on the line with his girlfriend when he died. It was further decided that the domestic disturbance and call had been unrelated to sixteen-year-old Wade Williams.*"

Smoke frowned and looked at Peanut. "Fuck kinda shit is that?" He was on his pro black shit and felt as if there was no justice for black people anymore. "We need to start killin' dem bitches."

"Leave it in God's hands," Peanut replied. He'd been trying to put his life in God's hands for the past few years, but with this business and his way of living, it all amounted to spiritual warfare.

"Ain't no God!" Smoke shot back. "How many times I gotta tell you that, shawty?" Smoke was an Atheist.

Peanut just shook his head and said a silent prayer for his friend.

"If there was a God, why would he let shit like this happen?"

Smoke tried to get him to see reason. "Those families are going through those trials to test their faith and—"

Smoke erupted with laughter. "Shut the fuck up. You sound stupid! The next black person come up dead, we gone start killin' white people," Smoke declared.

Peanut didn't know if the man was serious or merely venting. He didn't approve of either, but Smoke's word held weight, and Peanut could be killed if he didn't follow orders. Ken and Tez had turned Young Boss into a well-organized drug trade and hitman operation over the past ten years, and every member played their position to the *T*.

Smoke's phone rang, and he answered on the second ring. "Yea?" He listened a second, then got up and went into his bedroom. Peanut thought his actions were odd. They hid nothing from each other, and there was rarely, if ever, a time when he felt he couldn't take a call and speak freely in his presence.

Smoke returned to the living room five minutes later with a grin on his face.

"Who was that?" Peanut couldn't help but ask.

"God." Smoke burst into laughter.

"You gon' have to answer for all you saying when Jesus comes back," Peanut warned.

There was an armrest built into the center of the couch, which Smoke raised and pulled out a Ziploc bag with approximately thirty pre-rolled marijuana blunts. He threw them on Peanut's lap.

"Answer fa that," he said.

***

In the crowded, family-filled visitation area at Smith State Prison, Shakeena sat across from J-Bo, and both were unsure of what to say to each other. It had been nine years since her last visit to him in the county jail, abandoning him the second time, claiming to not want their son, JJ, to know of his father's past. J-Bo was hurt but he respected Shakeena's decision, and he was happy that she had come to tell him face-to-face versus disappearing, blocking and ignoring his calls the way so many females would. It was that courtesy which made him reach out to Ken with word to take good care of her along with his son.

Now, with J-Bo's release date approaching, he reached out to her requesting a visit to put matters into perspective; he wanted to know if they were going to be together again. More so, he wanted to put into place a plan to enter JJ's life. The fact that he and she were on good terms offered the possibility for both. He wasn't naïve to the point he believed she had been saving herself for him, or that she wasn't seeing someone. However, he was certain she cared, as she had often demonstrated throughout his bid.

Though awkward, he was happy to see her in person after so many years. J-Bo smiled. "What's up?"

"Hey." Shakeena was nervous and it showed.

"Come here." J-Bo leaned across the table, taking her hands in his. "Why you nervous? I look different?"

Shakeena gave a weak smile. "A little. Videos never do justice."

J-Bo laughed. "What? I'm ugly now?"

"No, that's not what I mean." Her smile brightened. "You just—your features have matured, but you look the same."

"Well, you know what they say—Chain-gang preserves you. A nigga ain't out there on all them drugs, eatin' fast food and shit. Just eatin' good, workin' out, readin', getting money and countin' down the days till they can be with the people they truly love." He kissed her hand, and her smile weakened.

Taking notice of her discomfort, J-Bo lost his smile and released her. "I'm—I'm sorry if I made you uncomfortable."

"No, you're fine. It's just—been awhile, you know?"

"Yea, I feel you."

A pregnant pause followed and gave way to an awkward silence.

"Do you want something to eat out the vending machines?" Shakeena pulled a bag of quarters from her back pocket. "I brought some change with me."

J-Bo laughed. "Shiiid, hell yea."

"What all you want?"

J-Bo told her what he wanted, and she got up and made her way to the vending machines, passing an older white lady with a Sprite and a tray of hot wings as she made her way back to her son.

J-Bo sat back, taking her in, silently contemplating how to say what he wanted to say next. He didn't know how to take her reaction to him kissing her hand. Was she really nervous or had she moved on? He pondered back and forth between the two as he watched her fetch him a chicken sandwich, a bag of hot fries and a pink lemonade, and on her way back to him, he decided the only way he was gonna find out was if he asked.

She made it back, sat the items on the table and sat down across from him. Somewhere on the other side of the room, a baby began crying.

"They didn't have any *Reese's.* If you want, I can get you something else when I go back up there. They have *Snickers, Almond Joys, Baby Ruth's, M&M's* and—"

"I want to get back together when I come home," J-Bo said, cutting her off. "I been gone all this time and through it all what made me strong was the desire to have my family back. I want to be a part of my son's life, Shakeena. I wanna be there—with him and with you. I want us back, and I need to know if you want the same."

Shakeena sat back, placing the bag of quarters in her lap. Pursing her lips, she glanced down and back up at J-Bo before responding. "I mean, Jerome, it's been ten years. You can't possibly expect me to—"

"Leave that other nigga you been fuckin' wit'?"

Shakeena cut her eyes away.

"Shakeena, I ain't trippin' 'bout no other nigga. Yo' pussy got wet when I was free. Me getting locked up ain't change that. You a woman. I get it. I understand. You ain't have no baby on a nigga, so it's all good. He had his time. It was fun. Now, I want you back. All I need to know is where yo' heart at."

Shakeena lowered her gaze and began playing with her fingers in her lap. "I—Jerome—you know—"

"Yeen gotta answer now," J-Bo said, cutting her off for the third time. "I see I got you on the spot, and that's not fair to you. I ain't tryna pressure you into making a decision. Just—think about it, okay?"

Shakeena looked up and nodded.

J-Bo smiled and held up the blue bag of *Andy Capp's* Hot Fries. "Want some hot fries?"

For the rest of the visit they caught up on how life had been treating them over the years, and Shakeena let him know how much his son was just like him. She shared different stories of JJ, and together they laughed and joked. J-Bo was cheesing hard with pride, and Shakeena's smile radiated with the joy of any mother when they spoke of their kids' innocent exploration of life. From the outside looking in, one might mistake them for a happy couple.

"C'mon, Bae. I mean—you know what I mean." J-Bo smiled. "Let's catch some pictures before it's time to go."

They had thirty minutes left.

He had ten picture tickets he'd purchased from the commissary order, and he planned on using them all.

The visitation area was a multi-purpose room adapted for education classes, GED graduation, religious service, and other events for inmates and the administration. The picture booth was set on a gray carpet podium with a painted background of palm trees and a setting sun. An inmate served as ticket collector and photographer.

On the podium, J-Bo popped his collar and posed for several solo pictures.

Shakeena smiled teasingly. "Boy, stop. All y'all look the same."

All Georgia inmates wore the same white uniform with a single blue stripe down the side of either leg and another down the shirt's front center. The belts provided were tan, the buckle gold, their boots black.

"That ain't how you feel," J-Bo said, gesturing for her to step onto the podium with him.

Photos taken, J-Bo returned to the table, and Shakeena went to the vending machine and brought back ice-cream. Their final moments together were spent down memory lane and sharing future plans.

“Visitation is over in five minutes,” an officer announced.

At the beginning and end of visitation is when they were allowed to kiss and embrace. Briefly in the beginning, but here at the end, most couples spent the entire five minutes within each other's embrace, kissing and sliding their hands in places that were against regulations.

J-Bo scratched his head. “Hey, uuhhh—I was thinkin’.”

“Mh-mm.” Shakeena gave him her undivided attention.

“Maybe I could have Ken swing by and pick JJ up. You know, take him out for a day of fun.”

“Of course,” Shakeena said, attempting to hide the large lump that was forming in her throat.

Soon after J-Bo was gone, he, Shakeena, and Ken all agreed that they wouldn’t tell JJ that J-Bo was in prison. They wanted to wait until he was old enough to understand the situation and why his dad had been absent for so long.

That didn’t settle well with J-Bo initially, but he allowed it because he wanted to make his absence as easy on his son as possible. He was already going to be missing for some time; he didn’t want him to worry about him possibly never coming back.

As a result, they came up with a story saying that Ken was Shakeena’s uncle. If anyone ever asked, Ken was her mother’s adopted brother, so JJ refered to him as Uncle Ken.

J-Bo may have missed nine years of JJ’s life, but that didn’t mean Ken had to, as well. Ken was a busy man, but he always made sure that JJ knew that even though his father wasn’t around, J-Bo and his people still loved him. Whenever Ken came around, he always went all out for his nephew.

It was because of that, that Shakeena was never able to have a logical reason to keep Ken away. She had to get more creative than that.

Her stomach felt hollow.

“Bet! I just want him to know that my people always had him, and that even from here, I gave a fuck. You know, for when I finally do get to build a relationship with him.”

Shakeena nodded. “I understand.”

J-Bo smiled.

"What?" Shakeena said.

"Nothing. I love you, girl." J-Bo closed the distance between them and wrapped his arms around her waist.

"I love you too," Shakeena said, sliding her arms around his neck.

J-Bo leaned in for a kiss. Without thinking, she opened her mouth to his as their lips met. The sensation was wonderful, and she was lost in his embrace. In that moment, she wanted nothing more than to give in and be his again. But if she wanted to have any chance at a life together with him, she had to act accordingly and put matters into perspective fast.

J-Bo pulled back and caught her nervous reaction. He smiled. "It's okay."

She nodded.

He sat down and watched her leave. He couldn't wait for the day to be free with her and JJ.

Shakeena had been there for J-Bo over the years. She figured it was the least she could do, considering he'd called upon Ken to take care of her and JJ until his release. She had a nice house and a couple of cars as a result. She hadn't worked in nine years. Although she had grown close to Nae, Ken made sure that Shakeena understood what was going on and that loose lips regarding who J-Bo was, why he was incarcerated, and his connection to Ken and Diamond would result in the deaths of her closest relatives. He hadn't said it directly, but the message was clear. She had been dealing with them long enough to comprehend the language.

In the parking lot, Shakeena contemplated the severity of her situation. The sun was shining but inside her head was a raging thunderstorm. She wished there was a simple fix to her dilemma, but there wasn't.

Why the fuck did I let it go this far? The question came to mind again, as it had for the last six months. *Why didn't I put an end to this a long time ago*?

Shakeena's phone vibrated as she went to the driver's side of the car. She deactivated the alarm and got inside as she answered the call.

"Where you at?" a voice asked.

"On the way back from visiting my brother," she lied.

"When you gon' let me meet big homie? And what my munchkin doin'?" he asked.

She was nervous, feeling as if J-Bo was watching her. "Soon," she said. "And he's at my mom's for the day, remember? Hey, the traffic is heavy. I'll call when it clears up. Love you. Bye." She broke the connection before he could question her further.

***

J-Bo was sitting on his bed, untying his boots when Savannah Mike appeared at his open door with an empty chip bag in his hand.

"What's up?" J-Bo acknowledged.

Savannah Mike was a thirty-year-old, slim, brown skinned man around six feet tall. He kept a fresh cut, and his clothes were always pressed. He was sentenced to serve twenty-five years for armed robbery. But his case was flawed. The right attorney could have him free by next year, at six years before his max release date.

"My bro ready to handle business whenever you are," he said.

"A'ight, I'ma make that call in a minute." He gestured at the bag in Savannah Mike's hand. "What'chu finna cook?"

"Just a lil' pocket," he replied.

J-Bo and Savannah Mike had been friends for five years and doing business together for three of them. The older man had become something of a mentor and big brother, offering advice on decision making and chain-gang etiquette.

"How's the lil' one?" Savannah Mike asked.

J-Bo smiled. "He good. Getting big." Having exchanged his boots for shoes, he went to retrieve his phone from the hiding spot, unconcerned about the man's presence in the matter; it was Savannah Mike who had helped locate the hiding spot.

"That's good, man," Savannah Mike stated. "When they let us out, this shit gonna be bigger than ever, baby boy."

"Yea, I know, homie." J-Bo put the phone to his ear, and was silent a second. "They ready, shawty—Okay, keep me posted." He hung up. "They said *okay*."

Savannah Mike gave J-Bo the thumbs-up. "I'm hungry as a fuck," he said before turning to leave. "I'ma halla at you later, dirty."

J-Bo shook his head, laughing at Savannah Mike's choice of words and dialect. *That's a country ass nigga, shawty.*

***

Smoking a Newport on the front porch of the Powder Springs home he shared with Shakeena, Shawn considered his array of old-school vehicles on the property. There was a 1990 Ford Mustang with a mighty mite C4 transmission, and 5,200-rpm stall torque converter, a '62 AMC Rambler American, a '75 Chevrolet Camaro, and a '71 Roadrunner. The most precious of them all was the pearl black '62 Chevy Impala with a 454 motor and TCL turbo trans. Neither were driven; they were collectables for his own pleasures.

The euphoric sensation he normally got from studying his collection was absent today, however. So distracted was he by Shakeena and her abnormal behavior of late. He took another pull from his Newport as her red 2014 Escalade pulled in the driveway.

"Whatchu got goin' on?" Shawn asked the moment her feet touched the ground. JJ got out from the passenger side and they approached. She had picked him up from her mother's house on the way home.

The question triggered an attitude "What you mean?"

JJ reached his arms out to hug Shawn.

"Hey, dea," Shawn knelt down and gave JJ a hug. He pulled back. "You have fun seeing ya grandma?"

"Yea, daddy," he told Shawn. "We ate chicken wings and French fries for lunch."

"Okay." Shawn glanced at Shakeena. "Next time tell her I said *hey*."

"Jerome." Shakeena only referred to her son as JJ when speaking to J-Bo or anyone in connection with him, but never in Shawn's presence. It was ironic, considering the fact JJ was no longer a Junior; Shakeena had changed the boy's last name. No more was he a *Dew* like J-Bo, he now bore Shawn's last name, *Grimes.* "Go in the house and get ready for school tomorrow."

"Okay." JJ ran into his house.

"What's up?" Shawn made a move to kiss Shakeena, but she dodged away with a frown.

"Yo' mouth got that nasty cigarette taste," she said. That was true, but so too was the fact that she felt guilty; J-Bo's tongue was in her mouth, hours earlier.

"You ain't been complaining 'bout that," he shot back.

"Well, I don't like it no more." She tried to walk past him but was stopped by his stiff arm.

"I gotta go home and handle some business," he said. "I'll be back in a couple days."

He often made trips to Savannah. This was nothing new to her, but she was under pressure and just wasn't in the mood.

She pushed past him. "Okay."

Shawn stared after her. Something was off. He just couldn't put his finger on it.

***

"Fresh meat!" the inmates in F-2 began yelling. Many ran to the door to see the newcomers. Bo-G was at one of the tables near the door. He and Bull were in the middle of their third game of chess. They were tied one/one, and it was looking favorable for Bo-G in the tie-breaker, though distracted while keeping an eye on the dorm's newcomers. It was his rule never to be so focused on one thing to miss another. Which is how he managed to spot Flip coming through the door. With that, he called for a pause in the game and went to greet Flip.

"What's up, G?" he said to the newcomer.

"What's up?" Flip replied.

"What room?" Bo-G asked, picking up Flip's mat.

"One thirty-three."

Bo-G laughed. "That's what's up, G. You in there with me. J-Bo in two forty-five."

J-Bo was in his room on the phone saying, "A'ight, folk. I'ma G wit' you," when his cousin entered. His eyes grew wide as he came quick to his feet. "Cuz, what's up, shawty!" J-Bo rushed him for a hug, almost dropping his phone in the toilet. His exclamation was loud, drawing the attention of some of the GD's closest to his door. And when they came running, so too did other members of the gang. They rushed into the cell, weapons drawn and ready, only to find J-Bo all smiles and excitement.

"Oh, my bad, fam" J-Bo said. "This my lil' cousin I been tellin' y'all 'bout."

Some nodded as they departed. Others grumbled, upset regarding the misperceived threat.

"You look good, baby. How you been?" J-Bo asked.

"I'm good, homie." Flip moved to the back of the cell and sat on the table seat. "I can't believe we just hit damn near ten years."

"I know, right." J-Bo extended the phone in Flip's direction. "Huh. You need to get out there?"

"Yea," Flip replied. "Lemme call my boo. You 'memba Daneisha?"

"You tawmbout the ugly bitch you met from Kentucky?" J-Bo asked, taking a seat on his bed.

Flip smiled. "Y the one from Kentucky but let's not refer to her as that."

Years ago, J-Bo would have clowned Daneisha for hours, but prison had brought about a sense of maturity. He also had a higher level of respect for his cousin. J-Bo nodded. "I respect that."

"She been holdin' it down. I mean she been there since the day we met and—" He paused. "Well, you know she's not the best lookin' woman."

Flip was serious, and J-Bo bit his tongue, trying not to laugh.

"But I don't wanna break her heart, man."

J-Bo frowned. "So, what's the problem?"

"It's just, you know. We kings and can have any woman we want and—"

"And you worried that you need to be with a better lookin' broad?" J-Bo finished.

Flip nodded.

"If you love shawty and she been there through this journey," J-Bo schooled his cousin, "she deserves you, folk. Because I'm a firm believer in karma. The last thing you should be worried about is how a muthafucka thinks yo' lady look 'cause I can guarantee you something, folk. A lot of these niggas' bitches is *bad*," he gestured with the words. "But dey ain't *loyal*." There was heavy emphasis on loyal. "And if she ain't loyal, she ain't shit! If that girl been holding it down, stick with her, folk."

Flip smiled. "You right, cuz." He dialed her number.

"But what you do outside of home is yo' business."

They both laughed.

Daneisha was a country girl that Flip met on *MocoSpace*, almost eight years ago. She was taller than him, with dark skin and long red dreads. She had teeth as large as those in a horse's mouth, and her build was almost masculine buff.

Flip had lost all his female friends almost immediately as a result of the life sentence. And having come across Daneisha, he'd only wanted someone to talk to. As time went by and Daneisha was still there for him, he fell for her. The fact she had no idea that he had connections with the owner of Young Boss Entertainment, one of the biggest and successful record labels around, made him even more attracted to her; she wasn't there for money. In fact, she threw a fit whenever he told her he didn't need any money, feeling as though he had another woman providing for him.

J-Bo stood. "I'ma give you a lil' privacy," he said, leaving the room. He called loudly for Bo-G, found him, and asked what room Flip was assigned to.

"My room," Bo-G said.

"Okay, that's what's up. Just making sho he wasn't in the room with the opps."

Bo-G shook his hand. "He good, G."

***

"It's possible we can take your offer into consideration," Ken said into the office line. He was on the phone with a representative from Gucci, seconds away from concluding the verbal preliminaries of an agreement that would lay the foundation for the written contract, which he couldn't wait to sign.

The clothing mogul wanted Psycho and Lil Dread to promote their Gucci clothing line in a commercial and wear Gucci attire while performing on tour; they were offering big bucks to have them do so.

"Yes," Ken played it cool, although he was excited. "Fax over the documents. We'll look them over, and if no discrepancies are found, you can expect them signed and returned to you by noon tomorrow." He thanked the caller, said goodbye, and placed the receiver into the cradle. He pumped his fist, unable to control his excitement. "Yes!"

"Mr. Griffith," Susie's voice cut through from the office com.

"Yes," he answered.

"You have a caller on line two," she informed. "Says he's from Block Runners."

Ken was even more excited. Block Runners was a multi-billion-dollar music group Ken was trying to link with. His adrenaline was rushing as he dismissed Susie's line to answer the call.

"Kenneth Griffith speaking," he presented his professional voice.

The caller laughed. "How are you, Kenneth?"

Ken recognized the voice and was furious for the game which had been played. However, the voice belonged to a boss bigger and more deadlier than he, and respect was due. The fact the caller had announced himself as someone Ken was looking to deal with said much for the caller's resources. “What’s up with the games, Higa?” Ken's disappointment was apparent.

Higa chuckled. “We can never be too certain, Ken. And games are a matter of perspective and perception.”

Ken understood that to be another one of the man's parables regarding caution. Ken had no way to reach Higa, and every number provided was changed within hours of its use. Ken sighed, shaking his head. “It's been nearly ten years, Higa.”

“To that and by that same token, we shall make it to see another ten."

“Right,” Ken said. “So what do I owe the pleasure?”

“All is well,” Higa stated. “You can meet with my nephew for the package.”

“Where?” Ken asked.

“Same place, Kenneth.”

“Okay,” Ken said, breaking the connection to make another call.

***

Outside Hartsfield-Jackson Atlanta International Airport, Tez waited with his luggage, agitated that his ride wasn't on point. He glanced at his watch and looked up and down the crowded bus lane. He couldn’t believe this shit. It was cold, it looked like it was about to rain, and he was already running behind schedule. His phone vibrated, and he answered without looking. “Where the fuck you at!?”

“That’s what the fuck I wanna know.” The voice belonged to Smoke, not the individual Tez was expecting.

Tez gave an aspirated sigh. “Why? What up?”

“We gotta drop off in Savannah,” Smoke said, “and I’m forty short.”

The individual Tez was waiting on arrived in a white A8 Audi. “A’ight, gimmie a few. I'ma call big homie and see what's the hold up.” Tez broke the connection just as his phone vibrated, revealing Ken's number.

He answered, “What’s up, big bra?” and placed a finger to his lips to silence the female who jumped out of the vehicle and rushed in for a hug.

“It’s time,” Ken said in his ear. “You can go pick it up.”

The woman kissed Tez's lips, and the phone was momentarily pulled away from his face. “What you say, homie?”

“I said the fucking package is ready!” Ken snapped. “What the hell are you doing?”

“I just got back in town.” Tez made his way to the back of the car, followed by his female friend. “I’m putting my bags in the cab now.”

“You smell so good,” the woman whispered in Tez's free ear before returning to the driver's seat.

He smiled, popped the trunk and place his luggage inside.

“A’ight,” Ken said. “Go handle that.”

Tez closed the trunk. “What the hell took so long? I thought you woulda already had it.”

“Fucking taco-ass-Mexican,” was all Ken had to say in regard to the matter.

They ended the call.

Tez hopped in the passenger seat, and his attention was caught by the woman's left hand and ring finger as she snapped on her seat-belt. “What I tell you ‘bout that?” he said, pointing at the woman's finger.

“Oh,” Nae said, sliding off her wedding ring, and placing it in the ashtray. It was a beautiful deep-set, cushion VVS diamond.

The sting of betrayal was felt at the sight of Nae's ring, and if it wasn't off before they came together, Tez always reminded her to remove it. “I have so much fun when I’m wit’chu, shawty.”

“When you say fun, do you mean sex?” Nae smiled, wishing he would say yes, but she knew that wasn't his objective. However, it would make matters much less complicated if it were.

“Nah, baby.” He leaned over to kiss her fervently. “You know how I feel ‘bout you, shawty.”

“How's that?” she asked between kisses.

“I love you, boo.”

"I love you, too, Martez." She put the car in gear, and pulled away from the airport.

Nae and Tez's disloyalty to Ken began close to a decade ago on the night he had come to her rescue with Ken. He'd seen her naked, had stared, and although briefly, she had stared back with no disdain. What they were doing wasn't right, and she hadn't intended for things to come to where they were now, considering her obligation to Ken. With Tisha's death and Ken hospitalized in critical condition, however, she was under a lot of stress. There were only a few who knew what had transpired on the night she was kidnapped, and only someone who had been present could understand and truly relate to her experience. Then her sister was murdered.

Tez had given Nae his number after dropping her off at her shop that night. From Jamaica they kept contact, setting the tone for sex at his return. Tez was conscious of his betrayal, more so after Nae and Ken were announced husband and wife. For a while afterwards Nae was faithful, but with Ken being so busy pushing Young Boss, he began to neglect her, and the affair began yet again. Now, Tez was stuck on Nae and couldn't let go.

"Yo, yo, yo, what's up? What you doin'?" Tez sat up, looking incredulous as they turned into the parking lot of some Decatur condo's.

Nae cut the blinkers on. "What's it look like? I'm dropping you off."

Tez looked around the parking lot. "Yea, but maaan, this shit hot. What if someone recognize yo' car? Or worse, you?"

"Boy, bye. They ain't stop making white Audi's when they made mine." She eased on the brakes and came to a stop. Throwing the gear in *park*, she smiled and turned to Tez. "Now, you gone give me a kiss or what?"

Tez leaned in and kissed her passionately before pulling back and getting out the car. He closed the door and walked around to her side. "Aye, nah. I'm serious. Why be reckless for no reason?"

Nae giggled. "I love you, too."

Without another word Nae pulled off, leaving Tez standing there shaking his head at her audacity. He did love her. He just hoped she didn't get him killed.

Chapter Three

Having gotten into a heated discussion with his girl, Smoke stepped out onto his balcony to continue the call in private. Below, he watched as a white A8 Audi pulled into the parking lot, driven by a female. Tez was in the passenger seat.

"Look, shawty," Smoke said, "I got some business to tend to. I'ma get at you later." He hung up without giving her time to object.

Dumb ass hoes always whinin' about some shit.

Tez was laying a lover's kiss on the woman. She looked familiar, but Smoke couldn't make out who she was. From where he stood, she looked white.

Tez got out of the car, and the woman drove off as he placed the phone to his ear.

Smoke's phone vibrated, and he answered, "Wassup, shawty?"

"I'm out here in the parking lot," Tez said. "Y'all come on so we can do this shit."

"Yea, I see you. We comin' out, now." Smoke hung up.

Alarmed, Tez looked up and saw Smoke leaving the balcony. *Fuck! Did he see me?*

Heart racing, Tez's life flashed before his eyes and his thoughts turned dark as he considered taking Smoke's life to save his own.

Moments later Smoke and Peanut came outside, and Tez made his way over to Smoke's Charger to meet them.

"What's up, what's up?" Tez dapped them up nervously and they all got in, Peanut in the back, Smoke in the driver seat, and Tez on the passenger side. Having enough reasons to get pulled over just for simply being black, they all put on their seatbelts.

"Who the hell was that broad?" Smoke crunk the car up, put it in drive, and pulled off. "I was like, damn, my boy done caught him a white girl."

White girl? Tez thought. "Y-yea, just a lil' hoe I c-caught a while ago."

"White hoes make you studder, huh?" Smoke asked.

They all laughed, and Tez realized that he'd gotten away by a gnat's ass. He couldn't afford those kind of mistakes. It served as a reminder of his betrayal, and the fact that he shouldn't continue with what he had going with the boss's wife. Problem was, he just couldn't bring himself to end it. While DJ had his child, Nae had his heart. It's the only reason they had carried on for so long.

They arrived at the U-Haul company, having rode most of the way in silence. Tez got out and went inside.

Peanut unsnapped his seatbelt and leaned forward. "Every time that nigga go to Haiti, he come back on some weird shit. I'm tellin' you. It's that voodoo. I think DJ got roots on him."

Smoke nodded. "Yea, shawty. Either that or he trippin' bout that white hoe."

They sat in the parking lot, observing the scene. Cars, people, and U-Haul trucks. Nothing seemed out of the ordinary, but Smoke kept the car running just in case. He was set to take the authorities on a chase if they were to arrive.

"Maybe the spirit is working on him and he's just tired of this work," Peanut said, doubting his own words.

Smoke screwed his face up in irritation. "Man, shut the fuck up! Matter fact, sit back."

Sucking his teeth, Peanut waved him off, sat back, and reconnected his seatbelt.

Tez walked through the doors of the U-Haul's office and saw a comely mixed woman seated at the desk typing on the computer.

"Hello, sir," she greeted. "How can I assist you?"

"Here to see Castro," he answered.

She looked him over in a way she hadn't at first. "Name?"

"Martez," he answered.

She disappeared through a door and returned moments later. "Castro will see you, now."

He followed her to an office that he'd been in several times.

"Martez!" Castro exclaimed when the secretary was gone. "What's up, my friend?"

He was tall, slim and looked very professional in his tailored Louis Vuitton suit. Castro was thirty-five years old and already a billionaire, thanks to his uncle Higa's operation. He played a major role as a Zeta.

Tez shook his hand. "I'm a'ight. How you doing?"

"Good. Good." Castro tapped Tez's shoulders. "How come you never buy cocaine, my friend? It's good, so good. Ninety percent coca!"

Tez smiled. "There's order in what we do." He was careful not to step out of his lane as a Young Boss. It's bad enough he was fucking Nae.

"Listen, Martez. You no tell your boss. I no tell my uncle."

Tez was certain that Castro would tell Higa. It was a family operation, and if Higa knew, Ken would know as well.

"You call me when ready, okay?" Castro passed him a business card.

"Okay." Tez accepted the card and tucked it in his pocket.

"Sit down." Castro sat behind his desk and pulled out a bottle of brandy. "Take a drink."

"Nah, homie, I can't. I gotta get this shit settled and distributed."

Castro nodded and pulled three keys from the drawer, offering them to Tez. "It's okay, my friend. Maybe next time."

"Yea, a'ight." Tez accepted the keys and turned to leave.

"Hey, Martez?" Castro called after him.

"Yea?" he answered without turning.

Castro smiled. "Don't be a bitch."

Tez's eyes narrowed to slits, and he scowled. Castro laughed. It was clear he referred to his refusal to accept the cocaine.

Tez looked him up and down and walked away. *Ain't neva been a bitch. Fuck wrong witchu pussy ass wetback!*

Tez reached the car and signaled *all good* to his soldiers. Smoke killed the engine and they both got out. Tez handed them tagged keys, and they wordlessly set out to find the trucks to match.

***

Nae turned into the salon's parking lot and was startled to see Ken's black Maserati parked next to the spot reserved for her. "Shit!" She felt around in the ashtray for her ring as she attempted to park. Unable to find it, she took her eyes off the road to look. She found it, looked up, and slammed on the brakes, nearly colliding with the expensive vehicle. A car blared from behind, unsettled by her sudden stop.

Nae took a deep breath and exhaled. The Nissan Murano sped around her, and the man behind the wheel shot her an incredulous stare as he passed. Usually Nae would apologize but she found herself at a loss for words, distracted by Ken's presence, the ring, and the near accident.

Nae didn't see Ken behind the wheel of his Maserati, nor did she see him get out. She slid the ring on her finger and was startled to find him at her window when she looked up. She jumped visibly, and he smiled.

"What's up, woman? I know these punk ass drivers ain't got you shook. They ain't crazy." He opened her door, she swung her feet out, and he kissed her the moment she rose to her full height.

"Hey, you," she moaned, kissing him again, wondering if he could detect Tez's cologne.

"I called you." He closed the car door. "What the hell was so important that you couldn't answer my call?"

He called twice while she was with Tez, but she let it go to voicemail. "I was on the phone with my dad," she lied. "You know if I click over it will disconnect."

It wasn't new to him. He nodded.

"Your hair is so sexy," she switched the subject.

"Uh huh," he replied. "You gone pick up KJ from school? I have a meeting in an hour."

"You on this side of town, Mr. Man. You might as well do it."

"I came because somebody wasn't answering." A noted client drove into the parking lot, and Nae pointed. "That's Ashley Tatum, Bae. I gotta go."

Ashley Tatum was a national favorite from the reality show, *Celebrity Widows*. Nae did her hair twice a week to keep her looking fresh on TV.

"I'll get him from school," Ken decided. "And why wasn't ya ring on ya finger when you pulled in?"

She was turning away and didn't stutter step or hesitate. “I took it to the jeweler today and got it cleaned.”

And you didn't immediately put it back on the minute it was done? he wanted to ask but decided not to make it a big deal. She was only human. “A’ight, bae, go get that money.” He slapped her butt as she turned.

“A lil’ harder next time, Big Daddy.”

Ken smiled. “I love you!”

“I love you, too!” she said without turning around.

***

Dressed as tourist, Smoke and Peanut rode the highway to Savannah in a RV with two hundred pounds of Kush secured in its body. The product was compressed, wrapped, and covered with a colored and odorless poison oil used to make pharmaceuticals and rocket fuel, the purpose of which was to render the weed undetectable by State Trooper devices. Marijuana was safe from the chemical as long as the plastic was washed before the vacuum seal was broken.

They rode in silence, with Smoke behind the wheel and Peanut in the passenger seat reading the Bible. There were other cars, trucks and RV's on the highway but not so many to the point where travel was difficult.

“Lemme ask you a question,” Smoke said. He kept his eyes on the road, but when Peanut didn't reply, he shot a sidelong glance at the man. “Real shit, shawty.”

Peanut never took his gaze from the pages. “What’s up?”

“How come you tryna be all godly and shit, but you still sell drugs, you still smoke, you not faithful to one hoe, and you kill people. So, what’s the point of talkin' ‘bout Jesus all the time and you not applyin’ it? You a hypocrite, bra.”

There was a long pause. Peanut felt the jab, but the statement and question was valid. “God is still working in my life. I plan on leaving this alone soon. Besides, there’s a lot of other things I don’t do that’s important to God.”

"Like what?" Smoke hit his blinker and switched lanes.

"I don't worship any other *God*," Peanut said. "I don't make idols that look like anything in or under the sky. I don't misuse God's name in vain and I give him the Sabbath day."

"What makes you so sure all that shit is real? I mean, what if none of that is real and it's just some bullshit white folks made up to keep us niggas under control, then what?"

"There ain't no *what if.* I know it's real."

"But how do you know?"

Peanut looked back into his Bible. "Because I live by faith, Smoke."

Smoke nodded then turned the radio up.

Peanut's relationship with the members of Young Boss had grown over the past twelve years. Their cohesion was great but he knew the moment he decided to walk away and devote himself completely to God, those ties, along with the relationships, could exist no more. The seeds to his transformation were planted four years ago at his mother's funeral. It was a day he would never forget.

At the sight of his mother's lifeless body in the casket and his rambunctious outburst, Peanut's aunt, Celeste, who he'd only seen as a child, pulled him into the bathroom.

"Listen to me, Peanut, and you listen good!" With her fingers, she lifted his chin. "I'm sorry she's gone, baby, but the reason I'm not crying is because she gave her life to the Lord before she died. Confess your sins and claim Jesus Christ as your savior or you will be thrown in the lake of fire for eternity! Matthew six verse twenty-four says *no one can serve two masters. Either you will hate the one and love the other, or you will be devoted to the one and despise the other*. Give your life to the Lord, Peanut. You cannot serve both God and money. We'll see her again."

The seed had taken root, and little by little he grew in the spirit of God. His living conditions following the death of his mother had led him astray, but it was only a means of survival. He had started back going to church on Sundays recently, and he would soon sever his ties to the game and walk fully with God.

***

Long after Peanut and Smoke were on their way, Tez remained at the warehouse. On the surface it looked to be a studio, but it was where the drugs were handled and stashed. With the fresh shipment, he was directing workers to unload, stash, weigh, pack, and prepare to ship. All the while, Nae was on his mind. He couldn't stop thinking of her to the point where he wouldn't even accept a call from the Haitian number that appeared twice on his caller ID.

***

The garage to Shawn's tire shop opened almost on cue as Smoke turned in. He drove through the opening and the door descended, closing behind the RV as he parked and killed the motor.

"What's up?" Smoke said. He was the first to exit the vehicle. Peanut followed.

"How y'all, dae?" Shawn said in his Savannah accent.

"We cool," Smoke answered.

Two men from Shawn's crew approached the RV to remove panels and access the hidden compartment, familiar with the routine.

"You wanna count it?" Shawn gestured at two huge duffle bags on the floor in the corner.

Smoke looked to Peanut for an answer.

"Nah," Peanut answered with slant eyes at Shawn. He didn't quite like the man. "I know it's all there." *It better be,* he thought.

Despite Peanut's lack of trust for Shawn, he was sure the money would add up because he had family behind the wall in the dorm with J-Bo. He wasn't stupid, and if he was, that would give Peanut a reason to do what he'd been wanting to do since the first time they met: kill him.

"Smoke?" Shawn said. "Let me halla at you fa a minute."

He flashed, what seemed to Peanut, a sinister grin as he stepped out of earshot with Smoke. Peanut stared, wondering what business could they have that didn't include him.

“What’s the plan?” Smoke asked.

“Fuck a plan,” Shawn said. “Let’s just take off. Listen, Smoke. We losing out by going through folks. I know you, you know me, fuck the middleman shit.”

“What am I supposed to tell my boss that’s hooked up wit’cha people?” Smoke countered. “And what about ya people doing time?”

Shawn laughed. “Tell 'em you got a bad vibe about me and you don’t feel comfortable working with me no mo’. I'ma tell my brother the same thang 'bout you.”

Smoke twirled his fingers together. “How our people that’s locked up gone eat if we box ’em out like that?”

Shawn retrieved a box of Newport 100’s from his pocket along with a lighter and nodded questioningly at Smoke.

“I’m straight.” Smoke refused to indulge in anything that clearly stated that it may cause cancer.

Shawn lit the cigarette and inhaled deeply. “Fuck em.” He shrugged. “When yo’ people get out, I’m sure he ain' got nothin' to worry 'bout financially.”

“What about ya brotha?” Smoke asked.

Shawn exhaled a heavy cloud, and Smoke fanned the air and put more distance between them.

“Fuck him,” Shawn said.

Smoke twitched at the cold words. It was normal for a man in the game to cross his friend for the compensation, but for a man to cross his blood brother and not give a fuck while he down and serving time was a different level of slime. He didn’t know how he felt about doing business with someone whose own brother couldn’t depend on to do right by him. I mean, to an extent what he was doing was slimey, too, but if he felt like it would seriously hurt Ken or J-Bo, he wouldn’t be with it at all. But they wouldn’t miss it. This move was small paper to them.

“They gave that boi twenty-five years. He ain’ coming home no time soon.”

And you just gon' leave him hangin'? Smoke gave no voice to thought and didn't question the man's sincerity regarding the matter.

They had been speaking about doing their own business on the side because too many other people had to get paid currently, but Smoke hadn't anticipated how doing so would result in hurting their very own.

Smoke caught Peanut's beckoning wave from the corner near the duffle bags. "A'ight, homie. I'ma make the call. Next time we meet, gone be just us."

They shook hands and Smoke walked away.

Peanut had to use both hands to lift one of the colossal bags, and he grunted audibly.

"It ain't that heavy," Smoke teased as he approached to take the second bag. He hefted it over his shoulder with one hand as they made their way over to the RV. "Nothing but paper, shawty."

"That's three hunnid and fifty bands of paper, nigga. That shit heavy."

For a total of seven-hundred thousand, Smoke thought. And when it was all distributed to the rightful holders, he would gain seventy-five for his efforts. J-Bo would come out the deal with a quarter million.

How the fuck a nigga that's locked up making more money than me and I'm out here workin'?

"Make sho y'all wash that shit off before opening it!" Smoke yelled out the window as he started the RV and put the transmission in reverse.

"What the hell he wanted?" Peanut asked, referring to Smoke's private conversation with Shawn.

"Nothing," Smoke answered.

Chapter Four

Behind the wheel of his Maserati, Ken pulled to a stop in front of Shakeena's house. JJ, on the porch awaiting his uncle's arrival, was down the steps and running along the walkway as Ken got out and came to meet him. He'd been in a meeting when the boy called and asked for new video games. Ken could have had them ordered and delivered, but he had given J-Bo his word that he would soon take his son for a day out. Besides, he enjoyed spending time with his nephew when the opportunity presented itself.

Looks more like J-Bo than Keena, the older he gets. Ken opened his arms to JJ. "What's up, buddy?"

"Hey, Kenny!" JJ was excited.

Ken smiled, then waved at Shakeena, who was on the porch in a green robe, before opening the Maserati's passenger door for JJ.

She watched anxiously as they drove away, recalling the conversation that she had just had with her son moments before Ken arrived.

"Okay, baby. You know the rules right? Lemme hear 'em."

JJ sighed but recited the rules his mom had given him years ago when she began letting Ken take JJ without her supervision. "Yeah, mommy. Don't mention Daddy because it will make Uncle Ken mad. Don't talk about ***my*** *Dad either, because it'll make him really sad, too."*

JJ knew he had another dad. He just didn't know where he was and was never told the situation behind his absence. He asked once before, but she told him that one day she would tell him when she believed he could understand.

Shakeena smiled down at her son, feigning as if she was calm when really she was a nervous wreck inside. She always was when she sent him off with Ken by himself.

She had taught him years ago what she did and didn't want him to talk about when he was alone with him, Shawn or the rest of her "uncle's" family.

Shakeena let out a loud sigh as she closed the door and said a quick prayer. *Please don't let this blow up in my face—*

***

Ken drove to Cumberland Mall. Of all the malls in the Atlanta area, this was one he rarely set foot in; too cheap for his taste. But he was pressed for time, and it was the closest mall to JJ's neighborhood.

"Get what you want," Ken told JJ as they walked into GameStop, and JJ was off with a childish squeal of delight. Ken busied himself with his cellphone and kept an occasional eye on his nephew as he brought several items to the register and went back for more. Their eyes met every so often as JJ searched for some sign of disapproval. Ken only nodded, and JJ continued gleefully, his expression like that of a younger kid in a candy store.

When he'd gotten all that he'd wanted, Ken smiled and approached the register behind him, looking at games, controllers, memory cards and several other items only the kid could identify.

"Sir," the shaggy haired white male store clerk said, "do you have both the PlayStation 4 and Xbox One?"

Ken looked to JJ, who shook his head by way of saying, *No.*

"Well," the clerk pushed his glasses up on the bridge of his thin nose and gestured to the pile of merchandise. "Most of what you have here is compatible with either one or the other."

JJ looked back at Ken, weary of what he would have to return to the shelf. His disappointment and reluctance to do so was clear.

Ken shot JJ the same smile he'd given him when the kid was piling items onto the counter. He gave the same nod as well. To the clerk, he said, "Do you have both those systems in stock?"

"Yes, but—"

"But what?" Ken cut in.

"Well, it seems that all of which you have here, along with both systems, will cost well over two grand, sir."

Ken grunted, raising both brows. The man was obviously oblivious to his status. Behind Ken and JJ, a father waited with his son, a mother was with her two daughters, and a married couple was with their son and daughter. Ken turned, greeted the parents, then addressed the kids with them. “Do you have PlayStation 4’s and Xbox One’s?” he asked.

The children looked to their parents before either shaking their heads or saying, “No.”

“You do now,” Ken faced the clerk. “Make that a PlayStation 4 and Xbox One for my nephew, here, and the same for each of the families behind me."

The clerk's cheeks were beet red, and he was at a loss for words. “Is this some kind of joke?”

“Yea.” Ken produced a No Preset Spending Limit American Express card from his wallet. “The joke's on you and your inability to recognize a boss. Now let's be quick. I have several matters that need my attention.”

The clerk's cheeks brightened as he lowered his gaze and proceeded to tally the cost of the items on the counter and those requested by Ken. Several shoppers had caught the verbal exchange from the beginning and had gathered around as a result.

The grand total appeared on display for all to see, and there were startled exclamations and murmurs of doubt. Ken merely smiled. A heavy silence hung over the store as Ken swiped his card. A chorus of ecstatic screams erupted at the approved transaction as the parents' mutual fear of their child's disappointment was assuaged and the kids understood their reality. Ken nodded as the clerked bagged the merchandise and called for a store assistant to distribute the remaining consoles to the families specified by Ken. Grateful parents and children gathered to offer thanks and words of appreciation to Ken, who accepted the praise graciously.

“Did you see that?” someone called as Ken and JJ took up their bags and made their way to the exit.

“Hell, yeah!” came another's reply. “He just bought, like, four PlayStation 4's and four Xbox One's and gave, like, six of them away!”

“Who the hell is he?” someone questioned.

“Um sayin', tho!”

"I recognize him from one of Lil Dread's videos," a female offered.

"You mean Young Boss?"

"Yeah," the female replied. "I think he's the head honcho."

Ken and JJ made several trips to the parking lot to drop merchandise to the car as they shopped one store after another. They were at it for close to three hours before they called it quits, and with more bags than they could comfortably carry, they settled into the food court to order Chick-fil-A for lunch.

"So," Ken said from his position across from the young fella. "You had fun with Uncle Ken today?"

JJ hurriedly swallowed the food in his mouth and sipped his lemonade.

"Yea!" he exclaimed. "I got the new DJI drone, the new Jordans, and all those new clothes!"

Ken bit into his spicy chicken sandwich. "If you were a lil' older, I would buy you a car."

"What!" The boy's eyes grew wide, and that tickled Ken, more so when the boy said, "You can still buy me one."

"Yo' daddy will buy you one when he gets out."

JJ frowned, trying to remember what his mom told him to say when Ken talked about his biological father. "Get out of what?"

Ken was confused by the boy's reaction, but quickly remembered that he doesn't know of his father yet. "Nothing."

"My other dad already has a lot of cars. He doesn't drive them, though. They're collectibles!" JJ said in an attempt to change the subject. He was feeling uncomfortable with the direction of the conversation. He couldn't remember what he was supposed to say, and he didn't want to get his mama in trouble.

Ken was taken aback. "Other dad? What you mean? The cars in the yard? Those are your mother's, right? Who you talkin' bout?"

In that moment, Ken noticed that JJ looked like a deer caught in headlights. "What?"

JJ looked conflicted. Like he wanted to say something but didn't know if he should.

"It's okay, nephew. You can talk to me," Ken encouraged, giving the boy his full attention. He decided to start with the easiest question. "Whose cars are you talkin' about?"

"My other daddy's. Shawn."

Ken's face went blank for a moment as he took in what was said, and when the realization hit, his blood began to boil. Keeping J-Bo a secret was one thing but passing someone else off as his father was another thing altogether and one that Ken could not accept. He needed clarification.

"So, you have two dads?" Ken asked.

JJ nodded. "That's what my mama said."

"What exactly did your mama say?"

JJ was speaking freely, wanting to speed everything up so he could go home and play his new game. "She said that my real dad died when I was a baby, and that Shawn was my dad too, because he takes care of us."

"That's not your dad. Your dad's name is Jerome. That's who you were named after. And he damn sure ain't dead." Ken was no fool. JJ was just a child, but Ken could read between the lines and knew exactly what the fuck Shakeena was doing.

JJ scratched his head. "I don't know, Uncle Ken. That's what my mama tell me."

Ken shook his head and rose to his feet. "Hey!" he called out to two guys walking past. "Carry these bags to my car and I got a hundred apiece for the both of you.

The guys looked at each other, shrugged and carried the bags to the car. Popping the trunk, Ken had them load up the car before paying them and sending them on their way. He was silent on the return trip to Shakeena's house, preoccupied with the idea of her having JJ believe his father was anyone other than J-Bo.

Upon arrival, several trips were made to and from the car, as all the shopping bags were carried to the house. Shakeena was used to the loads of stuff bought by Ken, but it never ceased to amaze her how the man took care of the boy. It still made her feel uneasy though knowing she was in the wrong.

"Wow!" Shakeena exclaimed, when they were done.

Ken gave JJ a hug. "I love you, buddy."

"Love you, too!"

Ken turned his attention to Shakeena. "May I halla at you outside, please?"

"Sure." Her expression reflected her concern. It was there in her tone as well. "Is everything okay?" she asked as she followed him onto the porch.

"Fuck no!" He stared deep into her eyes.

"What's the problem?"

"All these fucking years—All these fucking years you got that boy calling another man *daddy*?"

Fuck! Fuck! Fuck! Her nightmare had become reality. "Please don't tell J-Bo," Shekeena pleaded. "Let me tell him."

He looked at her in disgust. "Bitch, I'll neva cross my homie!"

Shakeena had never been disrespected by him before. Her eyes welled, and she felt small under his gaze. "It's not a cross by giving me a chance to come clean first, and you know it."

She was right, but he wasn't trying to hear it. "I don't give a fuck!" He walked away, and the tears fell freely down her face.

Shawn pulled into the driveway, catching sight of Ken's angry strut as he rounded the back of his Maserati, leaving Shekeena distraught and in tears on the porch. He threw his car in *park* and jumped out. "Wazzam, Bra?"

Ken, reaching for the door handle, spun abruptly. "The fuck you mean *wazzam*, nigga? Whateva you want to be happenin'!"

Shawn was definitely intimidated by Ken's size, but he couldn't let it show in front of his woman.

Shakeena hopped off the porch and was suddenly between them. She looked to Ken pleadingly.

Shawn asked, "Did he hit you, baby?"

"Hell no," Ken cut in before she could answer. "But I *will* slap a bitch, if need be."

Shawn pulled off his shirt. "Listen, Bra, I understand this ya niece, but you ain't finna come to our house and disrespect her like that. I won't condone that bullsh—"

Whap!

Ken slapped him like a bitch. Shawn floundered to the ground.

"Nigga!" Ken bellowed, coming to stand over him. "This my mothafuckin' house!"

Shawn was coming to his feet, but Ken's foot collided with his jaw and dropped him again.

"Pussy ass nigga!"

Shakeena moved to stop Ken's advance, but the man kept coming as if she wasn't there. Ken knelt over Shawn and delivered a bone crushing blow to his face.

"Tell this pussy nigga the truth right now!" Ken barked.

Shakeena cried hysterically as Ken punched him again. "Please, Ken!"

Shawn was trying to block, but Ken's ferocious blows cut through every time.

Ken looked to Shakeena as he rained blows to her boyfriend's face. "Tell him!" he barked.

"Ken, please! You gon' kill him!"

Ken delivered another crushing blow. "I said tell him!"

"Okay, Okay!" Shakeena finally relented. She took a deep breath "Shawn, Jerome is not your son!"

"Tell him who is!" Ken demanded.

Shakeena's tears ran more freely than before. "Ken, stop!"

Come clean or I'm beating this fuck nigga to death! Ken punched him again. "What the fuck did I say?"

"J-Bo!" she screamed. "His daddy's name is J-Bo!"

"And where he at?"

"He's in prison! Ken, stop. Please!"

"And he finna touch down, too, bitch ass nigga!"

Those were the last words Shawn heard before Ken delivered a blow to his mouth, knocking him unconscious.

Chapter Five

Ken lay on his back, staring into Nae's eyes as she lay with her head on his chest, caressing his swollen and bandaged fist. "She really had that baby believing Shawn is his daddy?"

Ken nodded. "Yea, man. That bitch ain't shit!"

"Have you told J-Bo yet?"

Nae didn't know J-Bo personally. According to Ken, the man was serving ten years for trafficking, and Ken looked out for the child and his mother. She and Shakeena were fairly close. Closer than she would have liked, but the woman had turned out to be an asset in her predicament. She also wanted to know just how much truth Shakeena spoke that night.

"Naw, not yet. I'ma tell him, though. Did Tez come here last night?"

Nae's heart leapt, and she jumped from her position across Ken's chest. "Ow!" she cried, clutching the back of her thigh. Nothing was wrong, however; it was all she could manage to justify the sudden separation, afraid he'd detect her accelerated heart. *Ain't no way he could have known it was—*

Ken giggled, fooled by her reaction.

"No," she proceeded with caution. "Why?"

"I left a message after I beat Shawn to sleep and told him to come by."

KJ came through the door, fully dressed with his backpack in hand. "I'm ready, mommy."

She went to the closet and slid on some jeans and a white tee with the *Young Boss* logo on front.

"What happened to your hand, daddy?" KJ asked.

"I burnt myself," he lied. "You gone be good in school?"

"Yes." KJ smiled and hugged his daddy.

Nae came out the closet and headed towards the door.

"Come on, KJ. Let's go before we late." She kissed Ken and headed out with KJ on her heels.

***

Tez awoke to his phone signaling a call. He had felt the vibrations moments before, but he was laid up with his lady friend and had disregarded the notice.

"Hello?" he answered sleepily.

"You got my message?" Ken asked.

"Nah, I just woke up, homie. What good, though?"

"Come by the house." Ken hung up without waiting for a reply.

Tez found Ken messaged from last night, listened to the urgent words, and was suddenly concerned. *Does Ken know anything about me and Nae?* He couldn't help but wonder. He got out of bed and the semi-naked woman stirred.

"Where you goin'?" she said.

He threw on a black short sleeve V-neck, pulled on some suade forest green Tru Religion jeans, and slipped on a pair of black, white and forest green Lebron's. "I'ma be back."

She made a demurring noise as he walked out.

***

Nae noticed Tez pulling into her driveway just seconds after she parked in the garage and the motorized door slid shut behind her. She loved being around Tez, but she got so nervous when they were together with Ken. She entered the house from the garage, and Ken yelled for her to open the door for Tez. She reached in her purse, popped a Winter Fresh stick in her mouth, and opened the door. She smiled, laying eyes on his chocolate skin. "Good morning, Tez."

He didn't return the greeting. He hated being this way with her but he played it safe whenever Ken was anywhere remotely near. "Where's Ken?"

Nae pointed to the stairs. Tez started past, but Nae grabbed his shirt. "I missed you."

Tez whirled with a frown. "Don't be saying no shit like that right—"

She cut him off with a kiss on the lips. He pulled quickly away with an indignant mug and went for the stairs.

Nae smiled. “I love you, too.”

Tez was disgusted by her actions. What they were doing was wrong already, but all up in the man’s house with it. *This bitch tryna get us both killed!* There were times when he wanted to end the affair, but her lips felt great on his; he wished he could wake up every morning to the softness of them.

Ken's bandaged hand was the first thing Tez noticed when he entered the master bedroom. “Fuck happened to you?”

“I tried to beat that fool Shawn to death.”

Tez gave him a pound on his left hand, then took a seat on the white leather love seat beside the bed.

“The fuck happened, shawty?”

Ken told him the entire story as Nae walked in and out on their conversation, casually shooting glances that Tez never returned. He kept his eyes locked on Ken, wishing she would stop playing the situation so close. Nae left the room with a couple of small boxes as Ken concluded the story.

Tez shook his head. “After everything J-Bo done did for her, even despite his situation. I can’t believe Keena played the game foul like that.”

“Martez—” It's been years since Ken had called Tez by his real name, and there was a grave look in in his eyes. “These bitches ain’t loyal no more. Don’t get caught up with a disloyal ass bitch. She’ll make ya bones rot.”

Tez’s skin crawled at the statement. He was suddenly apprehensive, uncertain whether the statement was directed at him, a warning perhaps. But considering the circumstances, there would be no warning. The idea didn't sit well, and with his budding relationship with Nae, an exit strategy was imperative.

“I want Shawn out of that house,” Ken ordered, and Tez relaxed. “All his clothes, shoes—everything—gone. The cars too; get them the fuck off my property!"

Tez nodded.

“And Tez?”

Tez’s apprehension rose anew.

"Keep doing what you're doing," Ken went on, "and you will take over."

Tez wasn't sure he understood correctly. He cocked an inquisitive brow.

"I'm thinkin' bout having some more kids and retiring from the streets soon. Only the office for me."

Tez smiled, pleased with the idea of being Young Boss's lead man. "That's what's up, homie." He could barely contain his excitement. His name and word held much weight with the team, but there would be none to contest or question his authority if he were to obtain the status implied; his word would be law.

Ken knew the treachery of the world he ran in; the lack of loyalty from those least suspected could land him dead or in the feds. He wasn't tryna go out like Irv Gotti. His legitimate exit was set; he would soon leave the game.

"Everything cool with Castro?" Ken asked.

Is that bait? Tez wondered. If so, he wasn't going for it. He nodded. "Yea, he asked why we neva buy cocaine."

Ken sat up. "What you tell him?"

"I ain' give no real reason. Just told him that I'll let him know if we become interested."

Ken nodded. "If you interested, just pump ya brakes for now. It's your call when I stand down. Right now, I don't want any part of that. There's a big difference in the time the Feds give for weed versus cocaine. You can have a million pounds of weed. Mr. Luis is gonna get you straight. You have a hundred keys, even with him, you might have to sit down for a while."

Tez nodded. "I understand."

"You hungry?" Ken asked.

"For sure." Tez stood, ready to go.

Ken laughed. "Take ya seat, my nigga."

Tez sat down. "Thought we was gon' get some to eat?"

"We are." Ken called Nae, and Tez immediately regretted wanting something to eat. Nae came in to stand in front of Ken.

"Will you cook me and my homie some breakfast?"

"Sure," she said and bent for a kiss.

Tez lost his appetite. Nae had cooked for him several times during their private encounters, but Ken's presence, here and now, was a constant reminder of his disloyalty. She turned to leave, but Ken grabbed her hand and pointed to the ring.

"Martez," he stated, "that's a hundred G's, my nigga. You need to get you something like that."

Tez smiled, trying hard to hide his discomfort. "Nah, man, I ain't ready for marriage."

Ken chuckled. "Why you say that?"

Because we have to end first, Nae thought. *Then he'll be ready.*

Tez shrugged. "The time just ain't right, homie."

Ken released Nae's hand, and she left them alone.

***

Shawn pulled out of the hospital's parking lot with vengeance on his mind. Yesterday, he'd been embarrassed when he regained consciousness, hurt physically and emotionally, having driven himself to the emergency room for treatment, where he was kept overnight. His face was set with stitches, he suffered a broken nose, and he was missing several teeth. He wasn't cleared by the doctor for release; he left at his own discretion.

The local police was there to see Shawn shortly after his nose was set and his stitches were fixed but he had given the officer a lie of having been attacked by three anonymous males, all of whom—he told the officer—he couldn't recall.

"We gon' handle this in the street," Shawn spoke aloud as he sped through a yellow light on Clampton Drive. He wasn't sure what fate he would bring to Ken, but the nigga was going to die a gruesome death for the humiliation he'd suffered at his hand. The actual beating paled in comparison to what he felt at Shakeena's claim that JJ was fathered by someone other than he, and that the man was in prison.

Shawn's vision was suddenly blurred by tears, and to wipe them away was excruciating. But that was equivalent to a candlelight in the face of the sun when compared to Shakeena's echoing claim. It was clear why he never met J-Bo.

Nasty bitch!

How could she have left him blind for so long? But even as the question came to mind, he knew it wasn't entirely her fault but one of his own as well. There were several things off in their relationship at one point or another. And the thought of a paternity test had come to mind on several occasions, but never had he followed through. And now, he could argue that he was sparing himself, then, the trauma he felt now.

Shawn shared a strong bond with JJ. He loved the kid to death and felt that a tie so strong could be nothing short of that derived from blood. With that came the question of Shakeena's sincerity in regard to her claim. Judging from the severity of the beating administered, he was inclined to accept her word as valid.

Lyin' ass bitch! Nigga probably ain't even ya uncle!

Even if JJ wasn't his son, why would Ken trip so hard? Was it because JJ's alleged father was on the way home and they wanted him out of the way? Shawn had a hard time accepting the matter, but so much made sense.

Nearly nine years ago, Shawn had run into Shakeena in Atlanta while in town for the weekend. The two had been talking off and on for a little over four years at the time, with half of that being as nothing more than platonic friends. She had come to him one night for comfort and emotional support, and the ordeal had led to sex, something Shawn had desired for so long but had always been denied as a result of her faithfulness to a boyfriend he never knew.

During that weekend, however, they had gotten with each other, and it was over dinner when he raised the question regarding the distance she'd placed between them, having lost all communication with him up until that point. It was in that moment that Shakeena had admitted to having had a child. She claimed he had gotten her pregnant the night she'd come to him for comfort.

"I didn't know how to tell you, once I found out," Shakeena had said. She told him about her trip to the abortion clinic, how she decided against taking her child's life and fled before going through with it. And by the time she decided to keep the baby, she had no way of getting in touch with Shawn. According to Shakeena, she began dating an old boyfriend who signed Jerome's birth certificate and was later killed in a sour drug deal by the time JJ was three months old.

Shawn had always been sweet on Shakeena, had always wanted her for himself but was kept at bay by her involvement with someone else. But the chance to claim her along with his son was more than he could ever ask for. He took them in, and at times, he felt like a sucker for love and second guessed everything he'd been told. However, it came to be less about Shakeena and more about JJ, as he grew more attached to his son.

Now, as Shawn drove aimlessly about the city, he was face to face with what he had feared for so long. While there was room to accept not being the boy's father, Shawn could still love and take care of the boy. But with J-Bo alive and soon to put in an appearance to lay claim, Shawn would be completely cut out of the child's life.

Shawn punched the steering wheel twice, angry at Shakeena's deceit, furious for the humiliation he'd suffered, contemplating bloody revenge.

Chapter Six

Two exotic strippers from a local strip club, Diamonds of Atlanta, danced in the nude for Peanut and Smoke in their living room. The two women had spent the night with the fellas after the big hot four-some they participated in last night. They were both red bones, medium height and on a scale from one to ten these bitches were twenties!

"You eva seen a bitch hit the weed wit' her pussy?" Asia asked, clapping her ass in Smoke's face.

Smoke glanced at Peanut, whose face was inches away from Tiffany's clapping ass. "Hell naw!" He pulled on his weed-filled Dutch again.

A huge colorful butterfly was tattooed on Asia's cheeks; the wings of which seemed to flap as her juicy ass clapped. She nabbed the blunt from his lips.

"Oh, that bitch fye!" Tiffany commented.

Peanut sucked his teeth objectively. "Man, she can't do no shit like that!"

"How much you wanna bet?" Asia asked.

Smoke was amused by the exchange.

"Two bands," Peanut said.

"Five," Tiffany joined in.

Peanut shook his head. "Naw."

"Broke ass nigga!" Smoke instigated, knowing he could get his lil' homie to bet, and the women's laughter was the icing on the cake.

"A'ight," Peanut said. "Five bands!"

"You can keep three," Asia said. "Just give me two."

Tiffany slapped Asia's ass. "Okay, Sexy."

"Just do the fucking shit!" Peanut barked impatiently.

Asia stuck the blunt past the folds of her labia, and with whatever else she did from within, the blunt's amber head brightened.

"What the fuck!" Smoke said.

Peanut couldn't believe his eyes. He dug in his pocket, but Tiffany stopped him. "Hold up, playa. She ain't done."

Smoke wondered what more was there. Tiffany took him by the arm and said, “Help me hold her.”

Asia stood on the couch, straddling Peanut’s face. She leaned back into Smoke and Tiffany's hands for balance as she positioned her pussy near Peanut's face and pushed out a cloud of smoke.

“What the fuck!” Smoke said. “I wanna hit that blunt now!”

They laughed as Peanut counted out the money to Asia. Smoke's phone signaled an incoming call, and he walked towards his room the caller's name displayed on his screen.

“Where you goin'?” Asia called after him, scratching her head with the same hand that held the blunt.

Smoke held up a finger before falling off into the room and closing the door behind him. He answered the phones. “Yo?”

“What’s up?” Shawn said.

“Shit, really. I’m cool. You ready already?” Smoke got right to it, ready to get back with the others.

“Nah.” Shawn cleared his throat. “But I wanna do some otha business wit’cha.”

Smoke’s brows were raised at that; the subject was now murder for hire. Careful with his next words, he said, “You need a clean-up crew?”

“Exactly,” Shawn answered. He had considered killing Ken himself, but with the recent events, he would be an initial suspect in the investigation. If Shakeena was questioned, there was no guarantee she would omit the incident between the two, which would make him high on the list. Shawn would have a rock-solid alibi when the murder took place; that which wouldn't be so if he were to handle it personally.

“I want him terribly terrorized before he goes,” Shawn said.

“Who?” Smoke asked.

“My baby momma’s uncle.”

“A hunnid G’s,” Smoke said. “We’ll meet later for specifics.” Smoke broke the connection with nothing further.

***

Yea, I got yo' bitch ass now, Shawn thought. He opened his phone's web browser to search a list of dentists with good reviews. He wanted something done to Shakeena as well, but he also wanted to know the truth. In a way, he felt her words were real but a part of him was hoping she'd only said what she said to stop Ken from beating his face in. He loved JJ too much to just walk away now. He was determined to get a blood test, and no matter the results, he wasn't leaving the boy's side.

Shawn considered the text she had sent the night of the fight: "*Shawn, I am sooo sorry for his actions. He was really on some other shit. I can't talk to you now because I feel terrible, but we love you with all our hearts.*"

The words were committed to memory. They were clear, but they didn't add up; Shakeena wouldn't answer his calls. If she loved him, then why not answer?

***

Depressed, lounged on her living room sectional. She felt terrible about Ken jumping on Shawn, and she hated the circumstances under which her secret had been revealed. She considered her son, in school now, and what he must be going through as a result of so much deception. She was disturbed even further by the fact J-Bo would be furious and may never want to be with her. She figured he knew all about it. *Surely, Ken had told him by now*, she thought.

Shakeena loved Shawn, but J-Bo was primary in her heart. She still couldn't understand how she had let the situation go on for as long as she had. Having met Shawn in the club a little over a decade ago, she had heard of him being a drug dealer. But considering the fact J-Bo was a young boss in the game, she wasn't impressed with his status. It was a mutual interest in cars that ignited the spark, and their interaction had grown from there. She'd slept with him soon after J-Bo was incarcerated. And later, assuming J-Bo would never get free for the triple homicide, she had convinced Shawn that he was JJ's biological father. Shakeena felt bad for her decision, and she didn't have the courage to face either of them. It was a selfish decision that she had made soon after J-Bo went away. At the time, all she could think of was securing a position where she felt she and JJ would be taken care of.

Shakeena was startled by three knocks at her front door. The knocks were hard, like those of a police officer, or of an angry man. Her heart skipped a beat, and she was certain Shawn had come to confront her about everything. She took a deep breath before getting up to answer. The encounter was inevitable. Looking out the peephole, however, she was surprised to see Tez standing on her porch. She opened the door and he greeted her.

"Hey." Shakeena squinted. The daylight was bright in contrast to the house's interior. A U-Haul was at the curb along with two black F-150 trucks. A brown-skinned male with dreads hopped out of one truck and began hooking a chain to one of Shawn's classic cars.

"Martez, what the fuck goin' on?" Shakeena started out of the door but was blocked by Tez's outstretched arm.

He pointed behind her. "Go sit the fuck down!"

Shakeena stared at him with pleading eyes but found no love or understanding. Reluctantly, she went back to the sectional. Tez waved, and three men hopped out of the U-Haul and approached the house with trash bags.

"Martez!" Shakeena screamed. "What the hell is going on? Who the fuck are these people?"

"Shut the fuck up," he shot back. And to his crew, he said, "Anything that belongs to a man I want it out. If you see a pair of socks that look unisex, I want that too."

The men nodded and went upstairs.

"Oh, hell naw! Y'all ain't finna go rumbling through my shit!" She shot towards them, but Tez was quick to block her path. He pointed at the couch. "Sit the fuck down 'fore you end up like Shawn!"

Again, she sat. She knew Ken gave the order for all of what was being done. She tried to stare in his eyes, but he broke contact.

"How did J-Bo take it?" she hated to ask.

"Stop talking to me, Shakeena," he warned.

She didn't say another word.

***

"I been went to war,
Like veterans,
Fuck wit me gon be regretting it,
Choppa leave yo ass acephalous,
Ain't gon be no re-attaching it!"

Rada was tuned in as Psycho tongued-twisted the verse in the studio booth. Rada was Young Boss' main producer and beat maker. He was the truth. Rada made beats for almost every artist in the rap game. He sat behind the glass that separated him and Psycho, working the sound board to correspond with Psycho's flow, until the rap concluded and the man exited the booth and came to sit next to him. The beat was still flowing, and Rada's chopped tag blared over the track. "It's Rada music!"

Rada was hyped. "This one right here gone do it, cuz. I swear!"

Psycho smiled, listening as Rada mixed and mastered his vocals to the instrumental. "It's a'ight."

"Man, you crazy, lil' nigga! It's more than a'ight!" Bobbing his head to the music, Rada put his hand on one side of the headphones and twisted a knob. "This gone generate some M's alone."

Psycho looked down. "Ain't like I'm 'em."

Rada worked the keys. "A lot of people gotta get paid, homie, but you'll get a nice amount."

"Man, I know my contracts ain't right. I know I'm 'posed to have more."

Rada took a break from editing the song. "You really think Ken would have you in a fucked-up contract?"

Psycho nodded.

"You know Ken love you like a lil' brother. Why you feel that way?"

Psycho sighed. "I neva really understand what's bein' said when it's time for signing paperwork and our net worth is what, two hunnid M's?"

Rada nodded.

"And not trying to sound cocky, but whose talent do you think generated that much?"

"You, of course."

"Exactly, so how much money do you think I should have in the bank right now?"

Rada racked his brain before answering. "I know you playin' wit' at least ninety mil."

Psycho shook his head in disgust. "More like forty."

Rada frowned. *Damn, Ken fuckin him.*

"So, if you know this shit why won't you leave Young Boss?" Rada began with the computer again. He was a bit upset because Psycho knew he wasn't getting paid right and he just allowed it to happen.

"Ken gave me a chance when nobody else believed or took me seriously, and I feel like I owe him for life."

Rada stopped working the keys and gave his full attention to Psycho. "Listen, lil' homie. Loyalty is important. I'm glad that you're trying to be loyal, but as a man, never accept less than you deserve." He paused to let his words sink in. "You never take less because you don't want to hurt a mothafucka's feelings. In this business, mothafuckas will chew you up and spit you back out. You deserve more, homie. Watch this." He pulled out his phone, dialed a number, and it rang on speaker.

"What's up?" a voice answered.

"Aye, listen." Rada winked at Psycho. "I was having a discussion wit' somebody about some of the hottest rappers leaving their labels. How much and how fast would they be picked."

"Okay?" the guy said.

"What if Psycho was to leave us and try to sign to you?"

"Thirty million advanced easy."

Rada laughed. "And you wouldn't care how I felt? I mean we boys?"

"This a business, baby. No hard feelings."

Rada laughed and told him he'd halla back.

"You been wit' Young Boss for ova a decade and you playin' wit' forty M's. You just heard the man say he would give you thirty just for signing."

Psycho looked down at his Young Boss chain. "So, what you saying I should do?"

"Talk to Ken, tell 'em how you feel, and I'll do the same."

"A'ight."

They dapped up, and Rada went back to engineering the track. Psycho was the hottest thing since fish grease, and he deserved more money. If Ken was to lose Psycho from his label, it's a guaranteed fact that the Young Boss net worth would drop. They would still be in business, but they would begin to lose money, and this Ken knew. That's why he was so tough on Psycho to keep up the good work.

***

Frank's name was called to the big floor as the dorm officer appeared to distribute the daily mail. Frank hurriedly retrieved his and returned to the cell to finish smoking the burning joint with Flip and J-Bo.

"Who wrote you, Unc?" J-Bo asked, peeping the envelope in Frank's hand.

"My daughter sent me some pictures." The bulk and feel of the envelope made it obvious.

"You gon' hook me up with her or what?" J-Bo teased. He knew how far he could joke with Frank.

"Her husband would kill both of us." Flip passed him the blunt, that which he hit twice and passed to J-Bo.

Frank blew a cloud of smoke as he opened the envelope and withdrew the pictures.

"Damn, they house huge!" Frank exclaimed.

There was a lot of pictures of the house. He handed them to J-Bo and after checking them out, J-Bo passed them along to his cousin.

"Damn, this a big ass house. Who the fuck is yo' daughter? Oprah?" Flip laughed. "All dese her cars?"

Frank laughed at his excitement, still going through the pictures. "Nah, her husband got the big bucks. Matta fact, here go a picture of them." He handed J-Bo a picture of his daughter, the husband, and their son together.

J-Bo chuckled darkly when he looked down at the picture and two familiar faces stared back at him.

"Fuck so funny?" Frank checked.

"Tell me if you know any of dese folks, shawty." J-Bo handed the picture to Flip.

Flip stared down at the picture, his face void of any emotion, then handed it back with a shrug.

Frank was baffled by their reactions. "Y'all know him?"

"Hell yea. He a big music producer, right? That would explain that big ass house!" J-Bo hit the blunt again and passed it to Flip. *What are the fuckin' odds of that?*

J-Bo looked down at the picture of Ken and Nae locked in an embrace. He mentally shook his head as he came to the realization that Ken's wife, Nae, was Frank's daughter.

It had been years since J-Bo had sent Ken on a mission to get rid of Diamond, a witness against him in his trial. In the process, Ken had fallen in love with her sister, supported her through her grief, and then married her.

J-Bo wouldn't have done it, but Ken was his own man. This new problem was a perfect example why he would have kept his hands clean. He had to call Ken.

The door opened behind him, and the noise from the dayroom followed.

"Say, folk?" Bull came in. "It's a new nigga in here tryna use the phone. I told him two dollars for thirty minutes."

"You put the tax on like that. He must be the opp?"

Bull nodded. "He a Blood."

"It's chargin' right now, but who is he?"

Bull opened the door and called the guy in. Both cousins immediately recognized the man. Unaware of this, Bull did the introductions. "Quan, this my brotha, J-Bo. He gone put you on when it come off the charger."

J-Bo asked. “Where I know you from, shawty?”

“Rice Street,” Quan shot back.

Flip heard the animosity in the man's tone and became defensive. “You good, folk?”

“Yea, I’m cool.” Quan walked out.

“Y’all must had some bad blood in the county?” Bull asked.

J-Bo turned to Flip. “You know who that is?”

Flip nodded. “Yea, we beat bra ass in the county for stealin’.”

“And how long ago was that?” Bull asked.

“Shiddd, damn near ten years ago,” Flip cut in. “He betta let that bullshit go before he gets put on the door!”

“Chill, folk,” J-Bo stated.

“Bull!” Bo-G yelled from downstairs. “Brang yo scary ass on so I can ‘mate you!” ‘Mate was short for checkmate. Bo-G was ready for him and Bull’s daily game of Chess.

“Y’all chill” Bull said. “I’ma halla at Bo about it.”

J-Bo and Flip agreed to fall back, and Bull walked out the room and downstairs to the table with Bo-G.

Bo-G was a black, short, fat mothafucka. He favored Mr. Brown from the Madea series, and had GD-related tattoos all over his face and body. He’d been incarcerated for over twenty years, and getting on the bullshit was natural for him. He was setting chess pieces to the board when Bull arrived.

“Sit down, young nigga.”

Bull took the opposite chair. “Aye, you know the new Blood that just came in here?”

“Yea, what’s up?” Bo-G bit his thumb like he always did.

“Him and J-Bo had some issues in the county. By the way he was actin', sound like he got some beef on his chest.” Bull took the first move.

Bo-G stood up, brow creased in anger. “He said something outta line?”

Bull restrained him and he took his seat again.

“Naw, naw,” he said.

"Well, as long as he acts right, he's cool. The first time he acts dumb, that beef gone get cooked by the Bo!" he exclaimed, moving his queen. "Check, nigga!"

Bull looked down, and realized he was in check. They had only moved twice.

"I think that's 'mate, young nigga!" Bo-G laughed hysterically while taking a slight glance at Quan.

I'll kill yo' lil bitch ass.

Bo-G had been GD since he was fourteen. He didn't take shit from anyone. He was one of the highest-ranking GD's at Smith State Prison. His first favorite hobby is stabbing people; his second is, talking cash money shit.

"Hey, F2!" he called to dorm. "I just checkmated this dumb ass nigga in three moves!"

Bull shook his head in chagrin.

"That nigga Bull dumb as a shit sandwich!" He laughed some more, took his seat, and began setting the board for a second round.

***

After a long hot shower alone, Nae stood in the bathroom naked, applying lotion to her skin. She looked at her wedding ring and admired how beautiful it was.

Damn, Ken, I'm sorry.

She still loved Ken, but she just wasn't in love with him anymore; that love had somehow transferred to Tez over the years. It shouldn't have, being that their relationship had been purely sexual at first. Now, however, their feelings were those expected from that of husband and wife.

A single tear rolled from Nae's eye as she thought about ending her marriage to Ken. There was no prenup, so she could easily keep the house, a couple cars and more millions than needed, simply because she would have custody of their son. However, she didn't want the house and cars, just some money, KJ, and Tez. She was getting wet just thinking about him.

Shirtless, Ken appeared in the mirror behind her. "You okay, Love?"

She hadn't seen him at first. However, she covered her surprise, nodded, and turned to him. "Just thinking 'bout Diamond," she lied.

He hugged her softly, caressing her hair, and she rested her head on his strong tatted chest. She adored his muscular build.

"She needs to be crying for you, right now."

Nae was confused.

"Babe, she's in a much better place now. She's living great. We're the one's going through hell on earth." She squeezed him tight as she really began to think of her deceased sister.

"You'll see her again, bae."

She knew he was right.

"That's why I love you, Ken." She kissed his chest. "You always know how to make me feel better."

He kissed her. "You're my fucking one and only female monarch; that's my job to make you feel betta."

She kissed him back.

"How much do you love me?" he asked.

"Too much to explain."

"Nae, if I ever was to lose you," he started.

Unaware of where he was going with this, she became a bit uneasy.

"I don't know if I could continue on in life. I would go crazy. You are my world, my everything."

"Aww, what made you say that, babe?" she asked with caution.

"Just saying."

She kissed his chest again, licking his nipple this time. Certain he didn't know anything, she wanted to change the subject.

"You know what you're doing, right?" he asked.

"Of course." She let her tongue travel down his stomach seductively, until she reached the top of his pants. Looking up with a smile, she said, "May I?"

Ken smiled. The view of his butt naked wife in a squatting position aroused him. "That's a big problem," he warned.

She giggled, unbuckling his pants. “I’m a big girl.” She pulled his dick out and began stroking it. “I gotta be careful when dealing with monsters,” she referred to the size of his manhood.

He leaned his head all the way back, as she took his dick into her mouth and massaged every inch with her tongue and throat until he was good and hard. Satisfied with her job, she pulled it from her mouth and bent over, holding the sink for balance. Ken gripped her waist with one hand and used the other to guide his dick inside of her. She moaned in ecstasy as he slid to the back of her walls. A few minutes in, and she had cum twice. She was already horny from thoughts of Tez. She pulled his dick from her moist cave and began sucking him again, causing him to cum quickly. She grabbed the base of his dick to spread the cum all around her lips and mouth, as the nut shot from the head, before licking it all up and swallowing it.

“Owww, you so nasty,” he moaned, pulling her up and tongue-kissing her.

Chapter Seven

Frank sat at the table in the library, writing Nae a letter. Even though he parlayed with her all the time on the phone, they liked to keep letters in rotation. She'd totally forgiven him for his actions, and for the fear and pain he'd caused her as a child. He promised to recoup for all the years of her life that he missed. Folding it and licking the envelope, he closed it. He would have been gone already and would have written the letter in the dorm, but all movement was stopped because the inmate headcount was inaccurate.

"It's almost over for you, right, Frank?" It was Tobe that presented the question. Tobe was an old friend of Frank's, a skinny, light, brown-skinned guy with silver hair. They had met and established a friendship approximately twelve years ago, and Smith State Prison was their third camp together. With that, they often met in the library to discuss new books, world events as they knew them, and their future plans for re-entering society.

"That's right, Tobe. A couple more months, and it's over. Twenty to the door."

Tobe let out a long whistle. "You got a plan, right?"

"Yea. Sit around and get fat."

They both shared a laugh.

"What about work?" Tobe asked.

"Well, I'm gonna get my CDL's. I want to drive trucks, but my daughter told me for the first couple months I can just lay up."

"She gon' take care of yo' old ass?" Tobe joked.

Frank laughed. "Well, I told you before that husband of hers is a big music producer. He got long money."

Tobe nodded. "Yeah, I remember."

A dark-skinned, heavy-set female officer came through the library door. "Count is clear!"

Inmates, impatient to be in there, began clearing out immediately.

"Alright, Tobe, you take care now."

"You too, Frank. Keep your head up, OG."

They embraced with a handshake hug and went their separate ways. Frank dropped his letter to Nae in the mailbox on his way out.

Can't wait to get out of this shit.

***

Ken had come to the office to assist Susie with a very important meeting. He hadn't planned to stay long after, but top producer, Rada, requested a meeting with him. Ken was at his desk, and Rada was seated on one of the Louie couches.

"So, what's up, Super Producer?"

"This new joint called War," Rada said. "The beat is bad, but Psycho's lines are crucial."

Ken smiled. "Like always, right?"

"Yea, but with tours and iTunes, I swear it's gon' generate a lot of paper." He took a deep breath. "I just think the lil' homie deserves a lil' more money."

Ken frowned. "And this is why you're here?"

Rada nodded.

"And what leads you to believe he's not making enough?"

"Because we spoke about it. He never expressed being unsatisfied," Rada lied. "But we talked numbers. Assuming they were accurate, we both know he's worth more."

Ken knew Psycho was worth more, but the percentage splits and other agreements had been put in place from the beginning because he was taking a huge gamble with him. Psycho was heavy in the streets, which posed a threat to his investment. He could have spent hundreds of thousands building him up, all for him to be killed and he would have to shoulder that loss. Most companies wouldn't have even dealt with him, but Ken came from that lifestyle, and he knew what it was like to want out with literally no hope. He didn't mean anything by it. He felt Psycho seemed happy and with everything going on, he never thought to go back and change anything. Besides, the duration of the agreement hadn't ended; and business was business. That was just real. Shoe on his foot, he would respect it because that's what he agreed to. Not to mention majority of the extra money that he capped went into building the label which ultimately increased Psycho's sales and brought him more endorsements anyways. All the same, if Psycho wanted more, he deserved it and Ken was willing to renegotiate numbers at the end of his term.

Ken nodded. "I'll look into it. Contract's duration is at an end anyways. I got him."

Rada smiled. "That's what's up, Bro. I'm sure he'll appreciate the news."

Ken stood up and they shared a brotherly embrace.

"Hell happened to your hand?" Rada asked, just noticing the wrapping on it.

"Had to show a nigga ass who's boss!" Ken playfully threw a right hook to the space between them two.

Rada laughed. "You need to calm down. You 'bout fifty, ain't you?"

"Nah, nigga, I'm thirty-seven with a hunnid bodies."

"You bullshittin'?" he asked.

Ken shook his head. "Unfortunately, I'm for real."

Rada's phone went off, and he stepped outside to take it in private, leaving Ken to contemplate their recent exchange. There wasn't much to consider. He'd made more than enough off Psycho. He was a hot artist, and he deserved a greater percentage than what he was seeing already.

Ken's iPhone alerted him to a call, and he answered without checking the caller ID. "Hello?"

"What's up, Bro?" J-Bo asked.

"Damn, my bad, homie. I'm supposed to have showed my face for a visit. Shit has been so busy around the office lately."

"It's cool, my nigga. You in the office, now?" he asked.

"Yea," he answered.

"Shiiid, you need me to hit you back?"

"Nah, I'm leaving out now. What's up?"

J-Bo got serious. "Aye, you know yo' wife is my roommate's daughter?"

Instantly, Ken sensed danger.

"Hello?" J-Bo asked from Ken's silence.

"J-Bo." Ken took a seat on the couch. He was cautious now. "Am I on speakerphone?"

"Hell fuck no! That nigga ain't een in here. What kinda sense would that make. Wassup?"

"He know you my people?"

"Nah, he showed us some picture yo' wife sent him of y'all. She sent 'em pictures of y'all, ya house, everything. When we seen the pic of y'all, we ain't say shit."

Fuck! Ken thought."This could be a big problem for me, J-Bo."

"You think?" There were three inmates in J-Bo's cell. He told them he needed a moment alone and dismissed them all.

"I told her you were gone for drugs." Ken adjusted himself in his chair. "Once her dad tells her his roommate's name is J-Bo, and that you're a friend of mine…" Ken let his words trail off. "and I'm sure he knows your charges, correct?"

J-Bo ran his hand down his face, releasing a heavy sigh. "Yea. Damn sho do."

"Okay, so yeah, she's gonna figure out it's you and wonder why I would lie about you having drug charges. Her dad's gonna tell her it was for murder—well, three murder charges. All she has to do is look back at the time her sister was killed, and the time I came into the picture, and it will all make sense."

"Tell her that you were under the impression I was down for drugs," J-Bo suggested. "Even if she does figure it out, you can play like you didn't know."

Ken felt that J-Bo's notion was ridiculous. He shook his head. "She's not stupid, J-Bo. Even if it were true, that shit is too coincidental."

"Ken, where were you when the homies wet her up and killed Diamond and her nigga?" J-Bo asked, trying to get his point across.

"I was in the hospital."

"Exactly. So how could you have done it?"

Ken released a heavy sigh of frustration. "Of course, she'll know I didn't do it, but she'll know I had something to do with it!"

"So, is it obvious what I need to do?" J-Bo asked.

Ken hated for it to be this way, but he couldn't under any circumstances let this one out. "Yes."

J-Bo nodded. "Say no more."

Hanging up, J-Bo stuck his head out his cell door and called Flip, who was standing right outside on the top range, one foot up on the middle rail, both elbows on the top of it, observing the dorm. "Pull up."

Flip entered the room and closed the door behind him. "What's up, bra?"

J-Bo sighed, running his hand down his face. "Ken wants my bunkmate dead."

Flip shrugged. "I'm not surprised." He hadn't even been around Frank that long, but the old nigga appeared to be a cool dude. He could tell his big cousin didn't want to do it, either, but they both knew what had to be done.

"So, what? He think she gone try to get dem boys involved?"

J-Bo sat on his bed and put his head in his hands. He didn't want to see Frank dead especially if he had to do it. One thing he knew for sure, though, was when the boss gives an order you execute it. J-Bo knew Ken could easily have him and Frank both killed, so he disregarded the thought of not doing it. Aside from that, Ken wouldn't be in this mess if he hadn't called for the man's help to get at Nae's sister to avoid going to prison in the first place.

"I don't know, shawty. I think it's more of him not wanting to fuck his family up."

Flip sat on the edge of the toilet bowl, took a deep breath, and exhaled.

J-Bo was racking his brain for a way out but kept drawing blanks. The only way he saw was the gung-ho route, but that was the route that got him where he is now. It had been his idea to knock off Jon and his pregnant girlfriend. He was the dominant of the two cousins, but he knew he wasn't the smartest. He looked up at Flip. "How you think I should do this, folk?"

"Listen, bra, we finna be getting out soon." Flip paused in order to let reality sink in. "Don't turn these ten years into the life sentence we just wagged."

"So, what you suggest?" J-Bo was desperate.

"One of these niggas in here that got life without. Give 'em a dot and let him do it."

J-Bo laid back and contemplated the move. Flip's idea was simple, but it made sense. It wasn't long before he had just the person in mind to make it happen. He slapped Flip on the leg, hopped up, and walked out the room. Flip was up and right behind him, pushing the door up on his way out.

They made their way down the range. The dayroom was noisy, and inmates were doing the usual: working out, watching television, talking on the prison wall phones by the booth or playing Spades at one of the many tables scattered about the dorm. Two GD's were posted on the range standing security, watching what was going on in the dorm. They both made an "L" with their fingers and put it to the left side of their chest when they locked eyes with J-Bo, and he returned the gesture before knocking and walking into Bo-G's room. He gave Bo-G the proper greeting of a Gangsta as Flip closed the door behind them. Formalities aside, he explained the seriousness of the situation to Bo-G as they sat in his cell. He knew Bo would be the shot caller of assigning Frank's executor.

"Damn, folk," he said. "Y'all think she gon' put the police on him?"

J-Bo took a deep breath. "Shit, I don't know, folk. I do know whoeva do it, I'll get 'em a five hunnid dolla dot."

Bo fanned his comment off. "We family, J-Bo. You ain't gotta pay nobody—"

"Yea, but I want to anyway," he stressed.

Bo-G bit down on his thumb. He wasn't the least bit nervous; it had just been a habit for years.

"Call and get the money, young nigga," Bo-G said.

J-Bo went to the door and yelled for Bull.

"What's up?" Bull was sweating when he pulled up, having been called from his workout.

"Go grab my phone from that Blood nigga. His time is up in like two minutes."

Bull nodded and went the opposite way.

Bo-G stood. "You gon' have to hide it good cuz CERT Team finna tear this bitch apart, G."

J-Bo looked back and nodded. "I know it."

The door opened in front of J-Bo, and Bull entered but stopped abruptly, surprised to see J-Bo standing so close to the door. He pointed his thumb behind him. "He say you owe him thirty more minutes."

J-Bo frowned. "Thirty mo'e minutes for what?"

Bull shrugged. "The fuck am I supposed to know?"

Bo-G glanced at J-Bo. "You owe him some more time, folk?"

"Hell naw," he answered.

Bo-G pulled his knife from its hiding spot. It was a foot long piece of metal about the same width as King Kong's finger. The base was wrapped with a sheet for good grip and the end was razor sharp. He tucked it in his shorts.

"Y'all gotcha guns?" he asked.

They all nodded, and Bo-G took the lead to Quan's room. When all the GD's saw the four of them walking in silence, they quietly went and strapped up just in case shit hit the fan. Bo-G tapped on Quan's door twice, then pulled it open.

"What's up?" he asked with a frowned face. J-Bo, Flip and Bull were on his heels.

There were five Bloods in the room obviously for the phone's usage.

"What's bangin?" one of them asked.

That pissed Bo-G off; he was GD to death. "Ain't shit bangin, folk! Come on wit' that phone!" he bellowed, taking a step in the room, showing them he meant business.

J-Bo, Flip and Bull followed.

"Aye, look, blood—" Quan was saying.

"We ain't cha mothafuckin blood, folk!" J-Bo bucked. "And I don't owe you no time, nigga. Fuck wrong witchu?"

One of the blood dudes whispered something to Quan then he handed the phone over to Bo-G.

"Simple shit like that is what start wars," Bo-G said as they exited.

"Man, nigga, fuck y'all pussies! Blood gang or no gang!" Quan lashed out. He acted as if he was trying to rush Bo-G, but he knew his homies were going to hold him back.

Bo-G laughed at his false attempt to fight.

"GD!" one of the Gangstas yelled from downstairs.

Bo-G held his hand to a halt the advance.

"These niggas ain't tawmbout shit, folk!" he yelled loud enough for the entire ninety-six-man dorm to hear him. "Let's go," he said to the GD's closest to him.

Chapter Eight

"You told him a hunnid?" Peanut asked from the passenger seat. Smoke was behind the wheel, maintaining the speed limit. It was dark, and aside from their head beams, the only light was from the occasional streetlamp they passed at intervals or gas stations alongside the road.

"Yea," Smoke said. He says it's his baby mama's uncle or some shit."

"Damn—he didn't say why?"

Smoke shook his head. "We finna find out now, baby boy." He turned into the Sheraton Hotel, parked, then dialed Shawn's number. He answered, said only the room number, then hung up.

They went through the big hotel and located Shawn's room. He was likely looking through the peephole because the door swung open before they could knock.

Smoke and Peanut looked past Shawn, saw nothing but darkness, and looked at each other.

"Turn the lights on," Smoke said.

They did good business, but when it came down to their lives, Smoke wasn't good at giving many people his trust. Shawn flipped the lights on, and they entered and took their seats on the sofa.

"It's yo' ol' lady's fam, huh?" Peanut asked, to fill the awkward silence.

Shawn nodded. He went to the kitchen area of the suite and returned with a bottle of brandy. He asked, with a gesture, were they interested.

Smoke frowned. "Naw, man. We ain't here for that shit. We here for this information and money."

Shawn nodded, taking a seat across from them. He hit the bottle, barely opening his lips, then placed it on the coffee table separating them. He pulled a small cotton sack from the side of the couch and tossed it to Smoke, who opened it and pulled the neat stacks out.

"That ain't a hunnid G's," Peanut exclaimed. It was obvious by the size. He knew what a hundred looked liked.

"It's fifty." Shawn sat the bottle on the coffee table and leaned forward, resting elbows to knees, hands folded one on top of the other.

Smoke twitched at the sight of his missing two front teeth.

"The fuck hap—" he began, but he stopped himself, figuring it had something to do with the guy he wants dead.

"Half now, half when he takes his last breath," he said, ignoring Smoke's reaction. "Just know that sonofabitch violated big time! I want that bitch tortured! I want his fingers cut off, and his dick cut off and stuffed down his throat."

The hate he carried for whoever had done this to him was evident. "Yea, he fucked you up," Smoke added.

Shawn stood and started pacing the floor.

"You say you not here for drinks," Shawn said. "That means you not here for jokes either, mothafucka!"

Smoke looked at Peanut, and Peanut shook his head, recognizing that Smoke wanted to kill Shawn and simply take the money.

"Just give us the info so we can leave," Peanut said softly.

Shawn grabbed a small manila envelope from the countertop and tossed it to Peanut.

"That's my baby mama's address, do not hurt her or my son!" he said. "But her uncle comes around a lot. His picture and phone number are in there."

Peanut tucked the pocket-sized envelope and stood to exit.

"Name?" Smoke asked.

"Kenneth."

Smoke nodded, and the two made their way to the door.

Shawn turned the bottle upside down and drank as if it was only water. He sat on the loveseat and tried Shakeena's line, but the results remained the same: no answer.

***

"That nigga beat the shit outta Shawn," Smoke laughed, putting the car in reverse, backing out of the hotel's parking space.

Peanut giggled. "Yea, buddy mutilated his ass."

Smoke laughed so hard he choked, turning into traffic.

Peanut pat his friend on the back. "Tighten up, nigga! You bet not crash this bitch."

"I'm good, homie," he continued laughing.

"So." Smoke adjusted the rearview mirror. "You gon' help me kill this nigga or you gon' leave it in God's hands?" He bit his tongue so in order not to laugh before Peanut answered.

"God bless, my friend," he bowed his head and prayed softly.

Smoke couldn't hold it in any longer. He laughed out loud. "You dumb as hell, shawty!"

***

Ken relaxed on the leather sofa in his living room with his family, his thoughts heavy. The thought of Nae finding out his deepest, darkest secret was repulsive. Sometimes he wished Smoke's shells would have killed his wife, but he regretted that thought when he remembered how peaceful and happy he felt with her and KJ.

In a way, he set himself up for this. Although he hadn't developed feelings for her until after the fact, he should've been more disciplined to walk away. He thought things would be easier to sweep under the rug with Diamond gone, but the world is small. Of all the prisons in Georgia, and all the cells at that prison, how could J-Bo end up roommates with Nae's dad.

If worst come to worst, she gotta die. And if—

Ken's phone brought him out of his dark reverie. "Yea?" he answered.

"Go get a five hundred dolla green dot," J-Bo instructed.

Ken played it cool, face an emotionless mask. He knew what time it was. He got up smooth, making his way to the door.

"That's all you need, homie?" He didn't want J-Bo to feel as if he was chumping him off. Then again, he practically owed him this body as much blood was on his hands because of him.

"Yea that's it," J-Bo answered, knowing he could get whatever he wanted.

"A'ight, I'll call you back in twenty minutes." He hung up, grabbed his keys and rushed to the garage.

"Fuck!" he squawked when he hit his right hand on the back of the couch. It caused excruciating pain.

Slow down, Ken, he told himself. He knew this was going to break Nae's heart, but he had to do what he had to do.

***

"Fuck wrong wit' dem pussy ass niggas, folk?" one of the gangstas asked.

They were piled up in Bo-G's room like sardines in a can.

"We gon' handle that, but you," Bo-G pointed to Fry. "You gotta bust somebody up."

Fry was twenty-four years old, and had been in prison from age seventeen. He was serving life without the possibility of parole for the murder of two McDonald's' employees during an armed robbery. He'd joined the GD organization while in the county jail.

This wasn't his first time being in the position to stab somebody. Besides, he enjoyed it because he liked proving his point to the brothers that's been gangbanging on the streets. Some street bangers had the notion that anybody who joined in jail or prison is scared to stand alone. Nobody believed this more than Bo-G, which was the reason he had picked Fry. That, along with the fact he was never going to be released anyway.

"And you gotta kill 'em, G."

The room was silent.

"Say no more." Fry was eager.

"We gon' wait til' this money come through, so if dey catch you, you can leave wit' some bread."

Fry nodded.

"After this shit die down, we gon' kill some of dem blood niggas." Bo-G looked around the room for any who seemed reluctant, but he found none.

***

"You wanna get started on this today?" Peanut held up the small envelope Shawn had given them. They were just coming through the door of their condo.

"We'll do it later," Smoke replied.

"But what we can do today is split that money." Peanut threw him the small sack and went in the bedroom to secure the delicate information, and when he returned to the living room, Smoke handed him a stack of bills. Peanut trusted the man, and he felt no need to count his share.

"Aye, Smoke. You know I love you, right?" Peanut sat across from him.

"Don't start that soft shit, Peanut," he stated.

"We ain't gon' be able to be homies foreva."

Smoke paused, then looked sharply at the man. "Whatchu mean?"

"Once I start walking wit' the Lord one hunnid percent, I'ma have to leave all of you alone."

"You is Young Boss to death," Smoke stated. You ain't leaving shit."

Peanut nodded. "Okay."

"So, what you gon' say when Ken tell Tez to knock yo' dumb ass off?"

Peanut smiled. "I'ma thank God for life and ask him to have mercy on my soul."

Smoke sucked his teeth and looked at Peanut sideways. "*I'ma thank God*—Nigga, you sound stupid! Thank God for *this*!" He lifted the couch's armrest and pulled out a bag of weed.

***

Fry lurked for hours, waiting for the right opportunity to present itself until finally Frank was walking along the top range in boxers and shower shoes, headed to the shower. Fry sat on the bench pretending to watch the TV program. Bull locked eyes with him and nodded.

I'm sorry, Frank, J-Bo thought as he saw how it was about to unfold. The tension was thick. Death was in the air for those who knew the smell. There were cold stares from the Bloods all day. It was likely they thought the others were afraid because the stares had gone unchallenged. Bo-G had something in store for them as well.

Fry went and retrieved his knife and headed to the shower. Frank was washing his hair when Fry pulled back the curtains and slid in on him. His eyes were closed, and he was singing Sir Charles' *Anybody Lonely.* Fry jugged him on the top of the head twice with the weapon, and streaks of blood began to pour from the wound. Frank choked on the lyrics and screamed. Blood spurted from the second blow, adding a red blend to the white foam of shampoo. Frank stumbled under the shower head and back against the wall, where he caught himself then swung back. His fist, however, was nothing compared to Fry's knife.

Fry went into a fury. "Nigga, shut up!" Fry snarled, stabbing him in the neck, face and head. Blood ran down the wall to mingle with the water on the floor, running a diluted trail toward the drain. Thick jelly clots falling from his body got caught at the drain. The clots bobbed between the grate, clung, and slowly dissipated from view.

"J-Bo!" Frank cried. "J-Bo, help!"

Weak from the assault, Frank slid down the wall to his naked butt with Fry jugging relentlessly. His cries were the first to stop, then came the end to his fight. His ragged breathing was the last to go. And to make sure his life was gone as well, Fry buried the weapon deep into his throat, wedging a jagged tear into his trachea.

Fry left Frank's shower and slid into the next one over.

Chapter Nine

There were but a few things to contend with preparing a family meal after having explosive sex with your husband. Nae was in bliss. She was at the stove with a plate, laying spice over an Italian plate of Risotto, as she contemplated Ken's recent performance. She was certain that he had taken something to assist with that session; he hadn't given her sex like that in some time now.

"You're the best daddy ever!" KJ exclaimed. He sat at the table across from his father.

The comment brought a smile to Ken's face. "Why am I the best daddy ever?"

"Because—You buy me toys, clothes, and you help my mama with all the bills."

The child was oblivious to Ken having mega bucks and being more than a helper to his mother.

"Oh yea," KJ said. "I want to play with my cousin. Can he come over this weekend?" he spoke of JJ.

"I'll see," Ken looked to Nae as she approached the table with two plates in her hand.

"Why daddy always get more food?" KJ huffed at the sight of his father's large plate.

"Because he's the boss." Nae scooted his chair closer to the table.

Ken smiled. "Damn right."

KJ giggled and covered his mouth with one hand and pointed at his father with the other.

"Daddy said a cuss word."

Nae adored her family. In some ways she hated having an affair, especially with Tez being her husband's right-hand man. However, it was utopia-like with Tez. That sonofabitch!

"Babe," Nae said. "You know my dad will be getting out soon."

Ken nodded.

"And," she hesitated, "I want him to come here for a while until he's ready to work."

He looked puzzled. "So, you're saying you wanna take care of a grown ass man until he decides to go to work? That's absurd."

Nae's heart sank. Her husband's objection to the idea was clear. She had hoped it wouldn't be this way.

"Ken, twenty years is a long time—"

"I don't wanna hear that sad shit. He didn't get twenty years for no reason, now did he?"

Nae noticed KJ was just finishing his dinner. "Honey," she said to him, "go upstairs and brush ya teeth. And get all ya stuff ready. I'll be up there to run ya bath water in a minute."

"Okay." He left his plate there and jetted upstairs.

"Why do you continue to cuss in front of him?" she pointed at their child as he ran.

He sipped his glass of red wine. "Because I can."

She knew she wasn't going to win that way, so she figured it was best to get back on subject.

"Ken, listen, my dad is an old man. Yes, he made a terrible mistake, but he's gonna need a strong support system. After twenty years, don't you feel he deserves to kick back for a while?" She stood and walked to her husband.

He had just taken his last bite. "I'm not going to allow my wife to coddle a grown ass man in my home."

She began massaging his shoulders.

"So," she sat on his lap and slow-grind, trying to feel his soldier stand up. "Not in your house. Well, can I buy him a small house around here somewhere?"

It looked as if she was riding his dick, only difference was they were both fully clothed.

"Yea, a lil' cheap house."

It didn't matter if she got him a twenty-thousand-dollar house or a two-hundred-thousand-dollar house. It wouldn't hurt Ken's pockets at all.

"They say pussy rules the universe," she stated as she began undressing.

Ken unbuckled his pants also.

"They say a lot of shit," he answered, anticipating what his wife was going to do first.

She dropped to her knees and took his dick in her mouth all at once, and Ken let his head back and bit his bottom lip.

"Aww, fuck!" he moaned as his wife gagged on his dick.

She pulled her head back some, so that he was still in her throat. She played with her clit while giving her husband some sloppy wet head.

"Oweee girl," Ken cried out in pleasure.

"Whose dick is this?" She pulled it from her mouth and slapped herself on the face with it as she spoke.

"It's yours, baby," he crooned.

"I can't hear you." She took him in her mouth again while quickly stroking it with her right hand.

"Aw shit, it's yo' dick, Nae!" he moaned a bit louder.

She pulled his dick from her mouth again and began flicking the tip with her tongue. You would have thought she had a motor in her mouth how quickly her tongue moved.

The house phone rang, and Ken cursed silently. Nae looked up and smiled. If they didn't answer it, KJ was surely on his way. She kissed the head of his dick.

"Be right back." Nae got up, got herself together and headed to the phone. "Hello?"

"Am I speaking to Nae Waters?" a voice asked.

She wiped her face with the balled-up shirt. "Yes."

"I'm Stanley Williams, Warden of Smith State Prison. I'm sorry to tell you this, but—your father was stabbed to death this evening."

She dropped the phone and fell to the floor, screaming. Ken rushed in the kitchen and found her on the floor sobbing uncontrollably.

"Who the fuck is that?" Ken asked, having caught her reaction. At the same time, he knew what it must be.

Chapter Ten

Ken awoke unusually early the next morning. He couldn't sleep well after Nae's nervous breakdown. Ken spoke to the warden and verified that her father was the victim by murder, and all night she went through hell accepting it. Dried tears could still be seen on her face. Ken licked his thumb and wiped them away as his cell vibrated.

"Yea," he answered.

It was Susie calling about a meeting he needed to attend, but he told her to attend in his place due to his wife's emotional state. However, Susie was quick to remind him that failure to appear in person could result in the loss of a fortune.

"Alright," Ken finally relented. "Have Mystro get the choppa ready. I'll be there in forty-five." He hung up.

"Please tell me I was just hearing things," Nae said softly. She referred to him and his plan to leave now, after last night's promise not to leave her side until she could deal with reality and go back to work.

"I'm sorry, love. It's a very urgent meeting in New York that I must attend in five hours."

"Ken, it's your fucking company," her voice cracked. "Why can't you make Susie go?"

He hated seeing his wife desperate for his presence. He leaned closer to her.

"Because this is going to be the biggest tour collaboration in history." He kissed her face and lips. "Block Runner and Young Boss, they don't want to meet with managers and reps. They want to see me personally." He planted another kiss on her lips as tears fell from her eyes. "Come on, Nae. Now is not the time to be weak."

She sat up to face him. "Ken, my mama, sister, and daddy are all gone, and you have the nerve to tell me to stop being weak?"

She broke down crying. He wanted so badly to show affection, but somebody had to be strong.

"Come here, Baby." He pulled her in for a hug. "You gotta be strong for them. They're good. To live in the hearts we leave behind is not to die. Don't let this steal yo' joy, okay. It'll get greater later."

Nae was still upset about him leaving, but she found the words comforting. She nodded, and he kissed her gently then took off to the shower. She laid back and her mind raced with thoughts of Diamond, their mother, her father and her own relationship with Ken. She disliked the fact that Ken's ownership of Young Boss caused him to travel a lot, but in some cases she enjoyed his time away; it was in those moments she enjoyed her time with Tez.

Every time her father crossed her mind, she thought of heaven, and it didn't hurt as bad. She'd learned that from counseling during the beginning of their marriage when she was going through it about Diamond.

Ken moved rapidly from the bathroom to the enormous walk-in closet. The sight of him clothed in nothing but a towel made her pussy throb. She knew he didn't have time to penetrate her, *but someone does,* she thought. She stood at the threshold of the closet in her pajamas, watching her husband dress.

"After I close this deal with Block Runner," he dropped the towel and slid in his polo boxers and socks. The sight moistened her. "We're gonna go to the Bahamas for six months and relax." He put on his Robin jeans and pulled a Gucci sweater over his white tee.

"You promise, baby?"

He looked at her. "I promise, baby."

"I'm horny, Ken," she whined.

He slid in his Gucci shoes, put his YBE chain on, then reached in a pink box and pulled out a dildo and tossed it to her.

"When I get back, I got you." He kissed her and rushed out.

The toy was great. It even had a switch on it for vibration and a prong that massaged her clit while she fucked herself. She endeavored to use the toy, but she wasn't satisfied. She wanted the real deal. She replaced the dildo to its box, grabbed her phone and made the call.

***

Flip entered the visitation room and looked around for Daneisha. He spotted her, handed her his ID card to the officers, signed the chart and approached his table. She stood for a hug, and it appeared she was almost a foot taller than him. Snacks and hot wings were already sprucely prepared for him on the table. Years ago, his pride would have denied her visit because of her poor appearance, but as far she could control, she was fine. Her hair, nails, brows and lashes were done. Not to mention she was fresh.

"Hey." She was happy to see her man. They hugged, kissed, and he gripped her ass before they took their seats.

"What's up, girl?" he stated, opening a bag of sour cream and onion chips.

"I called your cousin's phone a million times yesterday," she exaggerated.

He laughed. "A nigga got killed last night, shawty."

Her mouth dropped in disbelief. "You bullshitting?"

"Hell nah, our dorm locked down now. I'm surprised they allowed this visit."

"You be careful in here, Phillip," she showed concern.

He looked through his peripherals and saw Quan and his delicately beautiful woman visitor looking in his direction, laughing uncontrollably. Once Flip looked their way, they turned their heads, so it was confirmed that they thought something was funny.

***

Smoke was spooned naked in bed with Asia. Tiffany entered the room in the nude and smacked Asia on the butt.

"Wake up, Big Booty. We gotta go take pictures."

Asia smiled. "Oh, shit. I forgot," she yawned.

"That dick ain't that good," she pointed to Smoke's flaccid penis.

Asia laughed hard as Smoke sat up.

"Come lick it and see how good it is," Smoke's ego spoke.

"I did before and it was terrible," she joked.

The two strippers were best friends and they'd both fucked and sucked each other's man during the famous foursomes they had from time to time, but it was established that they don't fuck each other's man one on one. Asia grabbed his boxers from the floor and put it on top of his dick.

Tiffany rolled her eyes. "Girl, don't nobody wanna see his lil' dick. Peanut's way bigger," she exclaimed.

"A'ight now, keep talking shit and I'ma get Peanut in here to baptize yo' ass." Smoke smacked his forehead and made his body shiver, acting as if he caught the holy ghost.

The room erupted in laughter.

Tiffany waved him off. "Whatever, nigga. I'm going to hop in the shower. You coming?"

Asia nodded. "Put that up before I suck the skin off it," she playfully nabbed his penis, then she and Tiffany vanished into the bathroom.

Smoke stretched, put on his boxers and shorts, then got up and headed to Peanut's colossal living quarters. He was kneeled before the bed, praying. Smoke shook his head, opened the middle drawer of Peanut's dresser and procured the manila envelope.

Time to get to work, he thought. He put the envelope on the table and went in his bathroom to brush his teeth.

"I bet y'all won't kiss," he said as he watched them bathe each other through the glass door of his walk-in shower.

Asia laughed. "Get yo' freaky ass on!"

After brushing his teeth, he slid into his pajama pants and a white tee, then headed back to the living room. Peanut was on the couch drinking Cîroc straight from the bottle.

"You must got a hangover?" Smoke sat beside him and reached for the envelope. "It's time to go to work, Baby Boy."

***

This pussy ass nigga must wanna end up like Frank, Flip thought as he hugged Daneisha. Everybody who was there since earlier that morning visit was cut short due to a large amount of visitors and not enough chairs.

"Hopefully, next time I can stay the whole time," Daneisha said before kissing him.

"Yea, I know," he replied while shooting diabolic looks at Quan.

"I know I'm not the prettiest thing in the world," she looked down. "I just hope you act the same when you get out."

It was that statement that made him aware that she had caught some of Quan's teasing.

"We ain't finna go there. Come here. I gotchu." He kissed her like she was the prettiest girl in the world and went back towards the inmate exit.

Having been searched, Flip was on the way back to the dorm when he addressed Quan's offensive attitude toward Daneisha.

"Oh, that shit funny, huh?" He was close to flat out assault right on the walk, but he wanted to avoid the hole.

Quan smiled. "That bitch look like a fuckin horse."

They entered the dorm. "By the time we get off lockdown, I'ma have a video of yo' bitch playin' in her pussy and screaming my name."

Quan regretted not deleting his lady's phone number from J-Bo's phone.

"You call my girl, I'ma bust you." He threw up a gang sign.

"Y'all soft ass niggas ain't tawmbout shit," Flip challenged before the officer came in to escort them to their rooms. "I'm Young Boss to death, nigga."

Chapter Eleven

Just as the girls were coming from Smoke's room, he was emptying all the contents from the envelope to the table. They both stood to hug their woman.

"Y'all look great," Peanut complimented.

The condo was like their second home, so they always kept extra clothes and all kinds of girly shit over there.

"We putting on big tonight at the club. Y'all coming?" Asia asked.

"We gotta handle some shit," Smoke answered.

She sucked her teeth. "Uh huh, y'all prolly just want some otha bitches over here tonight."

"We grown," he shot back.

"And?" Tiffany remarked.

"And if we want some otha bitches ova here, ain't gon' be a secret," Peanut set them straight. "We ain't gon' lie and play games. We'll call some otha bitches while y'all ova hea."

"That's right," Smoke added.

They talked a little more shit then shot out the door.

"Fuck wrong wit' them hoes. Like a nigga gotta be incognito 'bout fuckin' off." Smoke reached for the face down photos, and Peanut poured himself a glass of E & J, grabbed the address and phone number and examined its context. Something about the information seemed slightly familiar to him. He took another sip.

"Bra, this is Ken," Smoke said.

Peanut nodded, lost in his thoughts. "Yea, he said the fool's name is Ken."

Smoke studied the picture to ensure he wasn't trippin. "Naw, Peanut. This is our Ken."

"What?" Peanut choked and began coughing, eyes wide in disbelief.

"This is our Ken," Smoke reiterated.

Peanut nabbed the small photo from his friend's hand and lo and behold, he saw a picture of Ken seated behind his desk. It was obtainable from the internet. Peanut dialed the written down number in his phone just to make sure the liquor wasn't playing mind games, but he knew it wasn't the liquor when the saved number showed up as *Big Homie Ken.* They sat in silence for a moment.

"This shit crazy," Smoke said.

Peanut inhaled deeply, and released a heavy sigh. "Yea, it is."

"Ken ain't got no fucking niece, do he?" Smoke scratched his head.

Peanut shrugged. "Shiiid, not that I know of. I ain't e'en know he had siblings."

Smoke grabbed the bottle and sipped. "A hunnid bands ain't enough to kill Ken."

Peanut frowned. "Nigga, ain't no amount enough to kill Ken."

"You know what I mean." A hunnid bands may not be enough, Smoke thought, *but for the right price, anybody can get it.* "I wonder what Ken fucked him up for."

"Hell, I don't know," Peanut said, but we need to call Tez ASAP."

***

After Ken's departure for New York, Nae called Tez then quickly drove KJ to school. Ten minutes after she arrived home, Tez was pulling in the driveway. She cooked him a big breakfast, they spoke of her father, their future together, and the rest of the time was designed for sex. She was positioned doggy style on the floor next to the bed as Tez provided long, slow thrusts. She desired to be on the bed, but he promised himself that he would never disrespect Ken to that degree. He was already crossing the line in a major way as it was. He knew if he was ever caught, death would be the punishment.

"Oh, my gawd! Tez—owww, that dick feels so good! Don't stop!"

Nae's moans made Tez feel like the owner of that pussy. Her butt wasn't too big or small; it was just right, and the sight of it could make a man cum. To have access to it was simply a blessing.

"Whose pussy is this, bitch?" Tez began to fuck her harder.

It felt like his dick was magnifying with every stroke. He dropped some spit on her butthole and forcefully stuck his thumb in it. Her head shot up in pain.

"Ow!," she winced, but as he fucked her pussy harder his thumb in her ass turned to pleasure.

Ken did it once, but it didn't feel this way.

"Look back at me, bitch," he demanded while speeding up his thumb's motion.

She loved when he spoke to her that way while they fucked.

"Tell me to put this dick in yo' ass!"

She loved the look only his eyes held. "Put that dick in my ass, daddy!" she yelled. He pulled his thumb out, bent down, and ate her ass in a way she's never had it eaten before. He got back up and put the tip of his dick in her asshole. Her lips trembled from the pain. He knew he had to break her in, so he put it all the way in her. Her eyes bolted open, and she squawked in pain.

"Bitch, whose ass is this?" he began stroking. It was so tight, Tez knew the explosion was gonna come soon.

Nae gasped. The penetration hurt like hell, but the pleasure soon began to override the pain. "It's yo' ass, Martez! It's all yours!"

"Can I come in this ass?" he asked.

He was gonna do it regardless of what her answer was; he just wanted to ask because talking dirty intensified the sex.

"Ummm! Come in my pussy, Martez!" she looked in his eyes again.

He wanted to so bad, but he didn't want to take advantage of her on that state. Having just recently lost her father, she could very well be thinking irrationally. "Bitch, I said can I come in this ass!" He fucked her harder.

Her head dropped. "Yes, come in my ass." *Maybe I can play wit' it in my pussy once it oozes out my ass,* she thought.

"I love you, Nae!" he stated weakly as he came in her butt.

He slowly pulled out of her, looking at the sticky mess slowly oozing from her anus. She began slightly jiggling her butt cheeks. He held his finger at her hole so all the sperm that came out landed on his index and middle finger. *Shit!* She thought in disappointment.

"Eat this shit," he commanded.

She turned around still on her hands and knees and began sucking his fingers like a dick, being sure to get every drop of cum. He took a deep breath and fell to his back.

She giggled.

"You a piece of work," he said as his phone rang. It was Smoke. He put his index finger to his lips and answered.

"What's up, homie?"

She wondered if it was Ken.

"I need to see you as soon as possible."

He frowned. "What's up, erthang a'ight?"

Nae crawled a couple inches and took his dick in her mouth. She sucked it passionately. He opened his hand, telling her to wait, but she ignored and tooted her ass in the air purposely. Smoke was talking, but Tez didn't hear a word.

"Hold on, Smoke," he said rapidly. He tried to push her head back, but her grip on his dick was like a vice. The big difference was this vice felt fantastic.

"What the fuck?" he asked her in pleasure. "I'm on the phone—" he was cut off by an orgasm.

"Ummm," she jacked him hard, repeatedly smacking her face with his dick.

There was cum on her forehead, in her hair, nose, lips, chin, and a small portion got in her mouth.

"Yea, Smoke, what's up, homie?" he asked after she went to the bathroom to get the nut from her face.

"Just slide through, man. It's Young Boss business."

Tez could tell Smoke was peeved by his lack of attention.

"Aye, my bad, homie. Talk to me." He stood up searching for his boxers. He found them on the stairs where they originally started.

"Can't speak of it on the phone. I said Young Boss business."

Tez nodded. "A'ight, gimme a few." He hung up.

I'm trippin, he thought. Whenever a member says Young Boss business, you're supposed to stop doing whatever you're doing and attend to it unless what you're already doing is Young Boss business. Tez was slippin'. Was he in a way putting Nae over Young Boss business?

"You're a fucking nympho," he said while dressing.

She took it as an expression of admiration. "You not gon' get in the shower wit' me?"

He looked up at her, considering the offer, but he refrained himself.

"Nah, I gotta handle something urgent."

She turned her back to him and bent all the way over, touching her toes. She used her hands to spread her butt cheeks and reveal her orifice. The view was enthralling, but Young Boss business came first.

"Clean this house up." He stood. "It smells like sex."

He kissed her then exited.

The love she had for Tez was inevitable after losing her sister and father. She was just ready to be happy. She knew her and Tez were compatible. *I gotta make this shit happen*, she thought, going into the bathroom to get the wedding ring from the counter.

"Yes, Martez, I will marry you," she said, slipping the ring in place. Her affectionate concern and passionate attraction to Tez was intense. So much so, that she was full steam ahead, even if it cost her life.

***

"That nigga Tez on some otha shit," Smoke hung up the phone.

"What you say?" Peanut was baffled as to what Tez had said. He knew Smoke was irritated on the phone by his facial expressions.

"Nigga putting me on hold and shit." Smoke pulled on the Kush-filled Dutch Master. "Then I say Young Boss business," he exhaled. "This nigga tawmbout *talk to me*."

"Talk to me? The fuck he mean? Nigga, you betta pull up." Peanut grabbed the weed from Smoke

"That's right." Smoke exhaled.

Peanut's phone beeped and he smiled. "Look, them hoes takin pictures fa *Straight Stuntin.*" He handed Smoke the phone.

Straight Stuntin is an almost nude magazine for exotic strippers, pornstars, and the baddest of the bad. High-class bitches only. Tiffany had sent him a few shots that they took so far.

Smoke cheesed hard. "Dem bitches turnt up!"

Peanut pointed to the photo of Ken so Smoke wouldn't get all worked up and fail to function effectively.

***

Tez's phone signaled a call as he parked next to Smoke's Benz. Stepping out of the car, he answered, "Hello?"

"I need a favor," Ken said.

He suddenly felt that Ken was aware of his treachery. "What's up, homie?"

"My wife."

Tez's heart accelerated as he began to imagine the consequences.

"What about her?" Tez played it cool, knocking on Smoke's door.

"Where you at?" Ken asked, having heard the knock.

"Smoke nem crib," he answered as Smoke opened the door and he entered.

"Okay. Tell the homies to keep up the good work. But she's goin' through hard times now. She just lost her dad, and I don't want her wallowing in sorrow." He paused.

Tez stood the entire time.

"I want you to take her a big bouquet of flowers. Tell her that I love her and will be home soon."

"A'ight, let me check on the homies, then I got you." He knew Ken was in New York from Nae.

"A'ight, Young Boss."

"Young Boss." Tez hung up and gave dap to Smoke and Peanut. "What's up, bra?"

"Boy, yo' hands smell like ass!" Smoke shouted, and him and Peanut laughed hard.

A grin covered Tez's face as he reminisced the reason his hand smelled that way. He went to the kitchen and washed his hands with dish detergent. Smoke was lighting another vanilla Dutch when he returned.

"Aye, Ken got a niece?" Peanut asked.

"Hell naw," Tez said.

"The nigga that we supply from Savann—"

Tez cut him off. "Hold up, why you ask me if Ken had a niece?"

Smoke held his hand to a halt. "Let him talk, please."

Tez nodded.

"The nigga that we supply from Savannah," Peanut reiterated. "He want us to knock somebody for him."

Tez shrugged. "And what's the point?" He was devoid of any moral compass in regard to murder for hire.

"It's his baby mama's uncle." Smoke pulled hard on the blunt and passed it to Tez.

"Maybe this weed gon' calm me down." Tez took a seat on the abandoned sofa across from them. "Cos if y'all on some sensitive shit, don't wanna kill a nigga 'cause he family with ol' boy type shit, y'all done really pissed me off!" Tez hit the blunt and exhaled.

The photo of Ken was faced down on the table.

"You know my heart cold to anybody if dey ain't Young Boss." Smoke ensured his ruthlessness.

"Aye, listen, man, cut all the bullshit right now. What's the problem?" Tez sat up and looked from one to the other.

Smoke turned the picture over. "This is a picture of the guy he wants dead."

Tez studied the picture in confusion. "What the fuck? Did he say any reason?" Tez wanted to cover the bases.

Smoke shook his head. "He said he violated or some shit like that. His face was kinda knotted up. He was missing his two fronts. I don't think that got shit to do with Ken, but I guess it could be a start."

Seconds after Tez passed the blunt to Peanut, he remembered Ken saying he fucked Shawn up. “Shawn.” Tez smiled. “I hate it because he spends good money. I love it because it’s minus another pussy ass nigga that’s plotting on a Young Boss.”

Peanut and Smoke looked at each other.

“Whatchu talkin’ bout?” Smoke asked, baffled.

“He gotta die ASAP,” Tez ordered. “We can’t afford to let him live because he might begin feeling froggy.”

They nodded, and he explained the story of Ken and Shawn’s physical altercation the way it was explained to him.

“So, you want us to go after him?” Smoke asked.

Tez shook his head. “No, he paid y’all half already?”

Peanut nodded.

“Tell him y’all completed the mission and go to pick up the other half. After he pays up, kill him.” The blunt was coming back to him.

“You can wait til’ he wanna re-up again and y’all just split that seven hundred cuz he ain’t getting no dope, then kill him.” He pulled on the blunt. “I don’t really give a fuck how it’s done; it just need to be done and fast.”

Smoke nodded.

“Y’all know we got Young Bosses all over Georgia and Detroit and y’all is in the top five of top dogs. I’m proud of y’all niggas. Ken says keep up the good work.” He stood and gave the weed to Peanut.

“Leavin’?” Smoke asked.

“Yea, I gotta do some shit for Ken, then I gotta halla at the Mexicans to meet the homies in the Midwest. You know dem punk ass Mexicans don’t like to travel.”

They stood and dapped him up.

“If you a real Young Boss, let me know how you feel.”

They put their right hand over their hearts and their words coincided.

“Young boss over everything. I love my Young Boss more than anything. If u ain’t Young Boss u lost. 25-2, I’ll neva cross.”

Tez smiled.

Chapter Twelve

Nae opened the door and immediately thought her mind was playing tricks on her, seeing her boo standing there with a big bouquet of flowers. She thought it was his introduction to their departure. She almost turned red once becoming knowledgeable who they were from. Chagrin could be seen on her face. She was ready for Tez to liberate her from her responsibilities as Ken's spouse. She asked for another session; he denied, then went to their trap spot on the Southside.

Damn, Shawn! he thought. He tried calling Ken three times, but he got no answer. He knew he was attending to business up north; therefore, he decided to call J-Bo.

"Yo?" J-Bo answered.

Tez knew that once J-Bo and Flip were released, Ken would appoint them superior over him within the Young Boss rankings.

"What's good, Big Bra?"

Tez relaxed on the couch.

"Ain't shit, we locked down now. What's up?"

"You know yo' peoples from Savannah that we serve?"

Silence.

"Yea, what about em?" J-Bo was curious.

"He tryna put a numba on Ken's head. I gotta do what I gotta do."

J-Bo was taken aback. He couldn't fathom why.

"What the fuck? Why?" he asked tentatively.

Shit! Tez thought. It was obvious that Ken hadn't put J-Bo up on game about Shakeena's diabolic ways, and he hated to be the one to tell him.

"You gon' have to get all the details from Ken. I don't know too much about it," he lied.

"A'ight, shawty, make sure it's clean." He hung up, wishing there was a way to spare Shawn on the strength of Savannah Mike. Losing the ones you love while doing time was the worst feeling ever.

That shit hit different.

***

After the meeting with Diezel and Pain, the founders and owners of Block Runner, Ken spoke to Psycho and decided to go halla at him since they were in the same city. A cab was responsible for dropping him off at the Hilton. He noticed a few missed calls from Tez after the meeting, but he feared it would be bad news or something within the street operation that would steal his joy. Therefore, he decided to speak to him at a later convenience. Psycho opened the door the moment his line began ringing again.

"What's up, boy?" Ken asked, hugging him excitedly.

"What's up?" Psycho responded in the same fashion.

Ken glanced back and saw Lil Dread recording with one of their audio engineers. Ken put up the peace sign, not wanting to interrupt his session, and pulled Psycho in the kitchen part of the suite.

"Nigga!" Ken emphasized that word. "Do you understand this tour is gonna be huge? Listen, homie." Their smiles coincided. "Psycho, this is a hundred-and-eighty-day tour— two hundred thousand a show—Block Runner get one, we get one."

Psycho's face showed a bit of unease, and Ken knew it was because of him and Rada's conversation about his finances.

"Look, homie," he put his hand on Psycho's shoulder. "After this six-month tour, I promise to modify ya contracts. You'll get half of every sell and every tour."

Psycho was ecstatic.

"Do you understand how much paper we finna make in six months, Psycho?" Ken was clearly excited.

Psycho shook his head

"Hell, I don't either. I need a calculator!" Ken exclaimed. They both laughed.

"Keep doing what you doing, homie." He looked at his watch, understanding that his visit had already been sustained long enough. "Check the move, though. I'm finna head out."

Psycho's face showed shallow disappointment. "Damn, you out already?"

Ken didn't want to leave so soon. "Yea, man. My wife needs me home."

Psycho threw a playful hook to his stomach. "Let me find out you getting soft."

Ken held up his unbandaged but still swollen fist.

"The fuck happened?" he frowned.

"Had to knock a lil' ruddy poot ass nigga like you out who thought I was soft.

Psycho tried to refrain laughing, but it was inevitable.

"I love you, lil' bra," Ken hugged him before leaving.

***

Ms. Smith assigned Flip to J-Bo's room after the officers packed all of Frank's property and took it to intake. She was J-Bo's mule. She brought anything he requested. He paid her, of course. She was a thirty-year-old slim, swarthy, Haitian woman. J-Bo gave her two five-hundred-dollar green dots. She's supposed to bring him a couple cans of tobacco, an ounce of weed, and give him and Flip some pussy tonight.

"You still got dem numbas that fuck nigga Quan called, right?" Flip asked his cousin, hoping he hadn't erased the call log.

"Hell yea. Why?" he asked, already having a hint.

After Flip explained, J-Bo smiled.

"We finna have that hoe screamin' both of our names."

J-Bo understood that money was the ruler of the universe. Nowadays you could make a bitch suck an AIDS dick for the right amount of ducats.

"Hello?" her voice blared over the speaker phone.

Flip went and looked through the small window on the door, ensuring that no police was in the dorm. It was clear.

"Aye, you the broad that Quan fuck with?" J-Bo calmly asked, laying back on his bed.

"Yea, who's this?" she asked.

"My name J-Bo," he smiled. "Quan show me pictures of you all the time and you are so fucking beautiful."

She giggled. "Thanks." She didn't quite know what else to say; it felt awkward.

J-Bo winked at his cousin.

"I got a proposition for you. What's ya name?"

"Shay, and what kinda proposition?" Listening, Flip could tell she was a bit alarmed.

"Play in that pussy for me and my cuzzo—"

She hung up on him before he could finish.

Flip laughed. "She wanna play tough, huh?"

"I got this, little cuz," J-Bo ensured while redialing her number.

She answered on the second ring and went slap the fuck off. "Aye, look, you perverted bitch! Stop callin' my fucking phone!"

"Listen, here." J-Bo endured her disrespect because he was on a mission. "I got a two-hundred dolla green dot for the video."

The line was silent. Thinking she had hung up again, he looked at the screen but she hadn't, which meant she was taking the offer into consideration. J-Bo reiterated the offer to push the issue.

She sucked her teeth. "How I know you ain't lyin?"

"Baby, I'ma boss." J-Bo pointed to his locker box, telling Flip to open it. "I don't play no games, Baby Girl."

He pointed to his small address book on the second shelf after Flip opened his property box.

"You gotta give me the money first," she shot back.

"Nah, we ain't rocking like that. Just shut up and listen." He called the green dot hotline on three-way and typed the fourteen digits in.

"To verify you will be loading two hundred dollars," the recording stated, then he hung up that line.

"Send that video and it's yours. I'm J-Bo, my cousin's name is Flip."

He was about to hang up until she said, "You betta not show nobody!"

He hung up, jumped up and dapped his cousin up.

"I'ma boss," he said.

Flip made a silly face and mocked him in a sarcastic tone. "I'ma boss."

***

Ken strutted from the hotel, stood at the end of the sidewalk, and waved for a cab. The sun was up in a cloudless sky, but it was a cool day. He smiled at the sight of the Big Apple. It was such a beautiful city to him. The cab slowed to a stop at the curb, and several other cars continued pass it. Ken opened the backdoor, climbed in and closed the door behind him. There was an Arab driver in the front.

He glanced at Ken through the rearview. "Where to, my friend?"

"Downtown Manhattan Heliport at Pier 6 & South Street. East River," Ken said.

"Okey-dokey, no problem." The driver hit the meter and pulled off into traffic.

Ken rode in silence, taking in the big city with business plans on his mind for the better half of the ride. Just as his thoughts shifted to Nae, his phone went off. Glancing at his screen, he saw that it was J-Bo and answered quickly.

"Yea?"

"Aye, folk, what the hell goin' on with my people from Savannah?" J-Bo got straight to the point.

"Nothing from my understanding." He searched his memory. "Is everything good with that guy?" He spoke of Frank, already knowing the answer, but this was their first time speaking since the hit, so he wanted to hear it from J-Bo's mouth.

"Yea, man, that's good, but listen," he paused, thinking of how to say this. Tez had told him to get the details from Ken, so how could he not know anything?

"Tez told me they gotta body him and told me to get the details from you."

The cab made a sharp turn into the heliport, forcing Ken's body to slide over. He stretched his arm out and held the door for balance.

"What the fuck!" he barked to the driver.

"Sorry, sir." The cab driver found a parking space and pulled to a stop.

Ken thought hard about what the hell Tez could possibly be talking about as far as killing Shawn, but he figured it had something to do with telling him of Shakeena's betrayal. He handed the driver one bill and walked to the chartered side where his helicopter awaited.

"I'ma find out what the hell he talking about, but since we speaking of that clown from S.A.V, there's something that you must know." Ken hated to tell him, but he knew it had to be done.

J-Bo was silent. Ken knew his words were about to rend his friend's heart whether he chose to express it or not.

"The fool Shawn—he umm—" his words were staggering. "J-Bo, you do know Keena been fucking with somebody, right?" First, he wanted to ensure that J-Bo didn't believe his baby mama isn't fucking.

"Of course, Ken. I've been gone damn near a decade. I'm not dumb, bro."

His understanding made Ken feel relieved for a split second.

"I'm gonna make a long story short," he said while approaching his helicopter.

"And give me the real deal," J-Bo let it be known he didn't want the uncut version of whatever Ken had to say.

"The fool Shawn is Keena's man." He boarded the helicopter and signaled to the pilot that it's time to depart. "I whooped his ass because he—never mind that." He was growing frustrated. "The bitch got JJ thinking that you're dead and got him callin' that nigga *daddy*. She also got Shawn thinking JJ's his." Ken laid it on thick.

Silence.

He looked at his phone to verify that J-Bo was still on the line, and he was. The pilot hit a few switches and made a call to the tower through the radios to clarify that it's safe for him to depart into the air.

"Ken, how do you know this?" He hoped like hell that his friend's information was inaccurate, but he knew it wasn't. One, Ken doesn't play games and two, Shakeena hasn't shown her face nor has she been returning his calls or texts. Ken told him what happened from the conversation with JJ in the mall all the way to him punching Shawn out.

"Damn," J-Bo said. The pain could be heard in his voice.

"Mr. Griffith, we're about to go airborne. Please turn off the device, so my frequencies won't be bothered," the pilot said.

Ken nodded. "J-Bo, I'm sorry bro, but I'm about to fly. I gotta hang up. I'll set up a visit as soon as I touch."

"A'ight, Young Boss." He ended the call.

The fuck Tez got goin' on with Shawn? Ken thought as his helicopter became airborne.

***

"Dammmn, folk." J-Bo flopped on his bed. He was hurt. He knew it was true, but there was a part of him deep down inside that refused to believe it.

"What's up, Cuz?" Flip asked from the toilet where he was taking a shit. His blanket was hanging between his property box and under his mat for privacy. They called it a "tent".

"This hoe Keena." The pitch in his words got louder.

Flip was confused. *Is this nigga ova there cryin'?* He concluded his business and flushed the toilet, able to hear the stuttering sniffles of a suppressed cry, even more so once the toilet completed its cycle.

"Cuz? Cuz, you a'ight?" He knew J-Bo was definitely crying now.

"Yea, folk." He wiped his eyes with his t-shirt.

Flip washed his hands, took down the tent, and went to sit next to his cousin. J-Bo's head was bowed, and the tears flowed freely. Flip grabbed the phone from his hand and checked the call log, finding Ken as the last caller.

The sight of J-Bo broken down in this manner disturbed him to no end. "What did Ken say, Cuz?"

"Nine years," J-Bo wept. "Nine fucking years and this bitch got another nigga thinkin' JJ is his."

Flip remembered J-Bo getting a blood test. In fact, he even read the results.

"What?" Flip asked. "Why would she do that?"

J-Bo shrugged.

"You know JJ is yours, cuz. Don't let that get to you, bro. You a boss."

He made it sound so easy.

Chapter Thirteen

Clear of the helicopter, Ken called Tez and told him to meet him at the office. He held a quick meeting with Susie, updating her on the status of the Block Runner and Young Boss tour, giving her instruction to ensure everyone and everything was prepared for the move. She left the office, and in minutes she alerted him to Tez's presence.

"What's up, Fam?" Ken greeted, extending his hand over the desk.

Tez shook Ken's hand and took a seat across from him.

"Talk to me," he said gravely.

"Obviously, Shawn don't know that Smoke and Peanut is our people," he paused. "He called himself hiring them to kill you."

Ken wore a baffled mask. He threw both his hands up as if to say, *Why*?

"Because you beat the shit outta shawty in front of his bitch. He feels like he went out bad."

"Wow, well, how did you respond upon learning this?" Ken needed to know that Tez did take action already.

"He'll be dead soon," Tez ensured.

Ken gave a nod. "I told J-Bo about Keena. He played it cool, but I know it fucked him up." That task left a lesion on his heart simply because he heard the hurt in his friend's voice. Also, he could feel it in the awkward silence they shared.

"He a man, he'll get over it," Tez said.

"Are the Mexicans gonna meet the homies in the D?" Ken switched to business. He was planning on making Tez boss. Therefore, he has to be 100% certain that Tez is on his shit and ready to handle the task.

"Yea, they said they'll go as far as Ohio, and the homies says that's fine."

He leaned back and locked his hands behind his head.

Ken chuckled. "My nigga."

Tez smiled. "I'm just doing my job, homie."

"Mr. Griffith," Susie's voice came over the system. "I'm going for lunch. Would you like anything?"

"No, I won't be in that much longer, thank you."

"Okay. Just checkin' on you." Susie hung up.

"What about my wife?" Ken asked, catching Tez off guard.

Tez lowered his gaze, and his heart skipped a beat, racing, beating so hard he thought Ken would note the vibration through his shirt. "W-what about her?" He cleaned dirt from under his nails.

The fuck? "The flowers," Ken reminded him.

"Oh yea," Tez took a deep breath. "She loved them. She was disappointed that it was me delivering them and not you," he lied. "So, how was the business in New York?"

Ken thought back to their conversation before taking off on the helicopter. He did tell Tez he was preparing to fly, but he didn't recall telling him where he was coming from.

"Everything was great, man. The tour will be very soon, homie." He rubbed his thumb and fingers together, making a money gesture. "A lot of money will be accumulated. But how do you know I was attending business in New York?" Ken leaned forward and locked his fingers together.

Shit, Tez thought as he began feeling sweat beads on his forehead.

"When I took Nae the flowers, she told me you were in New York at a meeting," he told a straight up lie.

Ken nodded. "Okay," he answered calmly.

Tez was trying to pick the reason for Ken's question, and he did the only way he could. "What? You think I'm spying on you, homie?"

"Nah, homie, I just wanted to know, nothing serious." Ken stood. "Before they kill that sonofabitch, tell him that I said I'ma beat his ass again when I see him in hell."

Tez knew he was speaking of Shawn. "A'ight." He stood and shook Ken's hand. He felt the man was onto him or his conscious had been slipping. Either way, it wasn't good. He needed to fall back. "Aye, homie, I need to shoot back to Haiti for a while."

Ken grabbed his keys, and they headed towards the door. "Okay, cool. Make sure Smoke and Peanut handle that before you leave."

Tez nodded and they exited.

***

Ken pulled in his driveway and smiled at the sight of his humongous home. *This crib is beautiful*, he thought, stepping from the vehicle. He approached the mailbox, retrieved the mail and found a letter from Frank as he scanned through.

Ken glanced at the house before returning to the car and placing the mail into the glove compartment, with Frank's letter on the bottom of the stack. He was certain it was the man's last letter before he died. He was tempted to let Nae have it, but he was uncertain of what info it contained.

The house smelled of vanilla incense. Everything was clean and spruce. He noticed the alarm didn't warn him to deactivate it. *Why don't this woman got the alarm on*, he pondered as he walked up the stairs. He opened KJ's door. He was on the floor eating Burger King and watching Cartoon Network.

"Hey, daddy," he said with a mouthful of fries.

It tickled Ken. "Hey, buddy, you were good in school?"

KJ nodded.

"I'm gonna check on mommy. I'll be back." He turned to leave.

"Okay, daddy." KJ gave his attention back to the TV.

Nae was in the tub enjoying a bubble bath when he entered the bathroom. She was relaxed in a laying position with her eyes closed.

"You know it's not safe to fall asleep in the tub." His sudden words caused her to quiver.

"Oh, my." She smiled and opened her eyes. "I wasn't asleep."

He took a seat on the end of the round Jacuzzi tub. "Uh huh." He kissed her lips. "Can I get in with you?"

She nodded. "Yea, sure."

"Did you like the flowers?" He placed his jewelry on the counter and took his clothes off.

"Yes, they were beautiful. Thank you."

He stuck one foot in the tub. "What all did you and Tez talk about?" He eyed her, then planted his other foot in and took a seat beside her.

"What were we supposed to speak of?" she rolled her neck.

"Don't fucking play with me, Nae." His deep stare made her feel like he was looking into her soul.

"We didn't speak of anything, babe." She hoped he wasn't onto them.

"Did you tell him I was in New York?"

She shook her head by way of saying, *No.*

Lying bitch, he thought.

***

Smoke and Peanut did a lot of talking about how and when to execute Shawn. Of course, it would be lovely to get the seven hundred thousand then kill him, but it wouldn't be that simple. In order to do that, they would have to go to Shawn's stomping ground. Peanut suggested they take a few of the homies along and just open fire the moment they pull into Shawn's tire shop. Smoke didn't feel like that plan was safe realistically. All of Shawn's soldiers were located in Savannah, and it would be suicide for a van full of Young Bosses to go there with that plan. Besides, a RV full of people is definitely a target for highway patrol.

"We just gonna tell him Ken is dead, meet him for the other fifty, then off him." Smoke shrugged. "Simple."

Peanut nodded. "It makes sense. So, when we gone do it?"

Smoke quickly contemplated. "Maybe in a couple days."

Peanut could tell his response wasn't permanent and the timing of Shawn's death was open for discussion. "How about we do it today."

Smoke frowned at him as he parked in front of their building. They took a quick trip to Lenox Mall to procure the new Jordans that came out earlier that morning.

"You moving way too fast, Peanut," he said in a serious tone.

"We hittin' the club tonight, right?" Peanut asked.

Smoke nodded.

"Okay, we'll tell him meet us at the club wit' the paper and knock him off in the parking lot."

Then we can stroll right back in the club like nothing even happened, Smoke thought. They exited the Charger.

"That make a lil' sense, 'Nut." He grabbed both their bags from the back seat, then they headed to the condo.

Peanut smiled. "I know it makes sense, fool."

"But what about people seeing?" Smoke remembered.

"Timing, brother," Peanut answered.

"Well, what about people hearing?" he shot back.

"Silencers. I'll get them from Tez." Peanut had it under control.

"Oh, okay, you on point today. God must have blessed you." He barely got the last words out before busting out laughing.

Stupid fuck, Peanut thought.

***

Shawn stood in the bathroom staring in the mirror at his new whites. He found and paid an authentic Savannah dentist five grand to replace his two fronts with false teeth. The surgery had just taken place hours ago, and his entire mouth was numb from the amount of lidocaine the dentist gave him.

These look betta than eva, he thought.

He tried calling Shakeena again, but he received no answer. He sent her a text and asked if he could come and pick up his collectables and his clothes. She replied and told him that Ken had all of his property removed from her home. He thought he was back in the game and tried holding a conversation, but she soon stopped replying.

He removed his shirt and stared at his physique in disgust. He flexed his muscles and thought of how flimsy he felt during his fight with Ken, though he knew it was no real fight; the man had nearly murdered him, that which he could have literally done. With that, he felt the need to get his weight up. He wanted to handle any future opponents the way he'd been handled.

Shawn's phone alerted him to Smoke's call.

"Hello," he answered.

"It's done," Smoke said.

A smile crossed Shawn's face. "Did you do him bad?"

"Yea," Smoke said. "Just how you said. I'ma be in *Diamonds* tonight. Slide through wit' the paper. I even got pictures of him all disfigured and shit. Be there at ten."

Shawn erupted in laughter. He knew he needed to leave Shakeena alone for a while because once she discovered her uncle was dead, he knew she would think he was the responsible party. He did the happy dance all the way to the living room, picked up his keys and headed out. *I'll be there way before ten*, he thought. He was at his spot in Savannah, but he knew he could be in Atlanta in as little as three hours, considering the way he drives.

"What's up, Shawn?" his elder neighbor who was planting new seeds in his yard yelled out once Shawn approached his vehicle.

He waved. "What's up, Mr. Lowethen?"

The old man stood. "Everything is great. How's the little one and that pretty girl of yours?"

Shawn lowered his gaze. He wished he could give a happily honest answer. "They're fine. I'm on my way to them now," he lied, opening his car door to end the convo.

"Okay, drive safe and tell them I said hello," the neighbor added before going back to planting.

Shawn nodded and drove away. Mr. Lowethen had met Shakeena and JJ a few times when Shawn brought them to Savannah to intermingle with his family and friends.

***

"Listen carefully," Tez said.

Smoke and Peanut sat on their couches while Tez stood.

"Do not play any games, do not hesitate, do not make yourselves hot," he schooled them. "Treat that nigga like the enemy that he is. Understood?"

They nodded. He knew they could handle the task, but on certain missions he had to prep them because a fuck up would fall back on him. He held up the two black silencers.

"These are highly illegal. That's why I don't let y'all hold them," he said with a seriousness in his voice.

We not babies, nigga, Smoke thought. He hated when Tez talked to them this way. As for Peanut, he understood exactly why Tez did it and didn't mind. He handed Smoke the silencers.

"Ken said, tell him that he's gonna beat his ass again in hell." He walked towards the door. "Tell him before you kill him of course," he said without turning to face them.

***

"Nae, this tour is gonna be huge," he told her again for the third time.

She lay back on their bed while he sat on the end giving her an oily foot massage. She smiled.

"I know, babe, you told me for the hundredth time," she exaggerated. "Are you gonna have to be gone with them?"

"No, not the entire time." He slid his fingers between her toes. "But I will show up to support the homies from time to time."

The sensation from his oily hands on her foot caused her to croon softly. It felt lovely.

"Why don't we go to the Bahamas while they're on tour?" she asked hopefully.

He shook his head. "There's still work to be done while they're gone. Just chill, I got you."

She poked her bottom lip out like a child.

"The only kid in this house is in there," he nodded towards KJ's room.

His phone went off. It was on the bed next to Nae. She looked at him for clarification before touching it. He'd established a long time ago that his phone is off limits to her due to the heavy amount of business. He nodded.

"It's Tez," she said.

"Put it to my ear."

She answered it, sat up and held it to his ear.

"Yea?" he asked.

She couldn't make out what Tez was saying, but she heard his voice and she felt overwhelmed.

"It's goin' down tonight at the club. Make sho you nowhere around," he warned.

He nodded. "A'ight, homie."

Tez hung up.

"Don't leave, Ken. You haven't even been in from New York that long." She obviously thought he was about to go handle something with Tez.

He tightened his grip on her feet. It felt so good.

"Ain't goin' nowhere, bae." He kissed her then she laid back.

"You hungry?" she asked with a crooked smile.

He nodded.

She pointed to her crotch. "Here, come have some of this."

Ken slowly pulled her panties off.

***

Ass fat (uh, bust it) / Yeah, I know, you got cash (mm, bust it) / Blow sum mo' (word) / Blow sum mo' (bust it)—

Nicki Minaj and Rae Sremmurd's new single—*Throw Sum Mo*—blared through the speakers in Atlanta's hottest strip club.

"Y'all throw some mothafuckin money fa the two baddest strippers in this club tonight!" the DJ's deep voice came through the speakers.

Asia and Tiffany came on the stage and instantly began popping their asses. They sported thongs that were buried in their asses, bras that revealed the lower breast and nipples. Their height was accentuated by six-inch *Red Bottoms*. The crowd went bananas, and dollar bills were coming from every direction.

Peanut looked at Smoke and smiled wide. They were seated among the crowd of people.

"Take that shit off!" Smoke stood and yelled right before throwing two hundred dollars in one's at them. Once him and Asia locked eyes, he knew they were about to turn up to the max.

Once Smoke took his seat, Peanut tapped his wrist with his index finger, indicating that it was ten o'clock. Smoke pulled out his phone, hoping he hadn't missed the call. He hadn't. He kind of knew he didn't because he had his phone set on vibrate and he hadn't felt it. He shook his head, telling Peanut that the call hadn't come through yet.

Asia turned her back to the crowd. Tiffany seductively slid Asia's thong down while Asia made it jiggle.

"Y'all broke ass niggas throw some moe!" the DJ yelled through the mic.

Once her thong was off, Tiffany got on her knees and crawled backwards, trying to come between Asia's legs, ass facing the crowd of people. Before she went completely between Tiffany's legs, Asia bent all the way over and pulled Tiffany's thong off. When she bent over, her pretty pink gold mine was revealed as well as Tiffany's. She placed herself totally between Asia's legs and they began shaking that ass like a pair of dice. Asia dropped down so her pussy was atop Tiffany's butt cheeks. The best part about it was: the shaking never halted.

Chapter Fourteen

As Shawn drove closer and closer to the club, he thought more and more of Shakeena and JJ. They were stuck on his brain like a tumor. He knew Shakeena was desperately going to be grieving once she found out that her uncle was cut up before being killed. *Maybe I can get in good again because she's going to need a shoulder to cry on,* he thought. *All I want is my family back.*

He turned in the packed parking lot of the erotic strip club. There were a few people outside, but nothing out of the ordinary. He drove to the back of the parking lot in a dark area and parked towards the exit. He retrieved the brown bag from under his seat which contained fifty thousand dollars in neat stacks. He dialed for Smoke.

***

Most of the men in the club were floundering to the stage to throw money at the girls of the spotlight. They were all intoxicated except for Smoke and Peanut. They were smoking weed and did a little sipping, but nothing major because they had to stay focused. Tiffany was on her stomach with Asia on her back. Asia's back was arched, and she looked back at the crowd of men and women as she made one cheek jump. At the same time Tiffany made the opposite cheek jump. There was a club full of strippers, but the attention was on them. Even the eyes of guys that were getting a lap dance were locked on the two stars. Of course, all the other strippers were jealous of Tiffany and Asia.

The stage was covered with money. Smoke was just about to throw some more when he felt his phone vibrate. He looked at it, then nodded to Peanut. They stood at the same time and made their way to the bathroom. The phone stopped vibrating, then started right back. Smoke answered as soon as they entered the club's bathroom.

"Where you at?" He listened, then nodded. "Okay, here I come." He hung up. "He says he all the way in the back. That's better for us."

Peanut nodded. "Bet!"

They exited the bathroom and headed to the door as they silently strolled through the club. Smoke peered over at their girls and how they were doing their thing, and he was proud.

They'll never notice we were gone, he thought.

"Aye, Gee, we gon' be right back," Peanut notified the security of the club so there wouldn't be a problem with them getting back in.

"Taka ya time, big homie," he said as they passed by. Gee was a cool guy and a loyal customer to the Young Boss operation.

Outside the club, Smoke pointed to the right. "Look, homie, you go around that way. Just in case anything goes wrong, he can't get away."

Peanut nodded.

"You loaded?"

Peanut nodded. They went in opposite directions.

Shawn sat in a dark area next to a few very expensive cars. *Maybe I need to go in and relax my mind*, he thought, but changed his mind because he'd only brought enough money to pay Smoke and Peanut. *Fuck it, I'ma go see my boo boo after this*, he said to himself. He figured by him already being in the area, another twenty-minute drive wouldn't hurt.

He saw a frame strolling his way and figured it was Smoke. The man stopped, looking this way and that. Shawn flashed the headlights to signal his location. Shawn's smile grew, anticipating the pictures and the story.

***

Ken felt goosebumps all of a sudden. He looked at his phone and he knew it was going down at that very moment. He and his family had just returned home from dinner and a movie. KJ was fast asleep. Ken and Nae had just changed into their night gear. He sat on the loveseat while she laid in the bed.

"Go get me a drink please," he said dryly.

Nae climbed out of their large bed to do just that. "You okay?"

He nodded.

She kissed his lips. "You sure?"

It was something in his eyes that said something she couldn't understand, but she knew something was bothering him.

He nodded, and she left to get the drink. *This is what happens when you fuck with bosses*, he thought.

***

Smoke staggered to the driver's window, acting as if he was under the influence.

"You a'ight, my boy?" Shawn asked.

"Man, I'm good," he slurred. "What's up wit' the money, homi-eee?" He rested his forearms on the roof of Shawn's car.

Shawn could smell the liquor on his breath.

"You fucked up, homie." He laughed.

Smoke feigned to be laughing with him.

"Tell me about that punk mothafucka." He referred to Ken.

"We did him dirty," Smoke lied.

"You said you got pictures?" he asked.

"Oh yea, homie, they right here." He reached in his jacket and pulled the Beretta with the silencer attached out, stuck his arm in the car, aiming the weapon on Shawn's chest.

Shawn's hands instantly went in the air.

"C'mon, Smoke, don't do me like this, baby. Here's the money if that's what you want," he tried to negotiate for his life. The brown bag was on his lap.

"Hand it to me—slowly," he ordered.

Shawn tried to talk as he handed him the sack of money.

"Please, Smoke," he begged.

"Shut the fuck up, Shawn. Ken is my peoples, you stupid mothafucka!" Smoke snatched the brown bag from Shawn's grip.

Shawn's eyes grew big. He couldn't believe how this shit just expanded. It scared him when he realized Smoke was sober. His mind roved everywhere, hoping this was a nightmare, but he knew this was real. He felt his heart beating. Sweat was rolling down his face, and he felt the cold steel resting on his collarbone.

"C'mon, Smoke, I'll pay you another hundred to let me live. Just tell ya peoples I didn't show up and if you catch me slippin again—" he was interrupted by a bone-crushing blow from the weapon to his head. That blow brought reality; this was no dream.

"Ken said he gone whoop yo' ass again when he meets you in hell."

Shawn knew the shots were on the way and he had to try. Smoke raised the gun to Shawn's head, and that triggered the terrified man's reaction. He placed his foot on the brakes, smacked Smoke's weapon with his left hand, simultaneously shifting the car in gear with the other. Smoke fired off a couple rounds, a few of which struck Shawn's torso. Shawn stomped the gas, running over Smoke's foot.

"Aw!" he cried out and dropped the money. He managed to limp behind the car and let loose several shots, shattering the back windshield but missing the target. Smoke limped back to where the money was, picked it up and jogged to the other side of the building that led to the back exit. It was up to Peanut now and he hoped the man didn't miss.

Clutching the wheel with one hand and his bloody stomach with the other, Shawn was near to panic. He hated the sight of his own blood. It was all over his hand and pants, having took several bullets to the stomach.

Peanut was lurking in the cut in between the back exit and a few parked cars. He was near to concern 'bout the job when he heard the approach of a vehicle under heavy acceleration. He drew his weapon, and his suspicion was confirmed as the car sped closer with Shawn behind the wheel, panic, pain, and fear written clear across his face.

Peanut said a silent prayer before he stepped out in front of the speeding vehicle and let loose four shots. The first two punched holes in the windshield, missing the target. The second two struck home: one in the center of Shawn's throat, the other in the center of his forehead. Peanut jumped out of the way of the speeding vehicle, and the car crashed into the stop sign.

Smoke rounded the corner with a limp, Peanut rushed towards him, expecting him to follow. "Let's go!"

Smoke ran past him in the opposite direction.

Peanut stopped and looked back. "What the fuck are you do—?" He stopped short as Smoke reached Shawn's car and emptied the rest of his clip into his lifeless body. Only then did he turn to follow.

He reached Peanut, and they began the jog back to the front door. "That pussy ass nigga ran over my foot."

"You got the paper?" Peanut ignored Smoke's pained foot.

He nodded and they entered the club.

Gee took notice of Smoke's limp when they returned but said nothing. He watched them for a minute, knowing they had just pulled a move. However, he wouldn't remember this moment if ever there was question.

Chapter Fifteen

Ken was slowly massaging his wife's feet when the call came through. The room was dimly lit by a few coconut scented candles, and R. Kelly was playing through the sound system.

She lay on her back in nothing but a silk robe purchased by Ken sometime ago. He unfolded the sprucely folded towel next to him and dried all the baby oil from his hands, and Nae began pouting as he reached for the phone. He paused. "What?"

"Baby, let it ring."

He knew the massage had gotten her horny and she wasn't ready for his touch to end, not even for a few seconds.

"Hello?" he answered.

She pulled her lubricated foot from his lap and went to the bathroom. He knew she had an attitude, and that just caused him to smile.

"Are you sure?" He asked the caller on the other end for clarification. His smile reappeared before hanging up.

"Come back, you big baby," he yelled to his wife.

***

Gee was responsible for escorting Asia and Tiffany to their cars after their time in the club had expired for the night. They both carried two trash bags full of money which was one night's earnings.

"Girl, we need to do that more often," Asia said. They were clearly satisfied with the day's earnings and gave each other a high five.

"Yea, y'all put on tonight," Gee stated. He quickly held both arms out in front of the girls so they could no longer pass. "Hold up," he said.

They followed his gaze and saw a vehicle crashed into the stop sign. From the back they could see the driver in the seat.

"He's probably drunk!" Tiffany exclaimed.

Gee pulled the club-owned Desert Eagle from his waist.

"Y'all hurry up and get outta here." He slowly approached the car with the weapon aimed.

Yes, it's possible it could've been a drunk driver, but as long as Gee had been working security at top-notch and exotic strip clubs, he'd seen it all, from bums trying to rob the strippers to drunk guys trying to rape them. The security of DOA used to be shallow until the Xtacy situation. Gee still remembered it as if it was yesterday.

"Nigga, you betta walk out here wit' me!" she yelled at Gee when he refused to escort her out.

"Girl, don't nobody want you but me," he remarked, letting their secret love life be known to whoever cared to listen.

"I'll be ova in 'bout an hour," he told her.

"You promise?" she asked, approaching him for a kiss.

"I promise," he kissed her. "Damn, them lips taste good," he complimented.

"If you don't getcho lazy ass up and walk out here with me, that'll be the last thang you taste," she teased and exited.

He knew she was all talk. She was chocolate, mid-height, and thick. She was one of the nightclub's main attractions. She was so good at what she did that strip clubs in different states requested her to dance for them. Gee was lucky enough to be the one screwing her.

That night was the last night he had tasted her lips. Xtacy was followed home that night, beaten brutally, raped, and killed. The man responsible had followed her from the club. He had been over-looked as a drunk sleeping in his car as he waited. Gee hunted Xtacy's executor down and happily killed him, but that didn't put his guilty feelings away. Him breaking up a big fight that night and getting hit with a bottle was why he didn't want to move; he was in pain. Never again, he promised himself as he reached the front side of Shawn's car. Asia and Tiffany were pulling out.

"Is he okay?" Asia yelled out the window.

Gee turned to face them. "This nigga dead, y'all get the fuck outta here," he ordered before jogging into the club.

Those words made her nervous and she stepped on the gas.

"I gotta message from Peanut, he says they at the hotel," Tiffany said as Asia flew down the street like a bat out of hell.

***

Peanut opened the door for Asia and Tiffany and threw his hands in the air in excitement. "There's dem superstars!"

They were smiling, but halfheartedly and he knew something was wrong. They walked in and he closed the door behind them.

"What's the matter?"

Asia rushed to the bed that Smoke was lying in.

"What happened?" she asked, looking at his swollen foot which was propped up by a few pillows.

He refused to tell her even though she knew the type of business they were in.

"Peanut ran over it," he lied.

Tiffany embraced Peanut then kissed his lips. "Somebody was dead in the parking lot." She studied his face, but his expression was blank.

"Well, I'm glad y'all a'ight." He sat at the table where an open bag of weed was and began breaking it down on the table.

She assumed his nonchalant attitude meant him and Smoke were the responsible party but she couldn't be sure. With her eyes Asia asked Smoke, *Did you guys do it*? Smoke just lowered his gaze. Tiffany took off her jacket and tossed it on one of the couches.

"So," she sat across from Peanut. "Why y'all niggas killing people at my job? Y'all had Asia scared as fuck!"

"We not finna talk about that!" Smoke barked.

"It's okay, baby, calm down." Asia rubbed his chest.

Peanut knew Smoke didn't approve of him talking about their bodies, especially with women. It didn't matter who it was. No woman. He felt like they were all wicked and couldn't be trusted.

"Nigga, we ain't the police!" Tiffany wolfed back in offense. She knew he was acting that way because she and Asia were present.

"Man, shut the hell up!" he barked back with flames in his eyes.

"Just chill, love, he just upset about his foot," Peanut tried to calm his woman.

***

"I'm just—I'm—I'm fine, Kenneth," Nae tried not to speak of why her behavior was the way it was.

She went back into the bedroom from the bathroom, and Ken followed. She slid in her slippers and searched for her keys.

"Where you think you goin'?" he asked.

"I just need some time. I'm going to Reshia's," she lied.

He stepped to her face. "Why, babe? What's the matter?" he asked fervently.

"You and your fucking jobs or whatever, you can't even let that fucking phone ring for thirty minutes while you spend time with your wife!" She snatched her keys from the dresser.

"Listen," he stopped her with his body as she tried to exit the room. "You can go to Reshia's, but you're going to get dressed."

She couldn't believe it. "Ken, move out of my way." She eyed him, but it did nothing.

"You're not leaving at this time of night in a fucking silk robe and house shoes."

She turned and went to the closet, and he went to flop on the bed, wondering what was really going on. He figured it was her father's death she was dealing with, and her response was the result of that. *I guess she deserves a lil' space*, he thought as she exited the closet fully clothed.

"I love you, Nae," he said softly.

"I love you too," she replied without stopping or looking at him.

Bitch goin' crazy, he thought before dozing off.

***

"How long will you be staying, sir?" *The Four Seasons'* receptionist asked.

"Just for tonight," Tez replied.

"We only accept MasterCard or Visa."

He pulled out a roll of hundreds. "I got cash." He'd been there over a hundred times. Therefore, he knew if you didn't want to use a card, a bribe would work just as well. He handed the woman three one-hundred-dollar bills. The cost of the room was only half that. She glanced around, took the money and handed him two key cards.

"Have a nice night, sir," she said as he strolled away.

***

"I don't giva fuck! Stop talking about it!" Smoke was irate. He wanted this talk of the dead body at the club to end immediately, but Tiffany took total offense.

"Nigga, fuck you! You ain't my fucking daddy! And we ain't no fucking police. You actin' like we gone tell on yo' sorry ass or something!"

Peanut was whispering in Tiffany ear, trying to pacify her before she went over the edge. There was fire in Smoke's eyes, and that look scared Asia.

"Please, baby, don't worry about her," she turned his face towards hers and kissed him.

Why is she enticing me? he thought before breaking the kiss and looking back at Tiffany. "You betta watch yo' mouth, bitch," he stated calmly.

Tiffany jumped to her feet and tried to attack Smoke, but she was restrained by Peanut's grip around her wrist.

Smoke calmly slid the pillow aside to reveal the Beretta.

"Baby, please," Asia tried soothing him with soft words. She knew he was really pissed, and he would do it.

Peanut saw the weapon and the look in his friend's eyes, and knew he had to act quick.

"Baby, let me halla at chu," he said as he stood to his feet.

"You gon' shoot me, pussy ass nigga?" Tears rolled from her eyes as Peanut pulled her towards the door.

"Step outside, love." He reached for the door.

***

Tez sat behind the wheel of his whip in the dark, smoking a Black & Mild. Scrolling through his phone's gallery, he found a picture of Nae in nothing but a thong. *Damn, my baby look so good*, he thought. She sent him that picture the day before. Tez wanted to be with her bad, but it wasn't that easy. *If only things were different*, he thought.

He saw the head lights flashing as she turned in. He put the Black & Mild out, retrieved a small bottle of Listerine from the glove compartment and gargled as she parked. He stepped out and spit the mouth wash on the ground. The alcohol burned his mouth as it cleansed away the smell of smoke. As she stepped out the car, he looked all around to ensure nobody was there who had no business there. It was clear of all persons except a couple in front of the hotel who appeared to be arguing.

Tez smiled at the sight and recited Jay Z's song, *If you having girl problems I feel bad for you son, I got ninety nine problems but a bitch ain't one.* He didn't notice Smoke's Magnum parked.

***

"Tiffany, baby, c'mere," Peanut said.

She tried to walk away. "No, fuck you, Peanut. You didn't take up for me."

He pulled her close. "Baby." He stopped once he noticed some movement in a black Expedition parked in the middle of the parking lot.

It appeared to be somebody sitting there smoking. The part that really caught his attention was, it appeared to be one of the *Young Boss* trucks.

"Baby, you know how Smoke is. You already know we don't talk about that stuff, so stop clowning." She turned to face him, and she knew he was right, but she wanted her man to be stout when it came to her defense.

"Why does he act like that? He went too damn far." Her voice was soft.

He wiped the tears from her eyes and pulled her in for a kiss. Peanut watched the man step from the truck and spit something out as another car pulled in and parked beside him. A female stepped out of the second vehicle, and the two embraced and enjoyed a long fervent kiss. Peanut couldn't see their faces in the dark, but they looked familiar.

"Baby, I'ma halla at 'em when it's just us alone, but when we go back in here, you gonna have to apologize to him because—"

"Apologize?" she cut him off, furious. "Are you fucking kidding me, Peanut? He pulled a fucking gun out and you want me to apologize? Stop acting like a bitch!" She threw a couple punches at him.

He blocked her blows, then grabbed her by the neck and pulled her to the sidewalk area of the hotel. The kissing couple was headed to the hotel entrance now. They passed under the light, and Peanut was startled to see they were people he knew, and that they were there together the way they were.

***

A wicked smile covered Tez's face as they entered their room. "You see that ghetto shit out there?"

She giggled as he shut the door, starting to undress. "Yea, they were fighting."

"That will neva be us." He took a seat on the end of the bed and watched her undress. She finished and came to stand in front of him in her *Victoria's Secret* underclothes. He rested his hands on each side of her waist.

"I want you, Martez," she purred and poked out her bottom lip.

"I'm right here," he pulled her closer.

"You know what I mean, daddy," she moved her body from side to side in slow motion.

The sight was hypnotizing to him. He shot a glance to her left hand to ensure that her wedding ring was absent.

"Listen, love." He planted a soft kiss on her stomach. He was just going to tell her to pack up and come to Haiti with him, but he knew it wouldn't be that easy. Ken would easily put two and two together. On the other hand, he thought of telling her to chill the fuck out and let him do the thinking, but he didn't want to offend her. Also, he was just as anxious.

"Start complaining a lot," he said, planting another kiss on her lower abdomen. "Tell him you're not happy, and when it's established that your relationship is over, I'ma fly you out to Haiti."

The words made her clit throb. She pulled her panties off, then assisted him in removing his own clothes.

"You tell him you want out of the business." She leaped on top of his naked body and took his bottom lip in her mouth. "Mmh, Martez," she moaned at the feeling of him becoming erect.

Chapter Sixteen

At Smith State Prison, F-2 was just coming off lockdown for the death of Frank. The cameras were faulty in the dorm, and in regard to Frank's death they could only say that Fry was near the shower area around the assumed time of the murder. However, it wasn't enough to have him dead to the wrong. They removed Fry from the dorm and placed him on Tier 2 until further investigation. Tier 2 is just an extended stay in the hole from nine to twenty-four months.

J-Bo gathered his towel, soap, rag, and boxers, then called for one of the brothers to escort him to the shower. It wasn't safe for a gang member to go to the shower without being accompanied by another member for protection. Flip laid back on his bed, watching Quan's girlfriend fill her orifice with her fingers while moaning and yelling him and J-Bo's name.

"Don't show nobody that," J-Bo said. "Wait til' I get out the shower."

***

I have to get out of the business and fast! All this snake shit goin' on, it's not safe, Peanut thought as he lay next to Tiffany. Smoke and Asia were on the other bed sleeping soundly, and he was the only one awake. After seeing Tez and Nae together, hugging and kissing, he knew there wasn't any loyalty in the game. He knew his affiliation had to be broken soon. Otherwise, he'd see things that would cost him his life. He quickly woke Tiffany and made her dress, so they could exit. She tried to take a shower and brush her teeth, but he insisted she skip that and do it at the condo.

When they left the room, the white Audi was pulling out of the parking lot. He shook his head at the sight of Nae leaving.

"Peanut!" he heard Tez yell out.

Peanut looked at him in disgust. "What's up, homie?"

They shook hands. "How long y'all been here? It's good to see you."

He spoke to Tiffany, but she just nodded because she knew her breath smelled bad. Peanut sensed instantly that Tez's excitement to see him was spurious. He was really trying to find out if Peanut knew anything he had no business knowing.

"We just came 'bout twenty minutes ago, had to handle something. We finna pull back out doe. I'ma catch up, homie," he tried to end the conversation.

"Cool, but are you sure everything went fine last night?"

Peanut nodded. "Yea, fasho."

Tez patted him on the shoulder. "A'ight, boss, stay up." He got in the truck and sped away.

There are so many women in this world. So, so many. So why must a brother be so sick to be fucking his homie's wife? Did Tez fully comprehend the consequences and repercussions for his actions? Young Boss had a motto: *Loyalty Is Everything*. Didn't he understand the motto was much deeper than being willing to kill for a brother or not snitching on him when the ship sinks? Peanut was racking his brain in search of answers to these questions, as he looked around the parking lot for his car until he realized he came in Smoke's car and Tiffany rode with Asia.

He reminded Tiffany who seemed distracted as well, and they called a cab.

***

Ken adjourned the meeting with Susie. They were preparing to begin the biggest tour in the history of new generation hip hop. He made sure she was on top of the stylist, make-up artists, barbers, and the graphic designers. During the meeting he was shown pictures of the tour bus, and he was impressed with the work: OG Awol's face blown up, over the faces of the younger homies. Over all in bold letter in the color of black and white, were the words: WE BLOCK RUNNING!

Awol was the youngest OG over his Blood set, and Block Runner's best artiste, toe to toe with Psycho, whose face was on the opposite side of the bus. The concept was the same, with Young

Boss's artiste depicted under him, and the words, "WE BOSSES!" in bold print above their heads. Ken, Pan and Diezel were depicted on the hood standing in a group hug on the words. The back of the bus portrayed Psycho and OG Awol dapping.

"Mr. Griffith," Susie called upon entering the office. "The bus will arrive in approximately two hours and forty minutes."

He was so busy sending out last minute emails and making calls that he ignored the fact she didn't knock. "Okay, will everyone from Block Runner already be present?" He pressed *Enter,* sending Rada an email to have some tracks ready.

"Yes, it's their drive," she confirmed.

"Okay, Sweetie, what I need you to do is get on the phone and get everybody here now! Where is Psycho?"

"He's here in Atlanta. I'll call now," Susie sped out the room.

Shit, he thought when he noticed his dreads were hanging. He called his wife twice, but he got no answer. It wasn't like her to miss his call, but he figured she was still a bit upset. *She'll be a'ight after the tour*, he thought as he dialed for Keke, one of the hair stylists.

"I'm on the way, now," she answered on the first ring. "I just got the email."

He smiled. "How far are you, Keke?"

"Bout ten min—"

"Hurry up, Sweetie. I need my dreads braided before these people arrive." He hung up without allowing her to respond.

***

"Do you want to get saved?" Peanut asked Tiffany as they entered the condo.

She giggled. "You already saved me, nigga," she was speaking of him cuffing her.

He closed the door. They entered the bedroom and stripped for the shower. He washed himself in silence. She knew something was on his mind and tried to ease it with sex, but he refused to engage. He ordered her to go cook after their shower, but she bucked and laid on their bed.

"Ain't cookin' shit!" she spat.

"Let me tell you something b—" he refrained from using profanity as he stood over her. "I'm a king. If you wanna deal with me, you gon' conduct yourself accordingly and act as my queen."

"I'ma fucking stripper, Peanut!" she screamed, cutting him off. "You ain't finna change my life with this bullshit!"

"*Was* a stripper, I'm not playin' with God no mo'e!" He pointed his index finger to her face. "And I'm not playing with you, either. I'll leave yo' ass just as quick as I got you."

She saw the graveness in his eyes and heard it in his voice.

She was suddenly aware that she had to either bow down and lock in or walk. "What you want me to do, Peanut?"

"First, seek a relationship with God. Second, get up and go cook."

She nodded and walked toward the kitchen.

***

J-Bo's shower was out the way, and now all the GD's were gathering for a meeting. Together, they agreed to start a war with the Bloods.

"Fuck dem pussy ass niggas," Bo-G said. "We Gangstas. We kill shit."

"So, you just wanna get to busting?" Bull asked.

"Nah, just chill, young dummy."

They all laughed. Then J-Bo announced, "Attention F-2! I got something for y'all to see! Attention in F-2!" He walked to the television, plugged the AUX cord into the back of it and the other end into his phone. Everyone gathered because he always did this when new music videos or new porn came out.

"What video this is, folk?" one of the bros asked, and he just smiled when he saw Quan amongst the group of people.

It came on and Quan's main squeeze, the one he calls bae, the one he plans to marry, appeared on the screen naked. Everyone knew it was his lady because he brags on her beauty and shows her pictures to anyone with eyes. His nose flared, his eyes turned red, his blood began to boil, and his heart and pride was mutilated as he saw his woman fingering herself while calling out J-Bo and Flip's name. She fingered herself with two fingers from the right hand, sucked two fingers from the left hand and moaned out.

"Mmh, fuck me, J-Bo! Mmh, Flip, yo' dick taste good."

The entire dorm was silent. The civilians went in their rooms and locked the doors as well as a few gang members who were afraid because they knew it was about to go down.

"I'ma kill y'all pussy niggas!" Quan yelled as he ran towards his room.

Bo-G ran directly behind Quan. He knew Quan was running to his room to retrieve a weapon. The moment Quan took off running, everybody began fighting, stabbing, or running to go strap up.

"C'mere, bitch," Bo-G wolfed as he forcefully grabbed the back of Quan's state shirt, causing his body to jerk back. He stabbed him in the shoulder with his eight-inch rod.

"Ahhh!" Quan squawked.

"Fuck nigga!" He stabbed Quan twice more before the man broke loose and staggered away.

It was a war zone in that bitch; blood was everywhere. By the time the officer in the booth realized what was going and could call a code, the floor was splattered. Flip was in a corner getting jumped by three Bloods, and the sight was heart breaking to J-Bo. He fought his way to his lil' cousin's rescue.

"You know I'm surgical with this bitch!" he yelled before jamming his knife into one of the Blood's necks.

One ran in the room to lockdown, and the other stood firm as J-Bo stabbed him while Flip punched and kicked him. The Bloods jammed on Soulja badly. Soulja was a GD that was in his bed asleep on the top range when it popped off. They ran in his room three deep and woke him up with punches and punctures to the face and head. He cried out, but so much was going; his cries went unanswered. He tried to grab his knife from under the mat, but the Bloods weren't letting up.

Covered in blood, Quan came limping out his room, a machete in hand. He felt his body giving out; he was losing more and more blood by the second. *Somebody coming with me,* he thought as he took a hard swing at Flip's neck. Flip threw his hand up just in time to protect his head from being chopped, but he lost his right hand. Bull ran towards Quan full force and punched him in the jaw, sending him unconscious.

Once he fell, Bull got down on his knees and said, "Ain't nobody playin' witchu, folk." He jugged Quan in the neck several times with his rod until he knew there was no life left in the man.

It was like Iraq in there, minus the bullets and mechanical weapons. The moment Flip's right hand was amputated, and he'd seen he was now an amputee, he went unconscious.

"Noo!" J-Bo rushed to his side. "Cuz! Cuz!" he slapped his cousin's face, but he got no response.

He pulled off his state shirt and tightly wrapped the nub of his cousin's wrist with it. Bull and J-Bo ran upstairs to check all their brothers' rooms to ensure no one was down bad. They reached Soulja's room, and it looked as if his room was decorated in blood. The Bloods were still punching and stabbing Soulja, but he wasn't moving. They knew he was dead the moment they'd seen it. It brought tears to Bull's eyes because he's the one that took Soulja under his wing and influenced him to join the organization. They rushed the room and went to war with the Bloods.

An extremely loud siren was set off by the dorm floor officer, alerting reinforcements to the situation at hand.

"Mr. McPharlan," an officer called into his mike. "Hurry! I think some of them are dead!"

"Hands on the ground!" Deebo came through the door spraying inmates off the rip, not even giving them a chance to obey his command.

The other CERT Team members were on his heels, and they were spraying inmates with pepper spray and shooting them with bean bags from high powered weapons. Deebo called a code for medical as soon as he saw Flip's amputated hand. Every person they sprayed and hit across the head with the baton, they hand cuffed. Ten dreadful minutes later, every inmate was cuffed. Medical came in and took out the injured living souls first. The inmates that were just lying there cuffed were yelling gang codes and disrespecting the opposition. Some were crying from the sight of their dead homies.

"This is a mess," Deebo uttered, walking through blood and over dead bodies. "We got about twelve dead," he said as the warden entered.

Chapter Seventeen

"Love you!" Ken yelled to Nae before rushing out the door in a hurry! He had to attend a meeting with Susie before he got on a plane and met up with Psycho and Block Runners in Fort Worth, Texas.

What kinda man don't even kiss his wife before he leaves? Nae asked herself. *I know somebody who will.*

He arrived at the office, retrieved his bills from the glove compartment and shot inside.

"Mr. Griffith, insurance agent on line two," he heard over the speaker as soon as he entered the building.

That's not Susie's voice, he thought. He approached his receptionist.

"Why isn't Susie on the call?" he looked baffled.

"I don-um-she's not in yet, sir," she staggered.

He looked at his watch. *At 8:23 a.m., why the fuck isn't she?*

"Tell him to leave a message," he told the speaker as he sped away to his office.

He dialed for Susie once behind his desk.

"Sorry, Mr. Griffith, I'm literally two minutes away." She apologized.

He hung up his line before he got upset. He searched his computer and chatted with Diezel for a while then decided to pay the bills.

Why the fuck am I doing this? Ken asked himself as he paid him and Nae's bills online.

The next envelope that he picked up was from Frank. *Damn, I almost forgot about this*, he thought as he opened it. As he reviewed the letter, he actually thought of giving it to her to have. Nothing was abnormal. There! Once he read that part, he knew he could not ever let his wife read it. Frank was speaking of how blessed his roommate is to be released from prison after ten years for a triple homicide. Yea, that's all good and dandy, but the part where he says, *he's a good friend of your husband* is the part that will make Nae wonder without ceasing, and Ken wasn't trying to have that problem. He plugged up his electric paper shredding trash can and just when he was gonna shred it, Susie came through the door.

"Pick up line two!" she rushed to the seat directly on the other side of his desk.

She went through her purse and retrieved a small tablet and one of the company pens.

"Who is it?" he asked.

"Mr. Griffith," she said, looking at him as if he's supposed to know the answer. "We have an eight-thirty conference call." She looked at her Armani watch.

"It's eight-fifty." He put Frank's letter back in its envelope, put it on top of the stack of bills and put them together in the last drawer of his desk. He tapped line two.

"Kenneth here, sorry we're late." After the verbal meeting, he and Susie went over some paperwork together in silence.

"Mr. Griffith, you have to get the hell out of here!" she exclaimed as she suddenly remembered.

Ken looked at her confused as to why she was talking to him like she lost her mind.

"I'm sorry for my language, but you have to get to Fort Worth."

"Shit!" Remembering the meeting in Texas, he tried to speed up with his work.

"I will finish, just go." Susie took the paperwork from him.

He smiled and rushed out the door.

***

Asia carefully washed and wrapped Smoke's foot. "How does it feel?"

"Better," he said. "You still ain't heard from Tiff?"

She shook her head. They woke up at the hotel. Peanut and Tiffany had already departed. They hadn't heard from the two of them ever since. Smoke tried calling Peanut several times only to be sent to voicemail and decided to leave him alone until he called back.

"Now, you sure you know the combo to the safe?"

Last night Asia told him how she was in the process of setting up one of Young Boss's rivals. She told him she'd been in his home on several occasions, and she clearly watched him unlock the safe several times and memorized the combination.

"I'm sure, love." She kissed him. "I'ma go check the food." She got up.

They got back to the condo, opened the door, and the aroma of breakfast smacked them in the mouth. They realized they were the only ones there and figured Peanut and Tiffany had come home and got cleaned up. *She must've cooked, and then they left shortly after eating.* He made Asia go cook, too. The way her ass jiggled in those boy shorts almost distracted him, but he quickly gained focus again on his plan to rob Big A.

Big A was a community drug dealer. He and Young Boss members had bumped heads on several occasions. Smoke was going to kill Big A awhile back, but Ken ordered him not to because he didn't feel that their petty argument should send Big A to his death. However, they've got into it again since then and Ken told them if the opportunity presented itself, kill him.

***

They exited the church building all smiles. Peanut sported a Gucci suit with the shoes designed for that suit while Tiffany wore a Gucci dress that he'd bought her a long time ago, although this was her first time wearing it. She looked magnificent.

"Did you enjoy yaself, young brotha?" one of the church ministers asked Peanut, coming to the realization that he's new to the church. He nodded and shook his hand.

"Yes, I did. Loved it." He glanced at Tiffany, and she agreed.

"Yes, it was wonderful." Something felt strange, but in a good way.

Tiffany had never been into the whole God thing, but that preacher said some things that ran chills down her back.

"Will y'all be returning for next week's service?" he asked.

"Yes, indeed," Peanut answered syllable by syllable.

They all shared a laugh. “They all call me Minister Mosley,” he said before departing.

“I actually liked the service, Peanut!” she exclaimed in happiness.

“That’s great. See how you was talking crazy this morning. Now, listen to you.”

Tiffany smiled. “I don’t know what it is, but it feels good.” He held her hand.

“It’s the holy spirit, babe.” They shared a kiss before his phone began vibrating.

It was Smoke.

“Hello?” he answered and listened for a while, said okay and then hung up.

“Who was it?” she asked, almost knowing.

“Smoke. He’s talking bout we need to talk and I’m ‘posed to answer, blah blah.” He looked at his call history and realized he had several missed calls and texts.

“So, we're going home?” Her tone dropped and she lowered her head.

“I like the way you look in this dress. Let’s hit the mall and buy you a few more.”

Tiffany looked up all smiles, and Peanut gave her a wink.

***

Nae awoke that morning feeling like Queen Elizabeth. She quietly got up and began cleaning the house up, making everything nice and spruce, then decided to prepare breakfast. Just the thought of her current situation brought joy to her heart. The only part that saddened her was *knowing this feeling was only temporary*, only until they did something about it. Yesterday, she had dropped KJ off at Shakeena’s house and spent the evening with Tez.

Tez awoke to sunrays sliding through the blinds and into his face. He yawned and stretched wildly in a bed that didn’t belong to him. He wiped the cold from his eyes, recouped, and became stagnate as he thought and had an emotional warfare within himself. *Ain't no way I spent a night over here*, he thought while lying in Ken's bed. He couldn't believe he had gone that *far. We want to be with each other. Ken don't own her*, he thought, trying to justify his actions. He discarded those thoughts and came back to reality. He couldn't go against Young Boss. He stood no chance.

"Good morning, Martez," he heard her sweet voice before seeing her come through the door with a silver tray full of food.

"What's up, Boo," he greeted her.

They ate in silence for a while. Then she asked, "What's wrong?"

He shook his head. She knew he was pondering on his betrayal.

"Martez, don't think about that. Just think of a plan."

He swallowed some orange juice. Feeling the frustration build, he brought the cup down hard. "I told yo' ass to start complaining!"

She knew he felt more guilty than angry, so she decided to let him have that.

"I promised myself I'd neva fuck you on this bed," he paused. "Now I'm fucking you and falling asleep with you in this man shit!" He shook his head. He was disgusted with himself.

Nae almost smiled, but she caught herself. She felt guilty at times, but the more time they spent together, the more she didn't care. She knew Tez was getting weaker, and he would soon be prepared to run off with her.

***

"What are we gon' do?" Tiffany asked as Peanut pulled from the mall's parking lot and merged in traffic.

"About?" he asked.

"I mean," she repositioned herself in the passenger seat. "Like are we gon' fall off the face of the earth or what?" She was scared, but she trusted him, and he knew that.

He stopped at the red light and looked her in the eyes. "Are you prepared to be my spouse?"

She giggled. "Nigga, I am your—"

"I'm not a nigga, don't call me that!" Peanut cut her off. "And you're not my wife yet." He gave his attention back to the road and put his foot back on the gas when the light turned green. "Do you believe you're ready to be my wife?"

She couldn't help but blush. She'd never been asked such a question before. "Yes, but I still got some ways that aren't gonna change overnight."

He nodded. "Yea, we gon' pray about it and live right. You'll break from them, but one thing you're not gonna do is go back to that strip club. If you do, then I'll feel my stay with you on earth is over."

Peanut's words offended her, but he was only expressing his feelings. They drove the remainder of the way in silence. He parked in his spot outside the condo, and they got out. She tried to grab her bags from the back seat.

"Leave it, we won't be here long."

She loved how he took charge, how he already had their next move planned out. He unlocked the door and they entered.

"Y'all look all cute. Where the hell y'all been?" Asia asked from the kitchen. Peanut said nothing. He went straight to the living room where Smoke sat. Asia frowned at Peanut. She didn't like being ignored. Tiffany joined her in the kitchen.

"What's up with him, girl?" Asia asked.

Tiffany shrugged. "He's just tired."

"Well, he needs to go lay his ass down somewhere." Tiffany smiled, shaking her head. It was clear that Asia didn't understand what her best friend meant based off her response.

"What's up?" Peanut was standing over Smoke.

"Boy, where the hell you been?" He was glad to see his friend.

"Church, what's up?"

Smoke laughed, held up his hands in surrender. "Okay. I got the combo to that safe in Big A's house. A few hunnid racks in there!"

"Not interested, Smoke. It's ova with for me," he said boldly.

Smoke felt like he was just going through a phase.

"Anyway." Smoke pulled a blunt from his ear and fired it up. "We gotta have a meeting today. A few of the bosses from Detroit coming down to help us organize the warehouses and build some shit to make sure we beat the police every time." He took a deep pull on the weed.

"Today is Sunday," Peanut replied.

Smoke shrugged. "And?" he searched his memory, trying to remember. If they had anything planned for this Sunday, he didn't recall.

Peanut took a deep breath. "It's the Sabbath day. I don't work on Sabbath days."

Smoke wanted to erupt in laughter, but he was already pissed about a lot of other shit, so this wasn't the time to be laughing. He stretched his arm out trying to hand Peanut the weed, but he declined.

"Sit down," Smoke said.

"No, thanks, I'm not gonna be here long," he continued standing.

"I see," Smoke took a pull from the weed and leaned his head back. "Tiff!" He propped his foot up some more with the pillows from the couch.

Peanuts brows creased in confusion; Tiffany stepped into the living room looking from Peanut to Smoke.

Smoke looked at Tiffany. "I'm sorry." He exhaled the smoke and looked at Peanut. "Now, are you ready to work?"

Peanut sighed. "It's clear that you're a lost soul. It's not about you disrespecting her. It's about me living for my God."

"Nigga, Young Boss is yo' God!" Smoke snapped. "The fuck wrong witchu!"

"I'm no longer Young Boss," he replied calmly.

The women stood there quietly and Smoke eyeballed Peanut in silence.

"Peanut, you know the rules."

Peanut knew he was speaking of death. "I also know the rules to my Holy Bible. This life is over with for me. I've spent too much time with y'all doing everything but the work of God, and there's no loyalty here."

"Peanut, you sound like a bitch. Loyalty is everything, nigga. Who ain't loyal?"

Peanut felt like he was too blind for him to continue conversing with. He turned to Tiffany. "You ready, baby?"

She nodded. He took her by the hand and walked to the door.

"God bless y'all," he said before leaving out.

***

"I want to start a family with you, Martez," Nae said.

"I want the same with you," he stroked her hair as she laid on top of him.

"We're grown. Let's do it," she whined.

"I gotta get outta this fucking house. Where you wanna go?" His conscience couldn't take it anymore. He gently pushed her off of him and sat up.

"I always wanted to go to the cabins." She looked down. "Ken's always too busy to take me."

His phone went off. It was Smoke.

He answered on the third ring. "Yo?"

"Anything you need me to do before we meet up wit' dem fools from the D today?"

Nae slipped the front of his shorts down and quickly put his dick in her mouth, but in the same instance he pulled away from her and stood up. She loved sucking his dick while he talked on the phone.

"Uhh yea, just go to all the spots and make sure all the basic shit taken care of. Make sure ain't no fuck shit goin' on. We don't need the Midwest bros thinkin' we down here bullshittin," he said.

"You right, but ain't we the ones 'posed to be goin' there making sho they got they shit together?"

Tez nodded. "Yea, Ken got a hell of a way of doing shit."

The fact that Young Boss began down south, but Ken had the Detroit members auditing them was something that never sat right with him either. It bothered him to the point that he had once asked him why this was.

"To lead is to take it upon yourself to be an outstanding member of Young Boss. To observe and analyze each member who claims and profess to be a part of the organization. The people put in position should not be chosen because you grew up with them or because you know them personally. But because they show loyalty to all teachings, laws and policies that govern this glorious organization," Ken had said.

Tez understood that to an extent, but he still wasn't with them checking them when they were the ones who had put the work in to make Young Boss what is was today. To hell with how organized they were!

He wasn't trippin, though. He knew he would be over the entire organization soon—*that's if this nigga don't get brand new when J-Bo and Flip come home*, he thought. "Just make sho you and Peanut on y'all shit, a'ight?"

Smoke was quiet.

"You heard me?" Tez asked.

"Man, Peanut playing a dangerous game." He didn't want to say.

"The fuck you mean?" Tez sat on the bed again, but Nae knew he was on an urgent call, so she didn't try him.

"He says he's giving his life to his Lord God."

Tez listened. "Okay. And? He can believe in God if he wants. What's the problem?" He was trying to get straight to the point.

"He said he ain't Young Boss no mo'."

The line was so quiet he had to look at his phone to ensure Tez hadn't hung up.

"Homie?" he asked.

"Yea, he uhhh—" Tez scratched his head, lost for words. "He must have just been goin' through something. I know he betta be at them warehouses today."

Smoke didn't reply.

"I'm gonna give him a call." Tez hung up.

He called Peanut several times and finally got an answer.

"What's up?"

"What up, boy? You a'ight?" he asked, trying to feel him out.

"Yep."

It was something about his answers that made Tez feel uneasy.

"A'ight, I was just touching bases to make sure y'all on point for today." He knew that comment would either verify or deny what Smoke just told him.

"Tez, I'm done. I'm done with Young Boss. I'm ready to live for Christ." He was bold.

"Shawty, don't you know I can have you killed based off what you just said?" he asked gravely.

"Don't you know Romans 14:11 says: *Every knee shall bow to me and every tongue shall confess to God*?" Peanut retorted.

Tez released a heavy sigh, and pinched the bridge of his nose. "Peanut, make sho you there, bro. I don't wanna be the one to decide what has to happen to you."

Tez hung up and turned to Nae. "Listen, I gotta go handle something really brief with Smoke. I'll be back." He put on his shoes. "Be ready for the cabins by the time I get back, okay?"

"Okay. I'ma swing by Keena's and drop off some money for babysitting."

"A'ight." He leaned in and kissed her soft lips. "You betta stop being nasty while I'm on the phone too," he pointed at her.

"You like it."

"No, I love it." He bit his lip.

Chapter Eighteen

The vibe was totally different as Peanut turned into a community of cabins called Hard Labor Creek. One hour and a half away from Atlanta. Tiffany was clueless as to where he was taking her the entire drive, but she lit up on the inside at the sight of these expensive cabins. Some were bigger than the other, but they all were at least fifteen hundred dollars a night. Some had big yards, decks, garages and some even had luxury cars apart of the package deal.

"Oh my God! Peanut, these cabins are wonderful." She wanted to hug him, but he was driving.

"Yea, it's nice. I've been here before." He parked in front of the leasing office and cut the engine. Getting out, he went in, paid his security fee for his four-night staying fee and got his set of keys.

He pulled up in front of the biggest cabin towards the back of the community. He liked being ducked off.

"Baby, do you need me to help pay for it?" Tiffany joked as they exited the car.

He almost said: *Girl, I'ma Boss!* But he caught himself. Instead, he just smiled and shook his head.

"Naw, love, I got it." He unlocked the door, and everything was neat, smelled good, and the setting was relaxing and calm.

"We're not gonna need those." He pointed to the first two sixty-two-inch flat screen TV's he noticed.

She looked at him as if he had lost his mind. "Why not?"

"Because we're not here for entertainment. We're here to clear our minds and start fresh as God-fearing people."

She nodded. "You're right, daddy."

That made him smile as they entered the kitchen area.

"When I wake up in the morning, I want you in here cooking for me butt naked," he told her.

"Your wish is my command," she said before hugging him and locking lips for a wet kiss. "Are they gonna kill you?"

He saw fear in her eyes and heard it in her voice. Everything was going well at first, but it just dawned on her what really happened. *What's really going on, how long will this last?* she thought.

He turned his head to the side, being sure not to break eye contact. He was gonna express how baffled he was by her question, but his wit kicked in and he knew she was speaking of the Young Bosses.

"Baby, listen," he grabbed her hand and led her to the couch for a seat. "They can't mess with a child of God and get away with it."

Her eyes began to water. "So, what does that mean, Peanut? Huh? You're telling me you're gonna die, but I'm supposed to be okay with it because God will take vengeance?"

She began crying. He wrapped his arms around her and rocked in silence as she continued to weep.

"I'm not saying I'ma get killed, but we both know it's a possibility," he said.

"Why can't they just respect your decision? Like, aren't they supposed to wanna see you doing better?"

"You know how the game go, Love."

She laid her head on his chest and closed her eyes. "Peanut, if they take you away from me, I won't be able to continue trying to walk with God. I know I'm gonna slip."

"I cast that down in the blood of Jesus." He tightened his grip. "Do you like nature?" he asked since they were in a cabin surrounded by wooded areas.

She nodded. "I want to record the deer running, the stars and stuff like that."

"Okay." He stood up and took her by the hand. "Let's go buy a camera."

"I can use my phone," she objected.

"Nah, I want you to have the best quality."

***

The meeting with the big bosses from Detroit had Tez pissed. They wanted to know Peanut's whereabouts and he had to lie for him because if he told the truth, they would've probably considered killing him for not killing Peanut. He told them Peanut's mother was sick, so he let him go spend time with her. After the meeting, they were ready to check out the warehouses. Tez didn't have to be present for that part unless he wanted to. He dialed Peanut's number and was sent to the voicemail on the second ring. He called again, and this time he left a message.

"You stupid mothafucka! Why the fuck weren't you there? You made me look bad. You betta get at me ASAP!" He was irate. "Oh shit!" he jerked the wheel to the right, almost crashing into a parked car as he looked down to end the call. He dialed for Nae.

"Yes, daddy?" she answered.

That made him smile.

"You ready?"

"Yep. Am I meeting you at the airport?"

Tez was confused. "Airport for what?"

"You wanna go to the cabins, right?" Nae laughed. "Don't tell me you changed your mind."

"Oh, naw. They have some really nice cabins in Madison, Georgia. That's only 'bout two hours away. I figured we could take your car."

"I don't mind."

"Okay, I'm only a few minutes away," he notified her.

"Alright, bae, I'm waiting on you."

"You talked to Ken?" His stomach hurt when he asked that question.

"Yea, he just called. He's still gonna be out for a few days."

"A'ight," he hung up.

Nae hung up wondering if it was possible to be in love with more than one person at a time? Was it safe to cheat on a guy like Ken with his lil' homie, his protégé? She was gambling with her and Tez's life and was very much aware of it.

***

Ken was having a ball in Fort Worth, Texas. He met several new possible business partners. They went by the arena and did a sound check for tonight's show. They shopped at the biggest mall in Texas for some new gear. They even showed love to one of Block

Runner's studios in Dallas. Now they were at a new technology convention at a private location hosted by a private party. There was a variety of fine women in attendance advertising their products to the paying customers. People were stopping them to sell all kinds of tech stuff.

A beautiful fair-skinned, petite woman with long hair approached him with a small box; it looked like some internal product. "Sir, this is a great product for such a busy man like yourself," the woman said.

"What is it?" Ken asked.

She smiled. "It's called *I Got You.* You see, it's something that I program in your phone. If you or your phone is ever lost, you will see the exact location and the exact amount of time it's been there."

"So, if I was to get kidnapped with my phone, how would anyone else know where I am?" Ken asked.

"From your laptop, iPad, or any phone that's on a group plan," she explained.

"So, any phone that's on my monthly plan, I can track the location of their phone?" he asked for clarification.

She nodded.

"Yep, after I activate yours. You type in the other phone number and you can begin tracking," she smiled.

***

On their way to Madison, Ken called Tez's phone. He had his phone hooked up to the AUX cord, so they could hear the music aloud from his phone.

"It's Ken," he said when he saw the name.

Nae pressed the green button, and Ken came on the car speaker. "Yo!"

"Hello?"

"What up doe, Tez? How's everything?"

"Shiiid, everything good, Big Homie. I'ma be shooting out for Haiti in the a.m."

Nae twisted her face up and looked at him. He felt her stare, but he kept his eyes on the road.

"Okay, okay, y'all already met up with the bros from Detroit?" he asked.

"Yea, they still here. They're doing their inspection at the warehouses. I already got the new chemical to beat the folks. They brought some chemicals from the Midwest that's better than the other shit. This stuff never touches the wrapping of the product, it touches the body of where it's at. Once they pressure wash the buildings with it, the police heat monitor will never go off. You can put twenty pounds on your back seat, wash the car with this chemical and drive straight past highway patrol and won't get pulled over.

"Okay, cool. Peanut and Smoke?"

Tez took a deep breath. "Peanut on some other shit. I don't wanna spoil ya day with it doe, so we'll talk about it later on."

"Sure it can wait?" Ken was concerned.

Tez switched lanes. "Yea."

"A'ight, Young Boss."

"Young Boss," Tez said before Nae hung up.

"What the hell do you mean you're going to Haiti in the morning, Martez?" she rolled her neck.

He didn't understand why that was a problem.

"Yea, that's when I'm goin'. I have a family there," he hated to say.

"So, what about me?" Nae's lips were pursed and her nosed flared as she waited for a response.

"We workin' on that. I told yo' ass to start complaining," he said.

"Fuck that! You think you can play with me!" Nae reached for his phone.

He grabbed her wrist with his right hand.

"What the hell are you doing, Nae?" he asked while looking back and forth from her to the road.

"I'm calling Ken. I'ma tell him straight up. I'm so tired of this being a secret!" she barked through teary eyes.

He tried to pull the phone from her, but she pulled in the opposite direction, causing him to swerve. He parked in the emergency side all the way to the right.

"Nae, chill the fuck out!" He snatched the phone from her grip.

"I love you," she cried with her hands over her face.

"I love you too, but chill. I told you I got you." Just as he kissed her lips, his phone rang again, and it was Peanut.

"Man, what's up with you?" he answered.

"Why are you leaving me messages calling me out of my name and threatening me, Tez?"

"I don't know what fuckin' drug you on, but wh—"

"I want out or else!" Peanut cut in, warning Tez.

Tez laughed. "So, you threatening me now, huh?"

"Yea."

"What the fuck you gon' do to me, nigga?"

"Maybe tell Ken you're screwing his wife."

The car was silent. Tez wasn't laughing anymore. Once those words came from Peanut's mouth, he and Nae immediately locked eyes. She hated that he knew, but at the same time she was ready to be happy.

"P-Peanut, why t-the hell would you say some fuck shit like that! You talkin' crazy. Where the hell you hear that at?" he stammered over his words.

His heart rate accelerated, and sweat beads formed on his forehead. *Ain't no way*, he thought. *When? How?* He thought he was doing a pretty good job of keeping things on the low.

"I didn't hear anything, Tez. I just want out, bro. Just let me be. I wanna live for God, man," he pleaded.

"Okay, okay," Tez replied quickly. "Peanut, I'ma talk to the homies over me and Ken. I'ma make sure you get relieved with no smoke," he lied. He knew that wasn't possible unless you've been Young Boss for so many years.

Peanut knew it too, but he believed that him and Ken had a strong enough relationship where he would let him go. Only Ken could make such a decision.

"Tez?" Peanut said.

"Yea."

"If I even think somebody's tryna harm me, I'm spillin' the beans." He hung up.

Nae was smiling.

"You think that shit funny?" Tez's eyes were squinted to slits and his fists were balled.

"No, I don't," Nae answered nonchalant.

Tez could feel his temples pulsing and it was taking everything in him not to slap Nae into Black History Month. "So why the fuck you smilin'?"

"Because I know you're gonna hurry up and make a move now."

Tez was convinced Nae had some loose screws up top. He ran his hand down his face, took a deep breath and exhaled. "Nae, don't you know Ken will have us both killed?"

Nae sucked her teeth and waved him off. "Stop being a bitch."

Pow!

He struck her with the back of his right hand. Then did so again between each word. "You—so—fuckin'—stupid!"

***

Peanut was kicked back on the California king sized bed in nothing but his sweatpants. Tiffany sat up beside him rubbing his bird chest. She had on a silk thong and a matching bra.

"I almost feel free now." Peanut smiled. "I feel great."

She looked down at him and felt joy from his smile. "You should. What did he say?"

She didn't know exactly who he was, but she knew it was someone in command within the Young Boss organization.

Peanut thought over Tez's words. "He said he's gonna speak to the homies over him on my behalf."

Tiffany continued stroking the center of his chest with her fingers. "Are you sure he's fucking your other friend's wife?"

He told her the entire situation before he phoned Tez.

He nodded.

"I caught them kissin' and huggin'. They didn't know I was there, though."

"That's a shame." She shook her head. "This girl must be extra fine."

"It don't matter how fine she is, Tiffany." Peanut was irritated because he felt like she was saying as long as Nae is really fine, it's okay to do. "She is Ken's wife! Ken took Tez under his wing. If it wasn't for Ken, Tez wouldn't be in the position that he's in now. Plus, it's millions of other fine women out there."

Peanut was out of breath when he finished.

Tiffany laughed and held both hands up in surrender. "You right, baby. Don't kill me."

He bear-hugged her and rolled on top of her.

"Girl, shut up." He kissed her lips.

"Um," she moaned. He kissed her again.

He rubbed her clitoris over the silk thong. It felt like she was fully naked.

"Umm, Peanut," she moaned as he pulled his dick out and slid it in her walls. She did a trick she'd learned over the years to make her insides tighten up while a man is inside her.

"Damn, girl!" he moaned as he felt his nut building up already. He continued to stroke her core, thrust after thrust, he fed her.

She pushed him off her when she knew he was seconds away from cumming.

"I'll be back," she said as she jumped up and grabbed the camera he purchased for her off the nightstand.

"Where the f—" He caught himself and laid back in bed with a hard-on. "Where you goin'?"

"Gonna go watch nature for a while. I'll fuck you to sleep when I'm done." She pranced off to the balcony. She loved teasing him.

***

Nae was naked on the cabin's bed. She had gone straight for the shower the moment they arrived. She fixed herself something to eat and rested. She hadn't said a word to Tez. She couldn't believe he'd slapped her the way he did. However, she found she kind of liked it. Tez stepped in the room. She rolled her eyes when he made eye contact. He turned off the lights and opened the huge balcony curtain, so only the moonlight lit the room. He slowly crawled on top of her.

"Nae," he whispered.

She looked up at him, and his heart ached when he saw her slightly swollen face.

"Baby, I'm sorry," he attempted to kiss her, but she turned her head. "Baby, I was just frustrated. I-I was," he stuttered before taking a deep breath.

She pushed him away. "Leave me alone, Martez." Her tone was soft. She turned on her side.

He got up, turned on the lights, snatched the blanket away from her, then quickly dropped to his knees and began eating her pussy sideways from the back.

"Oh my—" she moaned.

"I said I'm sorry." He began fingering her with two fingers while eating her pussy.

***

Tiffany turned the camera on while leaning on the balcony's railing.

"Hey, you," she said quietly as a deer ran past her camera's aim.

Tiffany's always been a nature type of girl, but the moment she got introduced to drugs, sex, and the pole, her desire for nature slowly went away. She smiled when she heard a wolf howling from afar. She aimed the Kodak camera up to the sky and admired the stars. When she was bringing her aim back down, she saw some strange movement from the window of the cabin next to them. It looked like someone having sex. *I need to mind my business,* she thought. Tiffany smiled, shrugged and aimed the camera at the window and held the zoom in button until the sight was vivid. There was a dark-skinned man fucking the shit out of a gorgeous light skinned woman from the back.

Damn, she thought, already wet from Peanut. *It gotta be good*, she thought. Based off the facial expression the light skinned girl was making, she knew she was in ecstasy. She felt her clit begin to throb and decided that nature could wait.

She turned the camera off and went back to Peanut. He was jacking off when she walked in. She rushed him, spit on his dick then began riding him.

Chapter Nineteen

The next morning Tiffany woke up early, showered, put lotion on and remained nude to cook for Peanut, just as he demanded yesterday. He entered the kitchen with sleep still in his eyes.

"Good morning, baby," she greeted him while she whipped the buttered cheese eggs. He hugged her from behind.

"Good morning, beautiful," he whispered. "Where ya clothes at?" He squeezed her ass.

"You said you wanted me to cook for you naked," she looked back at him.

He nodded. "I know," he released her and sat at the ten-person wooden table. Her camera was sitting there.

"Did you catch any deer running wild last night?" he asked.

She laughed. "Deer ain't the only wild stuff I caught."

"Say what? Whatchu talking 'bout, girl?" he asked, grinning.

She turned off the stove and packed his plate with cheese eggs, cheese grits, bacon, a chopped up Italian polar sausage, and four pieces of jellied down toast bread.

"Somebody was doing the nasty last night and I saw it." She laid the plate in front of him.

"You a trip," he said before taking a bite into the toast.

***

Tez woke up, penetrated Nae once more, hit the shower and sat on the couch pondering over the situation he was in. His gaze was deep in the air, staring at nothing in particular. *Damn, Peanut*! he thought. Those words hurt his heart; they kept replaying in his head. "*Maybe tell Ken you're screwing his wife.*" Even though he declared Peanut's liberation from Young Boss for him to be quiet, it wasn't tangible. Peanut may have thought it was an even swap, no swindle, but there's definitely some swindling going on.

Tez knew what he had to do; just the thought hurt like hell. He wondered if there was any way for Ken to find out about him and Nae after Peanut was dead. He didn't want to kill Peanut and then it comes to the light some type of way, but he was left with no choice.

***

Ken awoke in his hotel suite that morning with J-Bo and Flip on his mind. He'd had a dream about the three of them riding away from the courthouse in Lamborghinis. He frowned upon waking up realizing it was a dream. He called J-Bo's phone, but he got the voicemail. He left a message and then reluctantly called Shakeena. Surprisingly, she answered on the second ring.

"Hello?"

"Good morning," he said.

"Uh, hey, Ken," she was nervous.

"You spoke to J-Bo?" he asked.

"Um no, no. I—Ken, I'm scared. I don't know what to say."

"It's alright. I'll get y'all on the line one of these days." Ken cleared his throat. "Are you okay?"

"Yea, why you ask that?" Ever since her secret had been let out the bag, Ken made her nervous.

"I'm just checkin' on you. Even though I'm pissed with you, I'm still obligated to take care of y'all until J-Bo comes home," he said.

Awwww, she thought. "Thank you, Ken."

"Yea, anyway, how's my nephew?" he asked.

"He's good. Him and KJ played all day and night after Nae dropped him off yesterday. I'm 'bout to go wake them up for school." Her nervousness had her blabbering at the mouth.

The fuck?

Ken kept calm, not wanting to tip his hand. "All day yesterday, huh?"

There was a long pause. "Mhmm," she replied. "And I gotta get them up and ready for class now."

These bitches up to somethin'.

"Go ahead and do that," Ken said. "I'll talk to you later."

***

"Delete it," he told her after taking his last spoon of cheese grits.

"Noooo, Peanut," Tiffany crooned. "It got some beautiful sights on there," she said, holding the camera in her hand.

"You the only person I know that wanna sit around recording strangers have sex," he joked before downing a glass of orange juice.

She playfully slapped his shoulder. "That's not what I was doing, bae. Shut up." She blushed. "And they weren't having sex. They were fucking!"

He shook his head at how freaky she was.

"Let me see the damn thing," he reached for the camera.

"Oh, you tryna be nasty? Huh, Peanut? Are you tryna watch some strangers have sex?" she mocked him.

They both erupted in laughter, then he snatched the camera from her.

"How do you get to it?" he asked after trying to find the video.

"Let me see." She took it from him and sat on his lap. "Now listen," she said once she found the video.

He looked at her, giving her his full attention.

"I was curious as to what was going on and I zoomed in," she admitted.

He giggled, then she held the camera up so they both could see and pressed *play*.

***

"C'mon, Nae, you know I gotta be on this damn plane!" Tez yelled out to her.

She was taking forever to get ready. She came down the short flight of stairs.

"I was getting my make-up straight," she said sarcastically, indicating that she was covering up the black eye. What was a simple welt had got worse overnight.

"I'm sorry." He cursed himself for not being able to control his temper.

"Let's go, Martez." She grabbed her keys off the countertop, and her phone rang. She looked from the phone to Tez. He knew it was Ken.

"Nae, don't say shit crazy. When I get back from Haiti, I'm taking you back with me." She arched her eyebrow like she needed some security to his statement.

"That's on everything I stand for. Now, answer the damn phone."

She cleared her throat and put on her sleepy voice. "Hello?"

"Good morning, beautiful," Ken said.

"Morning," she said softly.

"I wanna tell KJ good morning before he goes to school."

Her heart sped up and she looked at Tez.

"He's, um he—" She coughed.

"What?"

"He's already in school. I-I took him earlier."

Ken squeezed his eyes shut. There was no further question that she was having an affair. He felt betrayed. He really did believe in his heart that she would never go that far. Mr. Higa's words replayed in his head:

If I can't teach you a lot, always remember to trust no one. I don't even trust my own wife.

He felt like a chump for trusting his wife after a man that's been in the business for thirty-two years told him not to.

"Okay, where are you?" he managed to ask.

"Home. I'ma go to the shop in a minute."

Ken dropped his head and let his dreads hang. His self-control was really being tested.

"Okay," he sighed. "Love you."

"Love you, too." She hung up.

"You a'ight?" Tez asked.

She didn't respond. Just stood there for a while. "Yea, let's go."

They grabbed the rest of their things and left.

"What did he say?" Tez asked as they approached the car.

"He wanted to talk to KJ, but it's just the way he sounded. I feel like he knows something." She got in the driver's seat this time.

"Nah, he don't know shit. When I get back, you coming with me," he stated with authority.

Nae smiled but remained quiet.

***

Peanut just looked at the camera as if he was bored.

"Just skip to the good part," he told her. He was tired of looking at the stars and deers.

She put the camera on the table and jumped to her feet.

"You so anxious to see it. How 'bout this," she began shaking her ass.

The view plus the sound it made was something else.

Clap!

Clap!

Clap!

Clap!

Instantly, it gave him an erection. He glanced back at the camera and when she zoomed in, he was in a state of shock. His erection turned flaccid as his mind raced with solutions to how it was even possible that his luck was this good. Tiffany noticed his sudden change and stopped dancing.

"That's the good part baby. What's wrong?" she asked.

He was lost for words; he couldn't think straight. *This is proof! This is solid proof to get me outta Young Boss*, he thought. The sight was disgusting. He knew they were messing around, but it's a totally different feeling to actually see them first-hand having sex. Well, more like fucking. Tez was power-driving her from the back.

"Is there a Best Buy close around?" he asked.

She thought for a split second.

"How the hell am I supposed to know! Matter of fact, I seen one maybe a block before we got here, baby," she said.

He grabbed the camera, his keys and rushed out the cabin.

***

I can't believe this shit.

Ken's head was hung low. He was so upset but he couldn't express it because this tour was humongous. His only consolation was in the fact the man was kept away from his son. A commercial for the *I Got You* tracker came on the TV. Ken had the subscription, and though he never intended to use it in the manner he now contemplated, he wanted to see exactly how the thing worked.

He used his phone and followed the instruction to activate the tracking feature, and it wasn't long before he found Nae's location in Madison, Georgia, having been the same since yesterday. A deeper search revealed that the address was linked to the cabins in Hard Labor Creek. Ken felt terrible; on several occasions Nae had brought to his attention a desire to go to the cabins. So caught up in business, he had never gotten around to it. Now here she was. And he was certain she wasn't alone.

"I give her whatever she wants, we're filthy rich, I fuck her good, what can another man have to offer?" he asked himself. He knew what it was. Time. That's also one of the reasons he wanted to step down because he wants to spend more time with his wife and family. *I will forgive her*, he thought. He promised himself that after this tour she will get all of his time and attention, he'll step down from the Young Boss rankings since he has enough years in to do so and be a family man. He sat wondering if it was too late for him to do what he thought it was gonna take for him to fix the problem. *I gotta get this shit off my mind*, he thought.

***

They pulled up at the primary terminal of the airport.

"Listen, Bae." Tez unbuckled his seat belt. "When I get back I'ma have shit planned out, shawty. DJ gone already be out the picture. Ken gon' get out the picture and it's gone be me, you, Gia and KJ, but—" he paused and grinned.

"But what, nigga?" Nae playfully pushed his shoulder.

"Y'all gone need to learn Creole."

Nae smiled.

"Oh shit, I almost forgot. He grabbed his phone from his pocket and searched for Smoke's name.

"Forgot what?"

"Peanut gotta go." He found Smoke's name and called. "He knows too fucking much."

"Hello?" Smoke answered.

"You 'round Peanut?" Tez asked.

"Nah, what's up, Big Bra?"

"Peanut D.O.S." Tez hung up.

Nae smiled. "So, you think you bossed up? You can just make one phone call and get niggas touched?"

He smiled. "I been bossed up. I can get the president touched, hell you tawmbout?"

"Whatever, Martez!" she laughed.

He kissed her. "Listen, shawty, I love you so fucking much and I can't hold it back no more."

"Just take me with you noooow," she pouted.

He thought about it. "Nah, I gotta handle some things alone first. When I come back to Atlanta from time to time, y'all gone be in Haiti. Ken ain't gon' know where you at."

"I love you, Martez," a tear rolled down her face.

***

"Welcome to Best Buy. How may I help you, sir?" the older white woman working there asked Peanut.

"I need a piece of a clip on a CD from this." He held the Kodak camera up.

"Say again," she didn't understand.

He took three deep breaths to calm himself down. *Maybe I was talkin' too fast*, he thought.

"My lady recorded a video last night," he paused to ensure she was following him.

She nodded.

"I want fifteen seconds of the video on a DVD," he continued.

"Ohh, okay that's easy," she plugged it up.

She pressed *play* after putting a blank DVD in the slot.

"Nice," she commented on the stars.

"Is this where you want to begin recording, sir?" she asked.

He shook his head. She skipped it a bit.

"Right there, start now." He almost jumped out of his skin.

She pressed *record* as Tiffany began zooming in. Once the sight became vivid, her jaw dropped, and she gasped.

"Sir, we don't do—" he stopped her when he slid a hundred-dollar bill on the counter.

***

Asia came in the room and caught Smoke staring off into space at nothing. She could tell something had him zoned out.

"Baby?" He didn't respond, let alone budge. "Baby, what's wrong?"

He ignored her. His phone was face up on the bed and she saw Tez was the last person he'd spoken to.

"Smoke, talk to me." She lifted his head up and made him face her eye-to-eye.

"Is your friend okay?" she asked.

My friend, my friend, he thought. Out of all the people within the Young boss rankings Peanut was his only friend. They grew up together, went to the same schools, joined Young Boss together and now this.

"Get the fuck away from me, bitch!" Smoke pushed her. As she tumbled down, she tripped over his foot, causing excruciating pain.

"Ahhh!" he squawked. He looked at her on the floor in tears.

"C'mere, baby, I'm sorry," his voice was soft.

***

They met with super producer Rada at a high-class studio in Austin. The city of Austin is Texas's capital and has a population of 16,986,510 people and still growing. Rada and Ken had established a lot of healthy relationships there. Everyone seemed to be enjoying themselves. Everyone, but Ken.

"You a'ight, homie?" Rada asked.

Ken wasn't speaking to anyone. He was in a chair on the end of the row doing something on his phone.

"Yea, I'm straight, homie," he looked at Rada.

Rada tried to hand him the rotating weed, but he declined. *Moe fa me*, he thought.

"Oh yea. Did you ever halla at da homie?" he asked when he saw Psycho bobbing his head to the beat he played.

It's Rada music! his tag on the beat turned the atmosphere up.

"Yea, we got an understanding. After the tour, I'ma rewrite his contracts," he answered dryly.

"Okay." Rada went back to his seat behind the computer.

The women came walking in the lab, and that's when shit got live. It was twenty of them and they all looked great. Dark- skinned, light-skinned, Cuban, white, BBW, thick, petite, skinny, big booty, little booty, big titties, little titties, whatever you liked. Ken took interest in a few of them, but he began thinking about Nae. He felt like if he just flat out cheated on her then he wouldn't have any rights being mad about her cheating. On the contrary, he knew he needed to keep his mind off Nae until he returned to Atlanta because he wouldn't be able to be as productive as he needed to be in Texas.

Ken had the idea to speak with Rada about more business and less pleasure. But as long as he's been in the game, he fully understood that pleasure is gonna come in their field, whether you wanted it to or not. And to give credence to the thought, a woman came and took a seat across from him. She sat a bit closer than a stranger should be seated. He frowned.

"Hi, I'm Zaya." She reached her hand out for a shake.

She had beautiful chocolate skin, wore her long dark hair in a silk press, and sported Gucci pumps, a Gucci necklace and a sky-blue skin-tight Gucci dress that stopped two inches below the knee.

He nodded his head. "I'm Ken."

She smiled and he took in her full lips. Her pink gums and Colgate smile let him know she took care of herself.

"I like your hair," she complimented.

He couldn't take his eyes off her lips; when she noticed, she blew him a kiss. He smiled, then put his phone away. She clapped for him.

"That's what I've been waiting for you to do."

"And why's that?" He expected her to respond like a groupie. They always did.

"Because I want your attention," she said.

That's a new one, he thought. "What do you do besides this?"

She looked around in a state of confusion. "Besides what?" She caught on quick and decided now was as good a time as ever to set the record straight. "I'ma tell you this straight up. I got my own everything, don't need a man for nothing, not even sex. The toys feel real these days. I've never been a sack chaser and I'm interested in you, but if you're not gonna respect me I'll gladly leave."

Ken was unimpressed. He decided to ask more questions to detect her motive. "Am I the only one in this room you find interesting?"

"Actually no, but you are the only one that looks like you have respect and knows how to treat a queen."

"All the sack chasers say that," he said.

"Bye, Ken." Zaya stood to walk away, and Ken grabbed her arm.

"Zaya, hold up." He stood up to talk face to face. "Listen, I apologize," he let her arm free. "I'm having a bad day."

She looked off around the studio. "I understand."

"You wanna stay a minute?"

Ken sat back down, and she did the same, this time not as close. He had never met a woman in all his years in this business that had an attitude like his possessions and presence didn't matter. They were usually all over his nuts like the hair that grew there.

"So, what are you doing here?" he asked.

"My friends asked me to come along," she pointed to a few women that were dressed hoeish and acting like groupies. Zaya almost felt embarrassed, but she was used to it by now.

"You ever hear the saying birds of a feather flock together?" he asked.

"Pardon?" she asked over Rada's loud beat.

He looked at Rada and motioned for him to turn the music down just enough to hear the person beside you. Rada complied, and Ken repeated the question.

"Yea, but it's only true to a certain degree."

He scooted closer and before she could object, he asked, "You think so?"

She nodded. "I know so."

"Explain."

"Well, I can tell that these guys in here have no respect for women and probably none for themselves." She looked at one of the homies all touchy-touchy with a girl. "They are thirsty for sex, slaves to money and some of them do things they don't have to do just to say they did it." She stopped.

"You just got off subject, Sweetie," he said, disappointed. He felt like she was another girl that thought she was so smart, but she was really a dumb ass.

"No, I didn't," she smiled. "You're flocking with these guys. You're all of the same feathers, but to a certain degree." She made him feel a bit silly.

"What makes you think I'm not the same type of guy they are? Maybe I'm a bit more laid back."

She had already began shaking her head before he finished talking. "I see through what you're saying now. I can see what the average person can't."

"So, what about me? Can you see what the average person can't?" Ken smiled.

"You're really sweet, but a lot of people ain't lucky enough to meet that side of you."

He laughed. She was correct, but he'd heard that a thousand times. She knew what that laugh was insinuating, so she took another shot at it. "You just want to be happy." She stopped to catch his reaction. He instantly thought of how unhappy he was right now, knowing his wife was cheating on him. He raised his left hand up to show his wedding ring. That was his best defense at the moment.

"I'm married. Been married for ten years," he said.

"It wouldn't matter if you've been married for twenty years. I know you're not happy. Y'all are having problems and I hate to say it, but it's probably not gonna last that much longer." Those words stung his heart.

"So, you're some type of psychic?" he asked.

She shook her head. "No, I'm a very observant woman and I can look in your eyes and see everything I just said."

He felt like she'd put her hand in his body and dug around in his soul to know the things she'd just said.

"What do you do?" He was fixated to her already.

"I'm studying psychology, but in the meantime, I'm a Registered Nurse."

"So, you're trying to be a psychologist?" he asked.

"That's right." She caught him staring at her lips again and blew him another kiss.

"You wanna kiss me?" he asked.

She nodded.

He leaned in, and she leaned back. "Just because I want to doesn't mean I'm going to. It's called self-control."

***

Nae rode to Shakeena's house in silence. There was a grin on her face. A grin of deceit and lies. The thought of knowing Tez was gonna make them official as a couple brought joy to her heart. *I love you, Martez*, she thought while looking in the mirror to see if the darkness around her eyes were noticeable, but her make-up did a great job of covering it up. She thought about how good it felt when Tez fucked her. The idea brought moisture to her slit, and she bounced in her seat, thinking of him inside her as she turned right off the Thornton Road exit ramp.

She could've taken the Bankhead route and got to Austell Road quicker, but she wanted to pass Birch Landing. Every time she passed Birch Landing Apartments, she got emotional. This time, instead of passing the apartment complex, she used her right blinker and turned inside there. She parked at the mailboxes because the security gates wouldn't allow her to pass without a code or a key card. After Diamond's death almost a decade ago, the owner was so scared of getting sued that he fired every employee, hired new ones and installed top-of-the-line security cameras as well as high-end security guards.

Nae sat in her car and wept. "Diamond, I love you, Sis," she said to herself. The more she thought about that day, the more overwhelmed she became. As she cried, she replayed that night in her head from almost ten years ago. But whenever she did, for some reason, she couldn't make out any of the perpetrator's faces

"Why!" she punched the steering wheel. The fact that she had never been able to identify her sister's killers ate away at her soul. She was the only witness, and a lousy, good-for-nothing one at that. She wished she could've done something about it, even if nothing more than trade places.

She thought about the severity of her death, and the tears became uncontrollable. She wanted to call someone, but her mom, dad and sister were all dead.

"I'ma catch those pussy mothafuckas!" she screamed.

Knock! Knock!

A large male knocked on her car window. He wore a black rent-a-cop outfit, so she knew he was some type of security. She rolled the window down.

"I'm Jeff," he identified himself. "Head of Birch Landing's security. Ma'am, are you alright?"

Nae sniveled and wiped her eyes. "Yes, I'm fine."

"Ma'am, I'm sorry, I know this is a bad time, but you have to leave now. My supervisors instructed me to ask you to leave if you're not a resident."

Where were you and your supervisors ten years ago, she thought. She gave him the look of death as she put her car in reverse. By time she pulled in Shakeena's driveway, her tears were dry, but they were still there. She pulled some wipes from her handbag, pulled the visor down so she could use the mirror, and wiped her eyes. She finished, got out and headed to the porch. Shakeena opened the door as Nae approached her doorstep.

"Nae!" Shakeena screamed in excitement. "Are you okay?" She pulled Nae in the house and sat her on the couch. "What happened?" Shakeena asked, concerned.

"It's my fault," Nae said solemnly.

Shakeena was confused.

"What's your fault, Nae? Talk to me." She wanted to help her friend.

"Diamond," Nae said, breaking down. "I knew testifying was a bad idea, but I wanted to be there for her and what she b-believed in."

Shakeena didn't want Nae to go into a state of depression and start demoralizing herself. She took her into her embrace. "I understand, baby, but you can't blame yourself. You're gonna build coal up in ya heart."

Little did she know, the coal had already built up in her heart and it's just expanding. Nae knew sooner or later it was gonna happen. She knew if she didn't get some stress relief or counseling, she would explode. She took some counseling after Diamond's death. It helped her get by for a while, but sometimes the pressure feels so thick on her that those "don't- think-about-it" tactics wouldn't work.

"Nae—Nae," Shakeena called her name while peering down at her."

"How the fuck can I not think about my little sister having her asshole blown out through her fucking face!" she yelled.

Shakeena just held on tighter. She knew Nae needed to vent. Sometimes it's best to just allow a person to vent in whichever manner they feel is necessary. Even though it comes out as an outburst majority of the times, those feelings are momentary sometimes. Kenna knew crying was good for the soul. Especially in Nae's case, crying can release all the poisonous toxins from the heart and mind if you allow it to.

"Where is KJ?" She wiped her face, forgetting today is Monday.

"He's in school, girl. Today is Monday," she reminded her.

A slight smile crossed her face, and she felt really silly not knowing the day.

"I talked to Ken a few hours ago," Shakeena stated, nervousness building in her as she thought about the bad news she was about to give her. She hated to add to her already heavy load, but she had fucked up.

"You called him?" Nae asked, hoping she wasn't mentioned.

"No, he called. He wanted to know if I spoke to J-Bo lately," she said.

Nae just looked at her for more.

Shakeena folded. "Girl, his ass had me nervous when he called, and I kinda forgot and told him that you dropped KJ off to me yesterday." She felt bad for getting her caught up.

Nae's heart dropped to her ass.

It was clear then why Ken had called and what she had heard in his voice.

Fuck!

"I gotta go," Nae said, handing Shakeena the babysitting money that she owed her.

Really the money hadn't been for babysitting at all. Shakeena and Nae had figured out years ago that they both had something to hide from the men in their lives. Neither of them knew the specific details about what kind of trouble that they were getting into, but they somehow came together in an effort to help each other get away with their dirt.

For years, Nae would drop KJ off with Shakeena when she needed to sneak away with Tez, and Nae always gave Shakeena a heads-up when Ken was going to be coming around for KJ so that she could make sure Shawn was long gone before Ken showed up.

Slowly but surely, all of Nae's dirty laundry was about to be aired the fuck out.

***

"So, you have to kill Peanut?" Asia asked nervously. The words were coming out of her mouth, but she couldn't believe it. She didn't believe such a time has come. Smoke and Peanut have been tight for as long as she'd known them. Besides, they were friends years before she even came in the picture.

Smoke nodded slowly.

"Bae, there must be a way around it," she said, hoping there was.

Smoke shook his head. "Bossman made an order. I gotta handle it."

Once reality overcame Smoke, he was drained, dehydrated, light-headed and everything else on those lines. He remembered when he got Peanut recruited to Young Boss—

The bell rang that ended school as Smoke hopped to his feet and shot out the door. Ms. E, his algebra teacher, was saying something about homework, but his ears were dead to that fuck shit. He hit the hallways and posted up with the other Young Bosses. Peanut walked up and shook his hand.

"What's up, bro?" he asked.

"Ain't shit man, just coolin' wit' the bosses, trappin, you know how this shit go," he replied.

"You might as well be Young Boss," one of the homies said to Peanut.

Peanut always hung out with them to the point everyone assumed he was Young Boss. Niggas wouldn't fuck with him just because they thought he was a member. Once, there was a big brawl between Get Money Squad and Young Boss, and Peanut rode with them.

He laughed. "Nah, I'on really care for gangs," he declined the offer without offending anybody.

"Peanut, we ain't no damn gang. We a family, a brotherhood. We got certain morals that we live by and rules to follow, but definitely not a gang," Smoke rectified.

After they kicked it a bit longer, Smoke took Peanut to the west side where the main trap house was to meet Tez.

"This my potna Peanut. Shawty solid," he told Tez.

Tez knew what he meant.

"So, you ready to be 25-2?" Tez asked, not taking his eyes off the money he was counting.

He nodded.

Tez made a call and began asking Peanut some personal questions while repeating his answers to the other party on the phone. He listened for a while then hung up.

"A'ight, shawty straight," Tez said as he got up to put Peanut through proper training.

Now, he was being sent to take him out. Maybe Peanut had been right all those years ago. What if Young Boss had never been for him?

"Babe—babe—Smoke," she tried to get his attention.

"What's up?" he asked.

"Try to talk to Ken," she said.

He shook his head. "Ken has no sympathy for niggas who wanna leave, unless they put in a certain amount of years or work."

"All the niggas he killed, does that count for something?" Her eyes became watery.

"It does but it ain't enough to leave. And don't cry." He wiped her tears.

She'd grown to really like Peanut beyond their sexual orgies. He pulled out his phone and called Peanut. With no answer, he was prompted to leave a message

"What's up, bro? I respect what you doing, my nigga, and I love you. I just wanna smoke one more blunt witchu before we go our separate ways. Oh yea, Tez said everything good witchu. The senior homies green-lighted ya leave."

He hung up, then he and Asia cried silently.

***

Peanut and Tiffany sat on the couch having a bible study amongst themselves. He explained to her in-depth the importance of the word. She understood some of it while a lot of it was brain-wrecking trying to comprehend, but she would learn and allow him to teach her. She laughed as he made nowadays examples to help her understand the parables from the King James Bible. She admired Peanut as he spoke the word; it was his graveness that caught her attention.

He's so serious about it. He was nothing like this six years ago when we first met, she thought.

"Y'all broke ass niggas betta throw some mothafucking money fa dese two bitches that's finna come out!" DJ SlickWitIt blared into the microphone.

Everybody sitting in front of the main stage began making noise. They knew the two bitches DJ SlickWitIt spoke of were the twins. Peanut sat silently among the crowd of people. As the twins put on a show, he watched Tiffany. Once she noticed, she gave him all the eye contact she could give. She mouthed some things to him, but he never replied. His lack of thirst made her pussy wet. After the performance, she made her way to the main floor where he was seated.

"What's up?" she asked in nothing but a thong.

He glanced at her titties then looked her in the eyes and nodded. "What's up, shawty."

"You want a dance?" she asked.

A thick, bodacious, dark-skinned chick walked by, and he locked in on her ass then looked back at her. Before he could answer, she sucked her teeth.

"Why you so fucking rude, man?"

She felt played and unwanted, but on the contrary she liked it. There were so many niggas that would love a dance from her, so when a nigga like Peanut gave off the 'you ain't shit' impression, she wanted to know why.

"I'm not rude. It's bitches in here, I'm not 'posed to look? The fuck they walking round naked foe?" he asked aggressively. She knew then she wouldn't turn back.

Peanut's phone rang while teaching his girl about the Bible, and it was Smoke. He let it go to voicemail and continued doing what he was learning to do best. His phone beeped, notifying him of a voicemail. He knew it was Smoke and decided to listen to it a little later.

"Sooo, Jesus never had sex?" Tiffany flashed her smile.

Peanut couldn't help but grin. He put the Bible down. "Is that all yo' lil' nasty ass think about?"

She slid her hand in his pants.

***

Fuck! Fuck! Fuck! Nae thought as she stumbled through the salon.

"You a'ight?" Reshia was wondering if her friend was drunk.

"I'm fine," she answered, going through the back door to her office. She flopped down in her rolling chair and put her hands over her face. She was trying to figure out what she would tell Ken. Honestly, she was ready to tell him the truth, but she promised Tez she'd wait til' he got back to handle it. She knew Ken wasn't a jackass, so she couldn't tell him anything and she knew he wasn't a pushover. *Yea, maybe it's best to let Tez handle it. Ain't tryna be on forensic files,* she thought as her heart rate accelerated.

***

Mr. Luis contacted Ken unusually early just to ensure he was in town. He wasn't, but he took the first flight back to Georgia. They had to have a private meeting with the crooked appeal judges and the new D.A. The deal was already sealed after J-Bo and Flip were first sentenced to life without parole, but a lot of shit can change in the span of ten years. Ken had a thousand different feelings running through him at once. He was overly excited about seeing the two cousins being liberated from prison after a decade. He was highly confused and disappointed in his wife. He shook his head. He still couldn't believe it, and time and time again he found himself asking why.

He just didn't understand. She wanted for nothing from the very moment they had made it official. He'd done nothing other than enhanced her life and make it easier. Women baffled him the way they wanted a man with money, then got in their feelings when the man didn't have the same amount of leisure time as the broke niggas they were used to. The time was coming where he could retire, but until then this was what it was: time or money. High quality men didn't have time to lay up on the regular. If he chose to do so and downgraded there lifestyle, or worse, fell off altogether, they would scream deadbeat.

He sat back and considered the possibility that this was his karma, that it was all a sign that he and Nae weren't meant to be together for life. What more could it be?

Zaya came to mind, and he considered her timely appearance. He felt the guilt of dealing with her, though he knew Nae wasn't being faithful. Yet, he couldn't help but smile as he evaluated his like for the woman. He was with her every day since the day they met. He got her a room close to his after she'd refused his offer to stay with him. But every day, there she was; at every show and studio with the team.

Psycho had noticed how cozy they were getting with each other, and one night had asked, "You ain't gon' take ya ring off?"

Ken laughed. "I'ma boss for real, young nigga. She knows I'm married."

He'd met a lot of women in this business, but none made him feel like Zaya did. None of them could hold intellectual conversations, and none of them rejected an invitation to his hotel suite. She was different. Didn't want his money; didn't want him to have her body just because of who he was. He knew she liked him for him, and it felt great. He rode to the airport as Zaya's passenger. She had a silver 2015 Infinity. He tried to kiss her before he entered the airport, but she didn't let him.

"I might give you a kiss if I ever see you again." She winked at him and blew him a kiss. "Call me when you get situated."

Smiling, she drove off. And as he made his way in the airport smiling and shaking his head, he knew that wouldn't be the last time he saw her.

***

"I guess I'll go smoke one last blunt with him," Peanut told Tiffany after numerous voicemails and texts from Smoke.

Tiffany put her hand on his arm. "Are you sure it's not a set-up?" She had stressed her bad feeling about the meeting several times already.

He nodded. "Everything is fine, baby, you know me and Smoke is a'ight. He would give me a heads-up if any funny business was goin' down."

Chapter Twenty

Nae pulled into the airport to pick up her husband despite all of her prior feelings about the whole Tez situation. She was overcome by a nervousness as she realized Ken was about to be seated next to her. It was easy to want to tell him it's over through the phone, but face to face was the part that took balls and she didn't have any.

He came walking through the electric sliding doors, talking on his phone and pulling his luggage. She was so scared that she made a big mistake. She didn't get out the vehicle and greet him. He took note of that as he threw his bag into the back seat and flopped down in the passenger.

"Okay, well, I'm literally just getting back in Georgia." He signaled Nae to proceed, and she glided into traffic. "I'm about to grab some of that paperwork and come directly to you," Ken went on. "Give me," he looked at his Rolex, "forty-five minutes tops—Okay, thank you, Mr. Luis."

He hung up, said nothing to his wife, then dialed for Susie at the office. "This is Kenneth," he said to the receptionist. "Get Susie on the line."

"This is Susie," she answered.

"Hey, that paperwork I had regarding J-Bo, put it all together and have it ready to go. I'm in a rush. I'll be there in twenty."

He hung up and shot Nae a disgusted look. Her actions brought a certain feeling to his stomach.

"Babe, I gotta tell you something," she almost sounded innocent.

He reclined in his seat and rested his hands on his chest.

"What's that?" he asked calmly. He didn't expect her to break down and tell him the truth.

"When I told you that I took KJ to school Monday, I kinda lied," she struggled to say while biting her bottom lip.

Ken was silent, so she continued while she had the floor.

"I just needed a break—"

"So where was he?" He cut her off.

"Keena's house," she was honest.

"And where were you?" he asked before she could continue.

"I was home, Ken, I just needed me time. I didn't want to be bothered."

He took a deep breath. "Well, unfortunately, when you're married and have a child, you don't get much me time." He emphasized the word *me*. "You have to be bothered. It's not all about you anymore, Nae, it's about us! Me and you became one the day you said *I do*, so what the fuck got you so stressed out that you go take my son to this bitch house? Why the fuck you haven't spoken to me about it?" She knew she couldn't talk to him about it now.

"Just thinking about my dad, Ken," her voice cracked. Her tears didn't hit home this time.

He sucked his teeth and fanned her off. She knew he wasn't going for her fuck shit. But she had to try. "You don't believe me, bae?" she asked, crying now.

"Why didn't you get out and hug or kiss me when you just seen me come out the airport?"

"I-I-I um," she was stuck.

"I-I-I my ass!" he mocked her. "You felt guilty, that's why. I'ma tell you one thing, Nae." He pointed his finger as he spoke. "This nigga you fucking better not be nobody I know. If he is, y'all might as well get together and blow y'all own brains out."

It was official. He knew, and she was still alive because he didn't know who she was cheating with. Nae was quiet. She was terrified by his threat.

He called Susie again when he was five minutes away. One of the graphic designers was standing outside with a cardboard FedEx box full of paper. The car came to a full stop, and he rolled his window down.

"Hey, Zach, put it in the back seat of my black Beemer," he said.

Zach nodded. "She told me to tell you that everything wasn't in order, so she just emptied the entire bottom drawer in here." Zach held up the box, Ken nodded, and Zach walked away to do what he was told to do.

Ken took a deep breath, contemplating what to say to Nae, if anything. He couldn't register in his mind the reason behind her betrayal.

He cleared his throat. "Nae, why are you cheating on me?"

She could hear the hurt in his voice and see the tears he fought back in his eyes. She was taken aback, but once it sunk in, she was in pain, she had a serious heartache. She couldn't face him, she knew he would find out sooner or later, but she had to give it a shot.

"Ken, why the hell would you ask me some shit like that? I'm not cheating on you!" she tried to snap.

"Come on, now, Nae. Kill the defensive attitude. That type of stuff don't work on me as you should already know. I'm willing to forgive you, move on, but you must be ready to move on. We should start with *why*?"

She frowned up. "I'm not cheatin—" she was saying before he rudely opened the car door to exit. She got out on the driver side and was right behind him hollering. "So, you mean to tell me you gone be that disrespectful?"

He turned around about to say something for her to think about then leave, but as he analyzed her, he noticed something extremely wrong. Her ring finger was missing a ring again. He approached her with fury in his eyes, getting close enough to kiss her. Her heart began skipping when he got so close.

"Ken, what the fuck are you doing?" she stepped back, frantically.

"Why isn't your wedding ring on your finger, Nae?" he sounded calm, but his eyes said otherwise.

She looked like a jackass as tears welled up in her eyes. It was then that she realized she hadn't had on her ring ever since the day he left for Texas. Her face began to redden as she was filled with embarrassment.

Ain't no way I'm slippin like this, she thought. She got so comfortable with it off for Tez that when he left, everything still felt fine. It wasn't hard to not be wearing a ring, because Ken was absent also.

"Baby," she said staring in his eyes. "I was cooking earlier, and I didn't want it to get dirty," she lied.

He so badly was restraining himself from reaching back as far as he could and slapping the piss out of her.

"I'm gonna leave before I do something I'll regret," he stated and went to the Beemer.

***

"You sure you don't want me to ride with you, baby?" Asia asked.

She had to work tonight, but if Smoke wanted her present at the scene for any reason she would call in and accompany him. She loved Peanut, but of course Smoke came first, and she knew how hard this was for him. He shook his head in sorrow thinking about when he told Peanut he'd get killed for trying to leave. He wasn't expecting to be the one to have to do it.

"Nah, you go to work, I'll prolly come through right after this," he said, standing in the full-body mirror adjusting his clothes.

He wore a black pair of 501 Levi's, some black Jordan's, number sevens and a long black sleeve thermal. He pointed to his .45 automatic lying on the bed. She passed it to him, he checked the magazine, put one in the head and tucked it.

Asia dropped her head in sorrows as she thought of what he was going to do. Just the thought of Peanut screaming and trying to fight for his life picked at her heart. Smoke's head was down too, so she knew he was pondering on the same thingt. She wanted to tell him after he killed Peanut to just pack up and they go find Utopia, but she knew his fate would be equal as Peanut's. She now understood how Peanut got Tiffany to feel the way she did, and why people wanted out after so long. There was no understanding. She was no longer sure she wanted Smoke to be apart of Young Boss, but she doubted she could get him to walk away even at her disapproval.

He turned for the door, and she leaped up and was on his heels.

"Smoke," she cried.

He turned around and kissed her.

"Talk," he said.

"Please end it quick. Don't make him suffer."

He nodded and turned for the door.

***

Peanut was still drying off from their shower while Tiffany was already dry and lubricating her skin with cocoa butter lotion. That was the only kind that worked for her. They had planned on going to meet Smoke then shooting out to dinner. They'd already made reservations at the small Italy. They looked at some houses online in Miami, Florida. Tiffany saw a picture-perfect three-bedroom home that sat on the border of the beach. She anticipated waking up early and watching the sunset, standing in the sand.

The property owner was contacted and Peanut had wired the down payment. They were going to head out in the morning.

Peanut pulled on his boxers and pants. "I'm ready to live a clean, stress-free life."

Tiffany smiled. "I know. Me too," she said, snapping on her bra. "You think I should go to Bible school?"

"It's not about what school I think you should go to. It's about what's on your heart, Love." He sat in the chair and put on his socks.

"Bae, I know," she admitted. "I just don't know what to do with my life."

"Don't try to do what you think will make me happy," He told her. "Do what makes you happy but find happiness in Jesus Christ's words. You'll kill yaself trying to satisfy me and you're not at peace."

All dressed, Peanut retrieved his keys from the table, and they headed out.

"Be careful, baby," she said as she got that bad feeling once again.

As Peanut turned into Sweet Water Park, he searched for Smoke's car so he could park next to him, but he didn't see him. There were only four cars parked out there, and Peanut's made five. He parked on the far end of the other three. The four cars were all luxury; he blended in just perfect. The cars were abandoned and nobody was outside, so the vehicles must have belonged to the staff of the park.

"You don't see him?" Tiffany asked, looking at the four cars.

Peanut scanned the area once more before answering. "Naw, but he'll be here." He stopped when he saw an all-black Charger cruising down the hill.

"There he goes right there, baby," he pointed at Smoke, who was parking an unreasonable distance away. Peanut opened his door, and Tiffany grabbed his arm. "What's up, Love?"

She squeezed tighter. "Be careful, Peanut."

"I will, Boo." He kissed her forehead.

"Take your gun with you," she pleaded.

"What?" he laughed at her suggestion. "Baby, you know I don't carry around a gun anymore. Are you crazy?" He couldn't believe she thought Smoke would kill him. "Listen, Tiffany, Smoke is and always will be my brother. If anything, he's about to warn me."

Something still didn't feel right. She looked up and trained her eyes on the full moon.

"Okay, I love you. Be careful," she said before kissing him and releasing his arm.

Smoke opened his door as Peanut approached.

"What's up, bro?" Peanut asked, slapping his hand.

Smoke just nodded and together they walked over to where the pavilion was. Once they were seated, Smoke lit the weed and inhaled rather deeply. He only pulled that way under stress.

"You a'ight?" Peanut asked.

He nodded as he blew the smoke out. Looking in his eyes, Peanut saw something strange. The same look Smoke has while killing somebody just mixed with some pain.

"So, what Tez was saying?" Peanut asked before inhaling the Kush.

Smoke thought about exactly what Tez said.

"Peanut D.O.S." Those words dawned on him and made him shiver.

Damn!

“Shiiid, he just told me that the homies made an exception for you.”

“That’s all he said?” Peanut asked, passing him the weed.

Smoke was waiting for the right moment, and he wanted the last four cars gone before he made his move.

Four Caucasian men made an exit to their cars, and Smoke took another hit of the blunt.

“I know that’s right, Jim," one man said to the other. "Tell Megan that I said hello.”

“Will do,” Jim said before entering his car and pulling off into the night.

The other two friends said their goodbyes and left.

“Hey, I’m locking up. My security will be here in exactly eight minutes.”

He nodded, knowing they knew what he meant.

“Alright, Mr. Sweetwater,” Peanut waved at the park’s owner.

“And stop smoking that shit here!” he barked before turning to them.

It was time, Smoke thought.

***

Ken laid back on his bed watching Psycho’s new video for his song, *Grizzy*. His business with the lawyer and appeal judges went well. J-Bo would be home next week, and he would be able to come home sooner, but he has to take a blood test for disease screening. He had his blood and other people’s blood on him during the clashing of the gangs, so they have to ensure he didn’t contract any blood borne diseases. The warden was gonna take out a warrant on him and Flip for every deceased person, but the moment Ken got wind of that, he offered a quarter million dollars. That dirty, money-hungry, bald-headed, sonofabitch—Stanley Williams—cancelled the warrant notion and took the two cousins’ names out of the report as aggressors. He made them appear as victims. It went swell.

He spoke to Nae again about her act. She continued to deny all accusations from him, but she told him how she wasn't happy anymore. He took it light. He could feel the end nearing as he felt the beginning for Zaya approaching. He smiled at the thought of her. Nae came in and got a pillow and a blanket.

"I'm sleeping downstairs," she said.

He didn't even acknowledge her. He was so upset with her, he wanted to get up and whoop her ass.

"Close my door behind you," he said as she pulled the knob as hard as she could, slamming the door.

He smiled as he dialed for Zaya. He looked at the time, ensuring it wasn't too late. *It's only 9:45 p.m., not too late*, he thought.

"Hello?" she answered.

"I'm situated," he smiled, rubbing his feet together.

She let out a soft heartwarming laugh.

"Where's ya wife?" she asked, wondering why they weren't in the bed together at a time like this.

"In Fort Worth, Texas," he flirted.

***

Asia was at the club working and all she could think about was Peanut being killed tonight by his best friend. She knew the stress was visible when the owner called her to his office.

"Look, Asia, I don't know what the fuck you got goin' on, but you need to tighten up! These niggas ain't feeling ya lack of enthusiasm."

She looked down, and the pain could be seen on her face.

"Go to the back and take a thirty," he ordered.

She thought about how Tiffany would feel if she found out she knew and didn't tell her. *Fuck that*, she thought before reaching for her purse.

***

Once Mr. Sweetwater pulled off, death could be seen in the late night's air and Tiffany had seen it.

"I guess this is it," Peanut said, standing from his seat.

Smoke stood next.

"Yea, but I wanna halla at you 'bout sum else," Smoke said weakly.

Peanut tried to think what else needed to be discussed between the two of them and why was Smoke avoiding eye contact.

"I love you, Peanut," Smoke said, discreetly pulling his .45 from his waist.

"I love you to—" he was saying before Tiffany's screams cut him off.

"Peanut! It's a set-up! Dey told him to kill you!" she hopped in the driver's seat of the 300C.

Peanut pushed Smoke down to the ground and took off running up the hill. Once Smoke got back to his feet, he stood still and opened fire. Peanut was hit six times as he finally made it to the car. Once he was in, she smashed out on the gas and peeled off. Smoke ran behind the car and began shooting again, hitting Peanut once more in the back of the head. Tiffany was all out of voice to scream. She quietly cried as she raced to the hospital.

Fuck! Smoke thought, jumping in his whip, following behind them.

Chapter Twenty-One

It had been a while since Tez reached out to Ken, and he was extremely pissed for his lack of communication regarding Peanut's execution. He felt like Tez was moving too fast and getting beside himself. Ever since Ken told him that he'd be in charge soon, it seemed as if his nuts had magnified. He hadn't heard from Peanut or Smoke since Tez left, so he hit up Smoke to check on them and he informed him of the previous event. Ken usually didn't call Tez's home phone in Haiti unless it was very urgent. After waiting thirty seconds for the international call to go through, DJ picked up.

"*Sak pase*, Kenny?" she answered because his number was saved in their phone's contacts.

He took a seat on the couch, frowned up.

"Hold on," she said in heavy accent.

"Hello?" Tez answered, knowing this had to be important.

"Nigga, what the fuck wrong with you?" he barked through his line.

Tez had to put space between his ear and the phone because of Ken's bass. Tez eluded responding for a second to think. He just knew it was over. Somehow, Ken found out about him and Nae. *How the fuc—* His thoughts were interrupted by Ken's voice.

"How the fuck you gon' call a hit on one of the homies without my approval? Who the fuck you think you are?" He was irate.

Even though he still had some answering to do, he felt a lot more relieved to know that this call wasn't about him fucking Nae. He let out a sigh of relief.

"You were on tour, Big Bra. I didn't wanna fuck up yo' business with our problems, so I handled it. That's what I was talking 'bout when I said we will talk later."

"What exactly happened?" he asked, already knowing the part Smoke told him. He wanted to hear what Tez had to say.

Tez told him everything that happened plus some. Ken was silent. He knew resigning was intolerable for the amount of years Peanut had in and the only answer for such a request is D.O.S.

Damn, Peanut! he thought.

"What's up with the funeral?" he asked, making a note in his mind to help pay for it and be present. *I gotta get in contact with his people*, he thought.

"Shiiid, ain't heard shit about his body." He didn't want to say those words at first because he didn't want things to appear as if he didn't have it under control. He knew Ken wasn't feeling his answer based on his silence.

"Listen I—" he stammered.

"Tez, what do you mean you haven't heard shit about the body?" He was perplexed. In all his years of killing and calling shots he'd never not known the status of the body. Unless, of course, he didn't die.

"Haven't been on the news or in the streets, but he had somebody driving so maybe dey took him somewhere to die," he tried to make sense of the situation.

Just then it dawned on him that Peanut was accompanied by someone. He hadn't thought much of it until now. *Why wasn't he alone? Was it the bitch he was with at the hotel that night?* he thought, not knowing if the driver was a man or woman.

"Are you positive Smoke's shots were successful?" Ken asked.

"Who you know got hit with .45 seven times plus once in the head and lived?"

"Okay, I'ma try to see what's up with him. Keep me updated if you hear anything."

"A'ight, bro, Young Boss," Tez said.

"Young Boss," Ken said before hanging up.

He shed a few tears for Peanut. He called at least twenty hospitals, seeking information on Peanut. After getting nowhere, he called to the streets, and still nothing. One thing he'd learn is that if anyone knows Peanuts whereabouts, it would be Tiffany.

He stepped into Diamonds of Atlanta, seeking her. He'd seen her before, but he couldn't quite put a face with her.

"You want a dance?" a skinny petite stripper asked, knowing who he was.

"I want a dance from Tiffany," he requested.

The girl twirled in front of him. *That hoe been M.I.A. for a week*, she thought. Based off the way he looked at her, she knew he didn't know if she was Tiffany or not.

"I'm Tiffany," she lied, turning her back to him and making her cheeks jiggle.

He stared at her, trying to remember.

"Do you remember me?" he asked, knowing he'd met Tiffany long ago.

She turned facing him and nodded.

"Yep, you're Ken," she answered.

He felt relieved to know he was getting somewhere. He had a feeling Peanut wasn't dead. He wanted to hear his side of the story, and she could be the power line to their reunion. Through common sense, he would've known that a lot of people knew him and by her telling him his name didn't mean shit. He relaxed in his seat.

"How's Peanut?" he asked.

"Fine," she responded quickly, not knowing who the fuck Peanut was.

He took a deep breath. *Yes!* he thought. He was glad she just verified his thought of Peanut still being alive. He smiled.

"I need to see him," he said.

She thought of a response as she danced to the music.

"I need some money and some dick," she said, bending over.

That comment threw him for a loop because Peanut's girlfriend should be paid and have enough respect to not ask his homies for sex. But he overlooked it; he knew how groupies could get.

"That's not a problem, but I need to speak to the little bro. I need to see what the hell happened," he said gravely.

She got nervous by his looks and just danced in silence. She didn't know what to say.

"Where is he?" Ken asked.

"Somewhere safe," she answered.

Another girl walked by with a silver plate full of drinks. Ken stopped her and took one off the plate and downed the vodka in a hot second. The dancing stripper grabbed his wrist and pulled him to a private section upstairs. Once they entered the room, he pulled out his black card and told her to go get five thousand dollars in ones. Once she left, he thought about this shit. Something just didn't seem right. He thought about how Tez was pausing and stuttering. Was Tez hiding something.

The stripper returned with a plate stacked up with one-dollar bills and his bank card. She danced for a while as he threw the money on her. He knew he would have to engage in a sexual act with her, but if that's what it took, so be it. He pulled out his dick, and she dropped to her knees and sucked it, taking it deep till he came. She made sure to swallow his cum.

"Where the fuck is Peanut?" he asked for the third time.

"I'm not Tiffany," she admitted, picking up her money. "I don't know Peanut. Tiffany hasn't been to work in bouta week."

He quickly grabbed his Desert Eagle from under the couch pillow he'd hid when she left for the money, and stuck it deep in her mouth, causing her to throw up.

"Bitch, you gon' help me find Tiffany or I'ma kill you. Understand?"

She nodded as tears rolled down and puke covered her chin, titties, and some of her stomach.

He pulled his weapon from her mouth and pulled his clothes up.

"See what you gotcha self into bitch?" he said with murderous eyes.

***

Ken pulled in front of Shakeena's home and honked the horn. He'd been scheduled to pick J-Bo up from the Atlanta Greyhound Station at nine that morning. He wanted to surprise him with JJ. *The fuck*, he thought, looking at his watch. JJ came running out with Shakeena on his heels.

"Slow down, boy!" she yelled. "How are you?" she asked as JJ climbed in the back of the Maserati.

He wanted to bring the Ferrari, but there wouldn't have been enough space.

"I'm fine, you?" He looked at her and saw sorrow in her eyes.

"I-I don't know," her voice cracked.

"We gotta go." He put the expensive vehicle in drive.

"Okay," she said softly.

"You know J-Bo is your dad, right?" Ken asked, looking into the rearview to see his nephew's reaction.

"Yes, mommy told me, but I miss Shawn. Mom said that he might not come back because he was mad at her," he said.

Those words hurt Ken. He would do any and everything in his power to make JJ happy, but he couldn't bring Shawn back.

"I hope he comes back for me," JJ said, his voice full of sadness.

Ken thought for a moment of what he could say to make his nephew feel better. He couldn't bring himself to tell him that the man he saw as a father figure was never coming back.

"Maybe he went on vacation. He might be back soon. I don't know," he lied.

"Maybe," JJ replied.

They were a few minutes late, but as soon as they turned in front of the station, J-Bo was standing there. Tears welled up in Ken's eyes as he saw his best friend in the flesh, in the free world after ten long years.

J-Bo didn't even notice the foreign car creeping up, but when he saw it, he knew who it was. Ken threw the car in *park*, hopped out and rushed J-Bo for a hug, and they both burst into tears, but nothing compared to seeing him embrace and love on his son for the first time.

J-Bo was having the time of his life being free again, but things still didn't feel right one hundred percent because Flip was free, but in the hospital still. He was scheduled to have surgery today. He's going to have a metal hand that's held in place by screws. This was the second J-Bo been out. Ken had already given him a car, a crib, a couple hundred thousand, a few pieces by Jacob and made him Chief over some of the Southside traps. They were in the mall shopping. Ken told him to get fifty thousand dollars' worth of clothes and shoes to get right. Once they were leaving the mall, Ken's phone rang. He listened for a while.

"Are you sure?" he asked, then hung up.

"Aye, bro, I gotta drop you off at ya spot and go handle some shit real quick," he said.

"You sure you don't need me to ride witchu, folk?" he asked, letting Ken know prison hadn't softened him up.

"Nah, I'm sure. I'm just doing a light investigation," he stated.

Twenty minutes later, he pulled beside J-Bo's 2015 Cadillac Escalade.

"I'ma get up witchu, folk," J-Bo dapped him.

Ken nodded then asked what he was about to do.

"Prolly shoot up here to this hospital and check on my cuz," he was concerned.

"That's what's up. Tell him to get well quick so we can celebrate." They weren't gonna party until Flip was home and well.

"Bet, Young Boss." J-Bo shook Ken's hand.

"Oh yea," Ken dug in his pocket, pulled out a single key and handed it to his friend.

J-Bo was baffled.

"What this go to?" he asked.

"Keena—well, yo' house that Keena and JJ lives in," he stated.

J-Bo smiled and accepted the key. Ken pulled off in the opposite direction.

***

Peanut laid in the bed catching some z's. Tiffany laid there for a while just admiring him, glad that he was still breathing. They paid a private doctor to tend to him. Things were looking pretty bad at first, but after two weeks, he started coming around. The only machine he still needed was the IV to provide a steady drip of opiates into his bloodstream to help with the pain. He was scheduled to begin therapy in another two weeks. Tiffany got out of bed quietly after looking at the time. She showered, got dressed, and woke Peanut. His head was wrapped up in a really thick bandage. He needed ten staples to close his head back and the doctor said if he hadn't had a driver that night, he would've died.

"Baby, I'm going to get my toes and nails done. Do you need anything of me before I go?" she asked softly.

"If I die, don't forget to sell that DVD to Ken, baby," he said very softly.

She didn't like him talking about dying, but she loved how he wanted to make sure she was a'ight by selling the DVD, so she would have some money to fall back on. She pouted.

"Baby, you're not gonna die, stop that shit. Do you need me for anything before I go?" she asked.

"Just gimme kiss," he said.

She leaned over him and kissed him deeply, making sure of taking her time to suck both lips.

"Why you so nasty, daddy?" she said when she felt him gently rub in between her legs.

She saw a bulge under the silk bed covers. She snatched the cover back to see if it was what she thought.

"Oh, my God!" she excitedly squealed.

His dick was hard. It hadn't got hard since the day he'd gotten shot. She started to fear that it would never reach its peak again. She looked at her phone, knowing she would be late from the time her and Lexus planned to meet and have girl talk, but she couldn't pass this moment up. She instantly got on the bed, being gentle because he was wounded.

"What I tell you that I was gon' do when it gets hard again?" she asked before spitting on his dick.

"Suck every drip of nut out it," he said slyly. She giggled and took him into her mouth.

***

Ken pulled into the nail salon on Austell Road right before you reach the East-West connector. He parked in the far end parking space. The exotic stripper got out of her car and entered Ken's passenger.

"Hey," she said, settling herself in her seat.

“Where is she, Lexus?” he asked. Lexus was the chick from the club that pretended to be Tiffany.

She looked around the parking to no avail.

“She was supposed to be here, ten minutes ago,” she said.

“Listen,” he mugged her. “If you’re playing games for whatever reason—”

She stopped him.

“I’m not playing, daddy. She’s on the way.”

His phone rang. It was Zaya.

“I’m telling—” she was saying until he held his hand up and told her to shut the hell up.

“Hello?” a sly smile was seen on his face.

They spoke for a few minutes then Lexus poked his arm and pointed to the Charger that just turned into the parking lot. He recognized it as Peanut’s whip.

“Hey, sweety, can I call you back in a few?” he asked.

Had she objected, he wouldn’t stamp on the line, but she agreed. They watched Tiffany climb from the vehicle and enter the salon.

“That her?” he asked, trying to remember her face one hundred percent.

Lexus confirmed.

He instructed her to go in, talk shit for a while, then exit, and he’ll handle it from that point. She nodded then looked at Ken.

“What?” he asked.

“You gon' hurt her?” she asked.

He was silent at first as he thought for a while. He shook his head, by way of saying: *No*. She said *okay* then entered the salon. He sat there for a while, contemplating on her question.

Did he need to hurt the bitch? He dismissed the notion. The real question is why did Peanut want to leave? Why would Tez call such a shot without checking with him first? Shit wasn't adding up. Killing a homie required a green light from one of heads.

Chapter Twenty-Two

Nae's emotions were mixed. She didn't quite know how she really should feel. Ken knew she was fucking around on him and actually agreed to forgive her as long as the guy isn't anyone he knows. She hated being caught in lies. She hated the feeling of knowing that he knew she was lying.

"I know what to do," she said to herself as she exited her office.

"You gone girl?" Reshia asked from her workstation as she saw Nae walking through with her purse.

"Yea, girl. I got some things to do," she said over her shoulder and exited.

Reshia knew whenever Nae left early, it was her time to take over. She would be the last one to leave, to clean and to lock up. As she drove home, she came up with a plan. She'd been stressing hard and doing a lot of complaining like Tez instructed. But she figured ain't no telling how long Tez would be in Haiti with that bitch DJ. She didn't just want to be in Georgia all mad and complaining, so she decided to clean up everything. She was planning to make a full confession to her husband and just play the happy role until Tez returned for her, then she would be out like a thief in the night and Tez would still have shit on lock in the States while she lived it up in Haiti as queen.

***

Smoke sat on the end of bed twisting up a spliff. He thought over all the events that's been happening and shook his head in disgust. He feared that Peanut could possibly be alive and if he was, he would definitely get in trouble for not carrying out a direct order.

Hell, I tried, he thought as he replayed putting all those bullets in his friend. He called Peanut's phone several times since the shooting, but only halfheartedly. He was really expecting him to answer. Even if he did, what would he say? If the tables were turned, he wouldn't answer either. He called Tiffany damn near every day since the shooting almost two weeks ago. She answered sometimes.

She said she hadn't heard from Peanut ever since the day they were at the cabins. He took note of the days she said they were in the cabins and reported it to Tez. However, he knew she was lying about not knowing Peanut's whereabouts because she would never agree to meet him anywhere. She's always busy and she hasn't been to work, and neither had Asia, until last night.

Smoke had been going by the club every day since he shot his friend. He knew it was that punk ass bitch, Asia, that warned Tiffany of what he was about to do to Peanut, and he was beyond furious with her. After the DJ made announcement for Asia's arrival to the stage, he got as close as he could. The moment she started shaking her ass, he grabbed a handful of her sexy permed hair and pulled her with all his might off the stage.

"Let's go, bitch!" he growled in her ear.

She tried to fight and scream until he punched her hard in the ribs four times. Once they reached the door, security and the club owner blocked his way.

"Let her go," one of the guys ordered.

Smoke looked at Gee. "Tell dese niggas to stand down, bra."

Gee whispered something to the other before they cleared his path.

"Asia, don't come back. You're fired," the owner said as they passed.

She was crying the entire time he held a fistful of her hair. In the parking lot he smacked her around as he questioned her about telling Tiffany, but she denied all accusations. He took some zip ties from his trunk, tied her hands behind her back, put her in the trunk and then drove home.

***

Nae cleaned up their home all by herself. She sent Ken a text saying, *Babe, I want to talk to you whenever you come home. I will be here all day. Love you.* He responded moments later and told her he was caught up and he would slide through later on. She took all of their cars to the carwash and to a very expensive detailer off South Cobb Drive.

"Where you gon' put all this?" the detailer asked Nae once he popped the trunk and saw a box and a bunch of loose papers.

Ken is so unorganized, she thought as she put all the papers in the box and tried to remove the box, but it was too heavy.

"Let me grab that, sweety," he offered.

She stepped back so he could remove it. Once he finished and returned Ken's mail to the trunk, she tried to leave after paying, but the nigga wanted to flirt. He was cute, but she had enough going on in her life, so she politely turned him down. She smiled at how smooth Ken's Beemer rode as she flew down Austell Road. She cracked the window and allowed the wind to blow in her face. She felt like her life was a movie. She actually contemplated saying fuck her move with Tez, but she felt like she would be a fool to do so. She turned into the Walmart on Floyd Road and bought some groceries to cook for Ken.

***

"Girl, what the hell took you so long?" Lexus asked Tiffany as they sat beside each other with their feet in the massaging tub. Tiffany smirked.

"Girl, do you need to know?" she giggled.

Lexus looked at her and slowly shook her head.

"Bitch, yo' ass is nasty!" she said as the Chinese people came and began doing their thing on their toes.

Lexus and Tiffany weren't the best of friends, but they weren't enemies either. It wasn't abnormal for Lexus to call her and ask for girl talk because they've done it before.

"Girl, my man had a lil' accident and his dick wouldn't get hard fa two weeks," she laughed when she saw Lexus' twisted up face.

"I know right, but anyway I told him that I was gon' suck every drip of cum out when it got back hard. As I was walking out the door, it got hard."

"How many times did he cum?" she asked.

The two frail Chinese men working on their feet looked at each other and mumbled something in Chinese. The girls knew they were talking about them in their language, but they didn't give a fuck.

"Five. And I swallowed it all. I wanted to ride him, but his body is fragile right now," she said.

"So, is yo' ass coming back to work? James has been asking about you." James was the club's owner.

"Girl, I don't know. It's a lot goin' right now." They moved on to their nails.

"What about Asia?" she asked.

Tiffany was baffled.

"I hadn't been talking to her. She ain't been working?"

Lexus told her of last night's event, and Tiffany felt sorry for Asia. They spoke for a little while longer before leaving. Lexus gave her eye contact as she pulled off. Ken walked behind Tiffany as she fumbled for her keys.

"Where's Peanut?"

She was startled as she turned around. "I don't know," she lied. She didn't know his motive.

"Listen, I'm Ken. Peanut is the lil' homie. I never green lighted a hit and I'ma handle who did. I know you know where he is. Don't make me do harm to you to get his attention," he said.

"He's in Alabama," she lied.

"How is he?" he asked.

"Fine," she mumbled.

He knew she was scared.

"Tell 'em to call me ASAP. I need to know what's goin' on." She said *okay*, and he turned from her.

***

"Oh shit!" Smoke said as he put on his shoes and ran downstairs to his Magnum and popped the trunk.

Asia was sleeping in the fetal position with her hands zip tied behind her back. She wore nothing but a thong. He pulled out a pocketknife and snapped the zip ties. She woke up from the force of her wrist being freed. They were beet red, and she rubbed them without making eye contact with Smoke.

"Get the fuck in the house," he wolfed.

Dried tears could be seen on her face, and she had bags under her eyes from being up all night hoping he would come for her.

"Smoke, I don't have on any clothes," she said.

Her voice was hoarse, obviously from screaming all night to no avail.

"Get the fuck in the house or stay out here anotha day or two," he said.

She jumped out and ran up the steps while trying to cover herself. While in the strip club, she didn't care about being nude of course, but in a residential area where there could possibly be kids outside was a different ball game. Once he entered the condo, she was in the bedroom applying cocoa butter to the big bruise on her left side. He walked up to her and smacked her to the floor.

"That was because I know you was finna lie, now!" He squatted beside her with his fist balled up. "Why did you tell her?" She denied telling Tiffany what he was up to last night after he snatched her out the club.

That's the reason he left her in the trunk all night. She wiped her tears and thought about lying again, but she didn't want him to hurt her.

"I'm sorry, Smoke. I felt so bad that I couldn't even function that night. Tiffany would've hated me if I wouldn't have told her,"She admitted.

He watched her cry and felt sorry for her. He unballed his fist and helped her to her feet.

"Have you talked to Tiffany since that night?" he asked.

She shook her head. He hugged her.

"I lost my job, bae," she cried.

He hated how she sounded hoarse. "Go get in the shower."

She nodded, kissed his lips, and headed to the bathroom.

***

Ken thought about what Nae wanted to talk to him about as he drove to the hospital to check on Flip. He received the message while sitting in the parking lot awaiting Tiffany. He was gonna follow her, but he didn't want to scare her, so that she wouldn't take him on a wild goose chase, nor did he want her to lead him into a trap for Peanut to off him. He was expecting to see J-Bo there, but he was on his way from checking on his guys at the traps that he assigned him over on the Southside.

Flip was sleeping when he entered the room. His wrist was bandaged up, but his hand was revealed. His hand looked normal until Ken touched it and felt the hard steel. He decided to call Rada and see how things were going on tour and to see where they were.

"Erthang good, homie. We in Olympia, Washington. Man, this shit is crazy out here, bro. Aye, we meeting in the morning wit' some people from these arenas. You gon' be able to make it?" he asked.

"Yea, I'ma catch a flight tonight, homie," he said.

"A'ight, bro."

***

A lot of shit was on J-Bo's mind as he drove from the Southside to the Greyhound Station. He thought long and hard about how Shakeena could have his son thinking he was dead and had another man raising him for all of these years, and it pissed him off. He had contacted Daneisha yesterday and scheduled for her to come out to support Flip.

"What's up, sis?" he said as she exited the Greyhound Station. He hugged her and then put her bags in the back of the car. *Damn, this bitch look dumb*, he thought as he entered his driver's seat and pulled off.

Twenty minutes later, they were pulling up to the hospital.

"Tell cuz I'ma pull up lata on," he said as she exited his truck.

"Okay, what about my bags?" she asked.

"You can get it later, silly," he said.

She laughed and closed the door.

"You need some money?" he asked, rolling down the window.
"No, I'm good, bra," she said and walked in the hospital.

***

J-Bo pulled up to the big house on Anderson Mill Road and walked towards the door. He felt like breaking down, but he had to be strong. He dug in his pocket for the key Ken gave him earlier and entered the house. He carefully searched the first floor. There were no signs of Shakeena. He looked at his phone before going up the steps. He wondered if she went to get JJ from school, but it was too early.

At the top of the stairs, he kept straight to the bedroom, hearing noise from Shakeena. She was laying on her stomach on the bed watching TV. He stood there watching, trying to decide whether to slap her around, to punch her out, or to simply shoot her.

***

Tiffany entered her Southeast Atlanta apartment where Peanut was hiding for the time being.

"Oh my gosh!" She rushed to Peanut's aid when she saw him struggling to walk down the hallway.

He used the wall for assistance and pulled the IV machine along which was still in his arm. She helped him to the couch.

"Baby, why are you up walking? You must rest." She was happy to see him walking because the doctor said he would need therapy before he could walk again, but she was furious because he appeared to be in pain.

"I just felt like getting up," he said softly.

She went to the back and got some gauzes and some antibiotic spray that the doctor left her with. She stood behind him and changed the dressing from the bullet wounds.

"How it look?" he asked as she did her thing on his back.

"Better. Do it hurt?" She applied a little pressure to his shoulder.

"Not really," he said.

She told him about what Lexus said about Asia last night. He told her to call and check on her, but she didn't answer. She told him about how Ken popped up on her.

"How you feel about it?" he asked.

"I don't know. He seemed sincere, but—" she shrugged.

"I'll call him lata," he said.

***

"What's up, Keena?" he asked.

She quickly turned towards the voice. *Oh my gosh!* she thought, when she saw J-Bo standing before her. She began receiving texts and calls about a week ago from him letting her know he was out. She never answered nor responded to the texts because she didn't know what to say. Would *sorry* be good enough?

"Why haven't you been answering me?" he asked, walking toward her and sitting beside her on the bed.

"I'm sorry," her throat was dry.

"Ken told me you have something to tell me," he said.

She didn't know if he was playing with her mind or what. She had figured Ken had already told him everything. Should she lie or not? Just to buy herself some more time.

"Jerome, when you left—"

She started crying hysterically. He wasn't trying to hear that shit. He only held his peace because he wanted to hear it from the horse's mouth. Hopefully, Ken was wrong somewhere.

"Shakeena, tell me what you gotta tell me," he said.

"Jerome, they charged you with triple homicide. I was pregnant and I didn't think you would ever come back to us," she cried.

He put his arm around her shoulder for comfort.

"I was fucking around with this dude from Savannah named Shawn. I'm sorry." He was baffled.

"Is that it?" he asked.

She nodded.

"Are you sure you don't have anything else to tell me?" he asked.

She ensured him that she didn't, and he hugged her. He'd seen a pair of handcuffs with pink fur on it inside the open drawer in the nightstand. He pulled them out.

"Can I handcuff you and fuck you all day?" he asked.

She wiped her tears away, tongued him down, stripped naked and laid on her stomach and put her hands behind her back.

"Ouch! Daddy," she complained. "That's a lil' too tight. Get the key from the drawer and loosen it a little."

He was about to do it, but his mind clicked. He thought of how he felt when Ken told him that she had his son thinking that he was dead. He went to the TV that hung from the wall and forcefully pulled the thick cable cord out the back of the TV.

"Jerome, baby, what are you doing?" she asked in a panicked voice.

He ripped the other end from the wall, then sat behind her. He looked at her curves and thought about fucking her, but his blood was boiling. He wrapped the cord tight around her ankles, then tied a knot through the handcuffs, so her hands and legs were tied together. He picked her up by the tight knot. She screamed as the cable and cuffs bit into her ankles and wrists, but he ignored her cries. She thought her arms and legs were about to pop out of place. He dropped her in the tub on her stomach.

"J-Bo, please don't kill me," she cried.

He engaged the tub's stopper.

"I'ma give you a lil' time to yaself to think if there's anything else you need to tell me." He smacked her on the ass, then turned the water on hot and exited the bathroom. That water was extras hot, and she was in excruciating pain the moment it touched her bare skin. She screamed at the top of her lungs for him to stop the water, but he didn't.

"Jerome! I'm sorry! J-Bo! Okay! Okay! I do have something to tell you !" she screamed as the water cooked her skin.

It was several minutes later when he came back to turn off the water. It had risen close to her nose; she was struggling to breath, squirming from the intense heat.

"P-P-Please, J-Bo—" her voice was weak.

He pulled her out the tub and dropped her on the floor. Though the water was hot, she would have been in need of medical attention had the water been set to run at its hottest temperature. However, it had been more than enough to bring about a confession. He listened to her excuse for why she'd played it the way she did. He understood somewhat, but he was still pissed.

J-Bo began pulling at the cord at her ankles.

“Ow!" she cried out.” And just as she was about to ask what was he up to, she felt his dick inside.

Her pussy was as good as he remembered. “I didn’t wanna hurt you,” he said while penetrating her. “Bitch, don’t you eva lie to me again. You undastand me?”

“Ummm—yes, J-Bo. I un-unda—” he cut her off with fast deep strokes.

“Whose pussy is this, bitch?” he barked.

“It’s yours, Jerome!” she moaned.

“Fuck another nigga again, bitch, and I’ma kill you!” he screamed as he came in her.

***

After cooking dinner, Nae texted her husband and asked where he was. It’s been hours since he said he’ll be there, and she was ready to get it over with. She remembered all of the unorganized papers and bills in the back of his Beemer and decided to put everything in order so things would be perfect. She put all the bills in one neat stack. Then she started to organize J-Bo’s transcripts. She knew Jerome Dew was Ken’s friend in prison for drugs, but here the papers claimed he was sentenced to life without parole for a triple homicide ten years ago, so she couldn’t understand why Ken had to meet his lawyer a few weeks back.

It wasn’t really her business, and she was about to move on but a letter with her name caught her attention. She pulled it from beneath a stack of bills and saw that it was from her father. She frowned. Was Ken aware of this? If so, why hadn't he given it to her?

Nae heard the engine of Ken's car and saw headlights wash over the house. She put all the papers back in the box, closed the trunk and ran back in the house from the garage. She put the letter in her purse and met Ken at the door.

"Hey, baby," she broke the silence.

He looked at how sexy she was in her white boy shorts with YBE printed on the back in pink, and her short t-shirt that revealed her stomach.

"What you wanna talk about? I'm finna shoot out to Washington." He followed his nose to the kitchen.

"Don't go tonight."

He smiled at the meal. She tried to kiss him, but he weaved it.

"Since you can't be honest with me—"

She cut him off. "Daddy, I'm sorry I have been messing around. Please forgive me," she sounded innocent.

"Why have you been fucking around?"

"Ken, you travel so much, and I just lost my dad. I need somebody," she faked a tear.

He pulled her tight to him.

"Where were you the morning that I asked to speak to KJ?" he asked to see if she was really ready to be honest.

"The cabins," she admitted.

He smiled.

"Who's the nigga?" he braced himself.

"A barber I met downtown. You don't know him. I swear I'll never do it again," she lied.

She hit her knees and rubbed his dick through his jeans.

"Are you goin' to Washington tonight?"

"I think I'll go tomorrow," he said before she pulled him out and took him in her mouth.

Chapter Twenty-Three

Nae awoke in the wee hours to pee. She looked over at Ken. He was sleeping soundly. She deeply wished it was Tez lying next to her. She went to check on KJ before using the bathroom. He was also sleeping soundly. Before getting back in bed, she looked at her purse that rested on their dresser and thought about the letter from Frank.

"Babe, what are you doing?" Ken asked sleepily once he reached for her and didn't feel her figure.

She had just unzipped the purse and was reaching in for the letter. "Nothing, baby." She sat the purse back onto the dresser and got back in bed. She kissed his lips then slid into his arms, wrapping her leg around his waist. He slid his arm around her back and they fell asleep.

***

"Hey, you!" Daneisha said as Flip opened his eyes.

He was surprised to see her. He stared at her for a while to make sure he wasn't tripping. He hadn't spoken to her since before the war between the two gangs went down. He rationalized that his cousin had contacted her or the other way around. However, it went, he knew J-Bo had something to do with it. He tried to hold up his left hand, but it felt like it weighed a ton. He sat up as much as he could and looked at his hand. It was bandaged up pretty thick and looked like screws were coming out. *Glad, I didn't lose my hand,* he thought. He hadn't realized that his hand was now metal. He figured his fingers wouldn't move because the medicine was still in effect.

"What's up, bae?" he replied.

"Your cousin called me, and I came out," she answered the obvious question.

He smiled, knowing she knew him like the back of her hand.

***

DJ drove down one of the poor streets in Haiti, witnessing some natives sleeping in tents. She hated seeing her people struggle. She was about thirty minutes away from Port-au-Prince, the rich part where they lived. She made a promise to herself and to God that she would visit the rugged parts every week and hand out water, food, and cheap clothes. It warmed her heart to know she was a help to somebody.

"Buzan Bitch," she said once she was cut off by a white van. The van stopped abruptly; therefore, she had to brake to a quick stop. She looked in the back at Gia to make sure the sudden stop hadn't disturbed her sleep.

DJ's driver door was snatched open, and she was suddenly staring at a buff, dark-skinned man with a nappy afro, holding a pistol in her face. He spoke quietly in Creole, telling her to get out of the vehicle. The white van had her blocked-in front, so she couldn't just smash the gas. And she couldn't dare try to go in reverse.

Another buff dude exited the white car. She figured they were just gonna throw her and Gia on the street and take the expensive car, until the second dude sporting dreadlocks tied her hands with a rope and put a blindfold over her face and threw her in the back of the white van. She kicked and screamed when she realized that her and Gia were being separated, and the van took off speeding.

Once the van stopped, the guy with dreadlocks got on the phone and said to somebody in Creole: "We here."

After ten minutes of wiggling her eyebrows, the blindfold had shifted just enough for her to see. They were in an abandoned parking lot. Her car was parked a few feet away. She could see Gia was still sleep. She knew she was safe when Tez's truck pulled up. He took Gia from her car to his, then returned with a shoebox and gave it to the dreadlock dude. Nappy afro pulled off, and *Mr. Dreadlocks* followed with DJ still in the back. Why hadn't Tez saved her? She was terrified, but too hurt for tears.

***

Back in the States, Tez was only minutes away from meeting with Smoke. He thought long and hard about what he'd done and what he was preparing to do. After paying the Haitians to kill DJ quietly, he'd paid five grand for a babysitter to live in the guest room and take care of Gia until another lady came to relieve her. Nae would be that lady. She had her passport already, and she could leave the country at a moment's notice.

Smoke pulled up and he got in. He would have preferred Nae as his driver, but she said she had to run a few errands and drop Ken off at the airport.

"What's up, my nig?" Tez said, shaking his hand.

"Coolin'," he dapped him up.

"You know J-Bo nem got out a few weeks ago."

"Oh yea? Erthang good with 'em?" he asked as Smoke merged into traffic. He'd been seventeen at the time the two had had caught their charge.

"Yea, Flip in the hospital. Dey say his hand got cut or some shit like that." He didn't really know the specifics. He only knew what Ken had told him. "J-Bo doin' his thang. And you know Ken gave him say-so over a few spots on the South and East Side."

Tez didn't like that shit because he's boss over all the spots on the South Side, West Side, and the one spot they recently started in Marietta.

"Eastside?" Tez frowned.

"We don't got no fucking spots on the Eastside."

Smoke laughed. "We do now. That boy J-Bo been out a little ova a week and got two spots on the East Side already and they booming," he said.

That comment infuriated him. He knew if what Smoke was saying was true, then Ken would definitely crown J-Bo king over the entire operation when he decided to stand down. He wanted to get his mind off it because his vision began to redden, and when he thought of J-Bo he thought of death. He looked at his phone, then at Smoke.

"So," he braced himself. "They found Peanut's body yet, bra?" He secretly had his fingers crossed, hoping and praying the answer to that would be yes.

Smoke's facial expression changed.

"Nah, bra, I been in the streets like tar and ain't heard shit," he replied, knowing he was disappointing his big homie.

"What about the bitch?" he leaned back in the seat and caressed his forehead.

"I been callin' her like every otha day. She says she ain't heard from him since earlier the day I shot 'em, but I know she's lying," he said.

"Why haven't you snatched the bitch yet, Smoke?" he asked in a 'use-ya-common-sense' type of way.

"Man, the bitch is laying low. That's how I know she's lying. I told her let's hit the streets together and if we don't come up with nothing, then we'll file a missing person report. She wasn't goin' foe it and my hoe don't know where she stays."

Tez thought everything over.

"How the hell they best friends and she don't know where she stay?"

Smoke laughed.

"I done tortured the bitch—I know she ain't lying," he ensured.

Tez told him to head to the south side so he could check on everything and collect some funds. Smoke explained every conversation he's had with Tiffany.

"Wait, wait, wait. Hold up, she said they was where?"

Smoke looked at him, then back at the road.

"The bitch said they was at a cabin," he repeated himself, not understanding why that part was so important.

"Are you sure that was the same day it went down?"

Smoke nodded.

"Did she say which cabins?" he asked.

"Nah."

Damn, could it be? Tez though. *Could we have been at the same cabins?*

"I know what's goin' on," Smoke said.

Tez quickly tried to read his face, but he couldn't. If he really did know, Tez would off Smoke as soon as he could get his hand on a burner.

"What's goin' on, Smoke?" his tone had lowered.

"If Peanut is alive, he prolly hiding out in the cabins still."

Tez chuckled at Smoke's bullshit ass theory of knowing what's going on. He was overjoyed that Smoke didn't really know what was going on between him and Peanut.

***

"You talked to Ken, babe?" Tiffany asked, reentering the bathroom with a blunt hanging from her lips.

Peanut was sitting in the tub. The doctor told him to take baths with a medicated oil to soak in his wounds and help them heal properly instead of a shower. He was about to say something about her bringing weed in there after they spoke of the things they would no longer partake in, but he felt like he needed it. She sat on the tub wall and held the weed to his mouth because his hands were wet. He took a deep pull, then coughed. He hadn't smoked weed since he'd seen Tez with Ken's wife.

"Nah, ain't talked to 'em yet. I'ma call today," he said, catching his breath.

After they smoked the blunt to about a quarter, she put it out, then began washing his back with the washcloth and soap in the tub that she had to feel around for.

"How much you gone ask for?" she asked.

He told her earlier that he would sell Ken the DVD. He thought about how much money he had saved up, half a mil. He was slightly disappointed in himself. He'd been fucking with niggas with millions for over ten years now and he didn't even have one saved. He knew he'd made a lot more than that; he just spent it on unnecessary shit.

"My life and five hunnid k," he answered.

She was silent as she gently scrubbed his lower back close to another wound.

"You sure he won't play along, and have you killed?" Her voice was full of concern.

He pondered on her question a bit before answering.

"It's possible. The type of nigga Ken is, though, he will definitely allow both parties to speak, then he'll judge it. Just like trial. Only difference is: niggas' sentence is brought by a gun." He thought of the few times he'd been ordered to knock a melon loose only after the brother spoke his peace in Ken's trial and lost. He knew Ken would not have him killed after he revealed what he had.

"Matter fact, grab my phone I'ma call him now," he said.

She grabbed his phone from the sink, searched Ken's name, pressed *call* and held the phone to his ear.

***

"What's up, beautiful?" Ken smiled at Zaya.

She seemed more sophisticated than he last remembered her, dressed in all-white casual gear with Prada shades matching her pretty dark skin.

After Nae dropped him off at the airport, he took a flight to Austin. He was headed to Washington but wanted to be blessed with Zaya's presence. They were gonna board a plane for Washington together.

"Hey," she cheesed hard, opening her arm for a hug.

They embraced for a few seconds, and they both felt great.

"You smell good," he complimented.

She looked up at him and smiled. "Do you still want that kiss, sir?"

He stared at her lips in a trance.

"Hell yea," he said after licking his lips.

She leaned in and kissed him soft and slow, carefully sucking both his lips. He slipped his tongue in her mouth and gripped her small, perfectly rounded booty. She pulled away from the kiss and smacked his hand from her ass.

"Tryna be nasty already, Ken?" she flirted, grabbing her bag that she'd abandoned to greet him.

"Nah, ain't nothing like that," he remarked, noting that she didn't approve of his actions so soon which made his fixation stronger to her.

"I hope not," she said, and they walked toward gate four where people awaiting the Washington flight, purchased or verified tickets and confirmation codes. His phone rang. It was Peanut.

"Excuse me, this is urgent."

She nodded and went to the counter.

"Peanut, what's goin' on bra?" There was urgency in his tone.

"Little bit of erthang," he said. "Ken, did you order Smoke to kill me?" Hurt was in his voice.

"No, Peanut, I was out of town. I'ma deal with him and Tez. So, you want out? Huh? Why?"

"I got some very sensitive info for you. I want you to spare my life and gimme five hunnid k—" Ken cut him off.

"What the hell makes you think I'ma do that bullshit? Unless you got a top secret!"

Peanut laughed. "I'll come by ya crib at nine. It's about loyalty issues. Oh, yea, and about ya wife."

He hung up.

Ken's head was spinning. Loyalty issues and my wife? What the fuck could he possibly have to tell me? Maybe he knew about the barber nigga that Nae was sneaking around with. Loyalty issues? He looked at his watch, knowing he wouldn't be back in time just as Zaya approached with two tickets. Peanut called back.

"Yea," he answered.

"I forgot to tell you. Please don't tell anyone about what I just told you."

Ken nodded. "Alright." He hung up.

"I got the tickets," she said. "Plane takes off in an hour."

He hated to disappoint her, but he had to meet Peanut.

"I'm so sorry, but I have to go back to Atlanta. Something came up that I can't miss."

She saw worry on his face.

"I'll reimburse you for those tickets later," he said before shooting to the counter to buy a ticket to Atlanta, hoping he could catch the flight that departed in twenty minutes.

***

Once her official document for traveling abroad was approved and stamped, she went to withdraw KJ from school. She wanted to pack up some clothes, but Tez told her to leave all that shit. He told her a new life means a new everything. He gave her the address to the house in Haiti and told her to order clothes next day delivery, so they'll be there when she arrives, which she did the other day.

"What's up, baby?" she answered the phone. She blushed hard. "Okay, daddy, love you, too." She hung up.

"Mommy?" KJ called from the back seat.

"What's up, baby?" She focused the rearview on him.

"Why did you just say *daddy* to my daddy?" he asked sternly.

"That wasn't yo' daddy, boy." Nae smiled.

Tez had just called to tell her he was about to FedEx some cash to their crib in Haiti, then come fuck her lights out before he sent her off. The rest of the ride was silent as she pondered on this big change she was about to make. Sure, it's the right move. So she thought.

***

After the nappy head Haitian and *Mr. Dreadlocks* raped DJ again for the second time, *Mr. Dreadlocks* pulled out a gun. They were paid to kill her quickly and quietly, but they decided to have a little fun with the fine ass woman. They took her to an abandoned house in one of Haiti's worst towns. Once they got her there, they never untied her hands. Only stripped off her clothes, threw her to the floor and took turns raping and sodomizing her, leaving her full of their sticky yucky cum. She begged *Mr. Dreadlocks* not to kill her, promising she would never report it to the police. She caught his attention when she said she had two hundred thousand cash.

"Where?" he asked.

She told him a spot that Tez hides his U.S. dollars until he can get it converted into Haitian gourdes. Nappy afro left. Thirty minutes later, *Mr. Dreadlocks* answered his phone.

"Sake passe? A'ight." He hung up, then cut the rope around her wrists. "I'ma gonna count to twenty. If I can still see you, you die," he said, and she got up and took off running butt naked.

***

Once Ken arrived, he rented a car from the airport. Calling for a ride would take too long, and he was super anxious to hear from Peanut. He went to the west side and tried to collect the money, but the homies said they sent it all off to be washed, so he headed to the south side. He wanted to just take five hundred grand from his bank account, but he already knew the Feds would be up his ass about why he needed so much cash.

"Damn, folk. What the hell y'all nigga tryna buy?" J-Bo asked after Ken told him to bag up five hundred G's right quick.

"I gotta handle something. And what you mean by y'all?" he asked.

J-Bo then told him that Tez collected $100,000 from every spot earlier today. Ken frowned. *Loyalty issues*—he thought of maybe Tez stealing is what Peanut was talking about.

"He said you told him to pick it up," J-Bo added.

"It's some fishy shit goin' on, J-Bo. Come ride with me."

They carried the bags to his rental and pulled off.

As they drove, Ken thought about what J-Bo had told him about Tez collecting a hunnid k from each of their spots. He called around to all the spots, and they all confirmed that Tez did come by today and picked up the money, mentioning that it was all for Ken. Ken gave J-Bo the rundown, explaining that he didn't want to jump to conclusions that Tez was stealing. Maybe it was for a just cause. But why in his name? He considered it all and finally gave the man a call.

No answer.

Ken got home, and found the driveway and garage absent of Nae's Audi. His cars were in the garage, so he shrugged it off and entered his home, J-Bo following close behind.

"So, you think he was talking 'bout Tez stealin' as far as the loyalty issues part?" J-Bo asked as he sat on Ken's plush couch in the living room.

Ken nodded.

It was almost nine and his house was empty. *Where the fuck is my wife and son?*

He dialed Nae's number and it went straight to voicemail. Not once, but twice. He knew she thought he was in Washington, and he couldn't help but wonder: *Did she always leave like this when I was gone*? *Is she with the barber nigga, now*? *Is my son with them as well*?

Just when he was about to go crazy trying to figure things out, he saw some lights flash from outside. Crossing the living room floor to the window, he peeked out the blinds to see that Tez had just pulled into the driveway.

He let the blinds close and turned to J-Bo. "He's here."

"Who?" J-Bo stood.

"Tez. He's here. Just pulled in."

They made their way to the front door and walked out just as Tez was approaching the door.

Tez's heart rate sped up when he saw J-Bo. He had planned on being out of the country by now, but there were still things to be handled. He had changed his mind about coming back and forth to handle shit, and he decided not to be greedy. He was just gonna take some money from the Young Boss organization and go live it up in Haiti. He would have some more babies.

"What's up, homie?" Ken dapped Tez up, then stepped aside for him to enter.

"W-whaddup, big homie." He tossed his head back at J-Bo, who stood behind Ken. "J-Bo, what's good?"

J-Bo stared him down with no response.

Tez's brows creased, feigning confusion. "You a'ight?"

"Come in," Ken ordered. "Have a seat."

"A'ight, yea, fasho." Tez walked past them, acting as though he hadn't a care in the world. Inside, he was terrified and scrambling for answers to the questions he knew were sure to come. He sat on the sofa. "Whaddup, Boss?"

"Why you lie to me, folk?" J-Bo asked straight up.

Tez looked at Ken, then back at J-Bo.

"Nigga, who the fuck is you to be grillin me?" he checked.

"He's yo' Chief, nigga. Now respect rank. You're now a baby boss for stealing, your violation will be tomorrow," Ken informed.

A baby boss was one of the first stages of being a Young Boss until you proved yourself and put in a little time, but he didn't give a fuck; he was planning to dip anyway. Tez dropped his head in shame.

"Tez, if you weren't the homie fa so long, I woulda had J-Bo end you right here, right now," Ken grilled. "Now where the fuck is that money at?"

"At the house, I'll go get it tonight," he lied. He had packed the money in big FedEx boxes and sent it to Haiti.

"What did you need it for, folk?" J-Bo asked.

"My intentions wasn't to steal. I was gone invest it." Tez mumbled.

"Sounds like stealin' to me. Then you lied on top of that." J-Bo shook his head. "Who's to say you ain't lyin' now? Invest in what?"

"Cocaine."

J-Bo narrowed his eyes in disbelief. "Cocaine?"

"Yea, nigga, Coke. Ken know." Tez pointed at Ken. "I told you 'bout Higa's nephew making me that offer. I know you told me to wait but I wanted to make the flip. I been puttin' in work and makin' shit happen for us for years and was worried 'bout bein' replaced by you and Flip when y'all came home. Figured if I could show I could grow the team's bankroll, I could prove my worth once and for all. No offense to you, J-Bo, but you gotta feel me. I been at this shit waitin' on my moment for over ten years in these streets."

The more Tez spoke, the easier the lies began to flow. Ken's face began to soften. He knew it sounded bad and he was still in deep shit, but at this point anything that made sense sounded better than what he was really up to. And if nothing else, the least he could do was gain some sympathy.

At least with Ken, anyways. J-Bo didn't look to be buying it.

Ken sighed and looked to J-Bo. "I'ma let you supervise his violation."

J-Bo nodded.

Just when Ken was dismissing Tez, a knock came at the door. J-Bo opened the door and Tez was hoping he was dreaming. *No!* he yelled in his mind. Peanut looked at Tez nervously then back at Ken, who ensured him that things were fine and told him to enter.

Peanut walked in slowly; that he was in pain was obvious. His head was still wrapped. The doctor had removed the staples earlier that day, but he rewrapped it so it could heal beautifully without any airborne bacteria getting in his head. J-Bo pointed at two duffle bags on the floor, the ones he and Ken had carried in.

"There's the money. Now what do you have to tell me that's worth that much, plus a pass?" Ken asked from the couch.

Peanut glanced nervously at Tez. Just then Tez pulled his nine and smacked Peanut across the face with it. Peanut crashed into the wall, then slid to the ground, blood gushing from the side of his face where the gun had gashed him.

Chapter Twenty-Four

J-Bo instantly pulled out his own gun at the sight of Tez's, looking at Ken for as little as a nod. Ken was calm despite Tez's sudden reaction because if his reasoning wasn't justified, he would die to-night. Ken looked at Peanut's blood on his fresh white carpet.

"Nigga, is you stupid?" Ken's eyes narrowed.

Peanut tried to say something, but Tez started stomping him, spreading more blood.

"Ken, I didn't wanna tell you this," Tez took a break from the stomps and decided to flip the script. "But the real reason I told Smoke to off him is because I found out he was in a cabin fucking Nae!"

Ken's heart broke in a million pieces. He remembered seeing Nae's location at the cabins in Madison, Georgia, and she had ad-mitted to being there with side lover. However, she lied about the guy's identity.

A barber, huh? Ken looked down at Peanut in disgust. He tried to talk, but Tez stomped him again, this time knocking him uncon-scious.

"Take 'em in the back and kill him," Ken ordered.

"Hold the fuck up, fam!" J-Bo barked when Tez tried to drag Peanut to the back. "That just don't make sense. See what fam gotta say the reason he wanted the bread."

Ken wanted to say fuck that and off Peanut, but J-Bo was right.

J-Bo kneeled down and started smacking Peanut back con-scious. "Ayo, 'Nut. Wake up, man."

The doorbell rang, distracting Ken. He grabbed J-Bo's gun, went to the door, and looked through the peephole. He opened it when he saw Tiffany. Peanut had left her in the car and told her if he wasn't out in three minutes to come in with the copy of the DVD. She saw Peanut on the floor bleeding and disoriented, trying to shake back. She could tell he was just waking up. She couldn't hold the tears back.

"Who the fuck is you?" Ken asked. She looked familiar, and it took him seconds to recall where he'd encountered her before.

"Baby, are you okay?" she asked Peanut.

He tried to mouth something, but nothing came out. It was bad enough he had yet to fully recover from his bullet wounds. Peanut was out of it. He nodded and pointed at Ken. She knew he was telling her to give him the DVD. Tez raised his gun at her.

"Bitch, he just asked you a question!" he sprung toward her, trying to knock her lights out with the gun, but J-Bo caught him in mid stride.

"Chill the fuck out, fam!" he yelled, pushing Tez back and snatching his gun away. "Matta fact, get the fuck out! I'ma get up witchu tomorrow," J-Bo ordered.

Ken didn't object, but Tiffany said, "No, don't let him leave." She pulled out a DVD case from her back and tossed it to Ken.

"Man, gimme my heat, I'm out."

J-Bo gave Tez his gun back, and he tucked in in his waistline.

Ken had been studying Tez's face all night and he knew Peanut had some dirt on him.

Ken opened it and saw a DVD. "What's this?"

"Watch it now," she said.

J-Bo got his gun from Ken and aimed it at Tez's head, as the man turned and headed for the door. "Don't go nowhere, fam."

Tez stopped dead in his tracks. "The fuck is this?"

Ken walked to his entertainment system and popped in the DVD, wondering what was on it.

"He—disloyal, Ken," Peanut whispered from the ground.

"Nigga, you gon' pull the strap on me cuz some hoe said don't let me leave?" Tez wanted to reach for his strap, but he knew J-Bo would blast him.

Ken grabbed the remote from the glass table, started the player, and what he saw immediately sent him into another state of mind. At first he couldn't speak as a result of what he saw. His heart began to race frantically.

"Aint no fuckin' way," he finally managed. He stood with tears rolling down his face as he watched the video of Tez fucking Nae in a way that he could never imagine.

"What is it, homie?" J-Bo turned to look at Ken.

Seizing the moment of J-Bo's temporary distraction, Tez cocked back and punched him square in the jaw with all his might, dropping him to the floor before runningr out the door.

Ken flopped down onto the couch, struggling to catch his breath.

To Be Continued...
Murda was the Case 3
Coming Soon

Author's Note

I really appreciate it if you've made it this far into reading my art. I'm really grateful for you all who enjoyed it. I want to let all the young people or easily influenced people know that when reading these type of books or listening to that wild music to only use it for what it's for: ENTERTAINMENT!

Please don't go tryna "be bout that life" because life is not a book or a rap song. Life isn't fiction; it's real, and real situations expose. I'm currently incarcerated now and have been for the last nine years of my life, for doing stupid shit. As fun as thuggin' may seem, I am a living witness to tell you all it's NOT worth the casualties nor the time you'll lose to the system.

Once you prove to them niggas that you hard, you gone have to prove to a judge and jury that you innocent.

Stay woke.

LDP SUPREME PACKAGE $1,500

Typing

Editing

Cover Design

Formatting

Copyright registration

Proofreading

Set up Amazon account

Upload book to Amazon

Advertise on LDP Amazon and Facebook page

***Other services available upon request. Additional charges may apply

Lock Down Publications

P.O. Box 944

Stockbridge, GA 30281-9998

Phone # 470 303-9761

Submission Guideline

Submit the first three chapters of your completed manuscript to ldpsubmissions@gmail.com, subject line: Your book's title. The manuscript must be in a .doc file and sent as an attachment. Document should be in Times New Roman, double spaced and in size 12 font. Also, provide your synopsis and full contact information. If sending multiple submissions, they must each be in a separate email.

Have a story but no way to send it electronically? You can still submit to LDP/Ca$h Presents. Send in the first three chapters, written or typed, of your completed manuscript to:

LDP: Submissions Dept
Po Box 944
Stockbridge, Ga 30281

DO NOT send original manuscript. Must be a duplicate.

Provide your synopsis and a cover letter containing your full contact information.

Thanks for considering LDP and Ca$h Presents.

NEW RELEASES

FOREVER GANGSTA 2 by ADRIAN DULAN

GORILLAZ IN THE TRENCHES by SAYNOMORE

JACK BOYS VS DOPE BOYS by ROMELL TUKES

MURDA WAS THE CASE by ELIJAH R. FREEMAN

Coming Soon from Lock Down Publications/Ca$h Presents

BLOOD OF A BOSS **VI**

SHADOWS OF THE GAME II

TRAP BASTARD II

By **Askari**

LOYAL TO THE GAME **IV**

By **T.J. & Jelissa**

TRUE SAVAGE **VIII**

MIDNIGHT CARTEL IV

DOPE BOY MAGIC IV

CITY OF KINGZ III

NIGHTMARE ON SILENT AVE II

THE PLUG OF LIL MEXICO II

CLASSIC CITY II

By **Chris Green**

BLAST FOR ME **III**

A SAVAGE DOPEBOY III

CUTTHROAT MAFIA III

DUFFLE BAG CARTEL VII

HEARTLESS GOON VI

By **Ghost**

A HUSTLER'S DECEIT III

KILL ZONE II

BAE BELONGS TO ME III

TIL DEATH II

By **Aryanna**

KING OF THE TRAP III

By **T.J. Edwards**

GORILLAZ IN THE BAY V

3X KRAZY III

STRAIGHT BEAST MODE III

De'Kari

KINGPIN KILLAZ IV

STREET KINGS III

PAID IN BLOOD III

CARTEL KILLAZ IV

DOPE GODS III

Hood Rich

SINS OF A HUSTLA II

ASAD

RICH $AVAGE III

By Martell Troublesome Bolden

YAYO V

Bred In The Game 2

S. Allen

THE STREETS WILL TALK II

By Yolanda Moore

SON OF A DOPE FIEND III

HEAVEN GOT A GHETTO II

SKI MASK MONEY II

By Renta

LOYALTY AIN'T PROMISED III

By Keith Williams

I'M NOTHING WITHOUT HIS LOVE II

SINS OF A THUG II

TO THE THUG I LOVED BEFORE II

IN A HUSTLER I TRUST II

By Monet Dragun

QUIET MONEY IV

EXTENDED CLIP III

THUG LIFE IV

By **Trai'Quan**

THE STREETS MADE ME IV

By **Larry D. Wright**

IF YOU CROSS ME ONCE II

ANGEL IV

By **Anthony Fields**

THE STREETS WILL NEVER CLOSE IV

By K'ajji

HARD AND RUTHLESS III

KILLA KOUNTY III

By Khufu

MONEY GAME III

By Smoove Dolla

JACK BOYS VS DOPE BOYS III

A GANGSTA'S QUR'AN V

COKE GIRLZ II

COKE BOYS II

By Romell Tukes

MURDA WAS THE CASE III

Elijah R. Freeman

THE STREETS NEVER LET GO III

By Robert Baptiste

AN UNFORESEEN LOVE IV

By **Meesha**

KING OF THE TRENCHES III
by **GHOST & TRANAY ADAMS**

MONEY MAFIA II

By **Jibril Williams**

QUEEN OF THE ZOO III

By **Black Migo**

VICIOUS LOYALTY III

By Kingpen

A GANGSTA'S PAIN III

By J-Blunt

CONFESSIONS OF A JACKBOY III

By Nicholas Lock

GRIMEY WAYS III

By Ray Vinci

KING KILLA II

By Vincent "Vitto" Holloway

BETRAYAL OF A THUG II

By Fre$h

THE MURDER QUEENS III

By Michael Gallon

THE BIRTH OF A GANGSTER III

By Delmont Player

TREAL LOVE II

By Le'Monica Jackson

FOR THE LOVE OF BLOOD II

By Jamel Mitchell

RAN OFF ON DA PLUG II

By Paper Boi Rari

HOOD CONSIGLIERE II

By Keese

PRETTY GIRLS DO NASTY THINGS II

By Nicole Goosby

PROTÉGÉ OF A LEGEND II

By Corey Robinson

IT'S JUST ME AND YOU II

By Ah'Million

BORN IN THE GRAVE II

By Self Made Tay

FOREVER GANGSTA III

By Adrian Dulan

GORILLAZ IN THE TRENCHES II

By SayNoMore

Available Now

RESTRAINING ORDER **I & II**

By **CA$H & Coffee**

LOVE KNOWS NO BOUNDARIES **I II & III**

By **Coffee**

RAISED AS A GOON I, II, III & IV

BRED BY THE SLUMS I, II, III

BLAST FOR ME I & II

ROTTEN TO THE CORE I II III

A BRONX TALE I, II, III

DUFFLE BAG CARTEL I II III IV V VI

HEARTLESS GOON I II III IV V

A SAVAGE DOPEBOY I II

DRUG LORDS I II III

CUTTHROAT MAFIA I II

KING OF THE TRENCHES

By **Ghost**

LAY IT DOWN **I & II**

LAST OF A DYING BREED I II

BLOOD STAINS OF A SHOTTA I & II III

By **Jamaica**

LOYAL TO THE GAME I II III

LIFE OF SIN I, II III

By **TJ & Jelissa**

BLOODY COMMAS I & II

SKI MASK CARTEL I II & III

KING OF NEW YORK I II,III IV V

RISE TO POWER I II III

COKE KINGS I II III IV V

BORN HEARTLESS I II III IV

KING OF THE TRAP I II

By **T.J. Edwards**

IF LOVING HIM IS WRONG…I & II

LOVE ME EVEN WHEN IT HURTS I II III

By **Jelissa**

WHEN THE STREETS CLAP BACK I & II III

THE HEART OF A SAVAGE I II III IV

MONEY MAFIA

LOYAL TO THE SOIL I II III

By **Jibril Williams**

A DISTINGUISHED THUG STOLE MY HEART I II & III

LOVE SHOULDN'T HURT I II III IV

RENEGADE BOYS I II III IV

PAID IN KARMA I II III

SAVAGE STORMS I II III

AN UNFORESEEN LOVE I II III

By **Meesha**

A GANGSTER'S CODE I &, II III

A GANGSTER'S SYN I II III

THE SAVAGE LIFE I II III

CHAINED TO THE STREETS I II III

BLOOD ON THE MONEY I II III

A GANGSTA'S PAIN I II

By J-Blunt

PUSH IT TO THE LIMIT

By **Bre' Hayes**

BLOOD OF A BOSS **I, II, III, IV, V**

SHADOWS OF THE GAME

TRAP BASTARD

By **Askari**

THE STREETS BLEED MURDER **I, II & III**

THE HEART OF A GANGSTA I II& III

By **Jerry Jackson**

CUM FOR ME I II III IV V VI VII VIII

An **LDP Erotica Collaboration**

BRIDE OF A HUSTLA **I II & II**

THE FETTI GIRLS **I, II& III**

CORRUPTED BY A GANGSTA I, II III, IV

BLINDED BY HIS LOVE

THE PRICE YOU PAY FOR LOVE I, II ,III

DOPE GIRL MAGIC I II III

By **Destiny Skai**

WHEN A GOOD GIRL GOES BAD

By **Adrienne**

THE COST OF LOYALTY I II III

By Kweli

A GANGSTER'S REVENGE **I II III & IV**

THE BOSS MAN'S DAUGHTERS I II III IV V

A SAVAGE LOVE **I & II**

BAE BELONGS TO ME I II

A HUSTLER'S DECEIT I, II, III

WHAT BAD BITCHES DO I, II, III

SOUL OF A MONSTER I II III

KILL ZONE

A DOPE BOY'S QUEEN I II III

TIL DEATH

By **Aryanna**

A KINGPIN'S AMBITON

A KINGPIN'S AMBITION **II**

I MURDER FOR THE DOUGH

By **Ambitious**

TRUE SAVAGE I II III IV V VI VII

DOPE BOY MAGIC I, II, III

MIDNIGHT CARTEL I II III

CITY OF KINGZ I II

NIGHTMARE ON SILENT AVE

THE PLUG OF LIL MEXICO II

CLASSIC CITY

By **Chris Green**

A DOPEBOY'S PRAYER

By **Eddie "Wolf" Lee**

THE KING CARTEL **I, II & III**

By **Frank Gresham**

THESE NIGGAS AIN'T LOYAL **I, II & III**

By **Nikki Tee**

GANGSTA SHYT **I II &III**

By **CATO**

THE ULTIMATE BETRAYAL

By **Phoenix**

BOSS'N UP **I , II & III**

By **Royal Nicole**

I LOVE YOU TO DEATH

By **Destiny J**

I RIDE FOR MY HITTA

I STILL RIDE FOR MY HITTA

By **Misty Holt**

LOVE & CHASIN' PAPER

By **Qay Crockett**

TO DIE IN VAIN

SINS OF A HUSTLA

By **ASAD**

BROOKLYN HUSTLAZ

By **Boogsy Morina**

BROOKLYN ON LOCK I & II

By **Sonovia**

GANGSTA CITY

By **Teddy Duke**

A DRUG KING AND HIS DIAMOND I & II III

A DOPEMAN'S RICHES

HER MAN, MINE'S TOO I, II

CASH MONEY HO'S

THE WIFEY I USED TO BE I II

PRETTY GIRLS DO NASTY THINGS

By Nicole Goosby

TRAPHOUSE KING **I II & III**

KINGPIN KILLAZ I II III

STREET KINGS I II

PAID IN BLOOD **I II**

CARTEL KILLAZ I II III

DOPE GODS I II

By **Hood Rich**

LIPSTICK KILLAH **I, II, III**

CRIME OF PASSION I II & III

FRIEND OR FOE I II III

By **Mimi**

STEADY MOBBN' **I, II, III**

THE STREETS STAINED MY SOUL I II III

By **Marcellus Allen**

WHO SHOT YA **I, II, III**

SON OF A DOPE FIEND I II

HEAVEN GOT A GHETTO

SKI MASK MONEY

Renta

GORILLAZ IN THE BAY **I II III IV**

TEARS OF A GANGSTA I II

3X KRAZY I II

STRAIGHT BEAST MODE I II

DE'KARI

TRIGGADALE I II III

MURDAROBER WAS THE CASE I II

Elijah R. Freeman

GOD BLESS THE TRAPPERS I, II, III

THESE SCANDALOUS STREETS I, II, III

FEAR MY GANGSTA I, II, III IV, V

THESE STREETS DON'T LOVE NOBODY I, II

BURY ME A G I, II, III, IV, V

A GANGSTA'S EMPIRE I, II, III, IV

THE DOPEMAN'S BODYGAURD I II

THE REALEST KILLAZ I II III

THE LAST OF THE OGS I II III

Tranay Adams

THE STREETS ARE CALLING

Duquie Wilson

MARRIED TO A BOSS I II III

By Destiny Skai & Chris Green

KINGZ OF THE GAME I II III IV V VI

Playa Ray

SLAUGHTER GANG I II III

RUTHLESS HEART I II III

By Willie Slaughter

FUK SHYT

By Blakk Diamond

DON'T F#CK WITH MY HEART I II

By Linnea

ADDICTED TO THE DRAMA I II III

IN THE ARM OF HIS BOSS II

By Jamila

YAYO I II III IV

A SHOOTER'S AMBITION I II

BRED IN THE GAME

By S. Allen

TRAP GOD I II III

RICH $AVAGE I II

MONEY IN THE GRAVE I II III

By Martell Troublesome Bolden

FOREVER GANGSTA I II

GLOCKS ON SATIN SHEETS I II

By Adrian Dulan

TOE TAGZ I II III IV

LEVELS TO THIS SHYT I II

IT'S JUST ME AND YOU

By Ah'Million

KINGPIN DREAMS I II III

RAN OFF ON DA PLUG

By Paper Boi Rari

CONFESSIONS OF A GANGSTA I II III IV

CONFESSIONS OF A JACKBOY I II

By Nicholas Lock

I'M NOTHING WITHOUT HIS LOVE

SINS OF A THUG

TO THE THUG I LOVED BEFORE

A GANGSTA SAVED XMAS

IN A HUSTLER I TRUST

By Monet Dragun

CAUGHT UP IN THE LIFE I II III

THE STREETS NEVER LET GO I II

By Robert Baptiste

NEW TO THE GAME I II III

MONEY, MURDER & MEMORIES I II III

By **Malik D. Rice**

LIFE OF A SAVAGE I II III

A GANGSTA'S QUR'AN I II III IV

MURDA SEASON I II III

GANGLAND CARTEL I II III

CHI'RAQ GANGSTAS I II III

KILLERS ON ELM STREET I II III

JACK BOYZ N DA BRONX I II III

A DOPEBOY'S DREAM I II III

JACK BOYS VS DOPE BOYS I II

COKE GIRLZ

COKE BOYS

By Romell Tukes

LOYALTY AIN'T PROMISED I II

By Keith Williams

QUIET MONEY I II III

THUG LIFE I II III

EXTENDED CLIP I II

A GANGSTA'S PARADISE

By **Trai'Quan**

THE STREETS MADE ME I II III

By **Larry D. Wright**

THE ULTIMATE SACRIFICE I, II, III, IV, V, VI

KHADIFI

IF YOU CROSS ME ONCE

ANGEL I II III

IN THE BLINK OF AN EYE

By **Anthony Fields**

THE LIFE OF A HOOD STAR

By Ca$h & Rashia Wilson

THE STREETS WILL NEVER CLOSE I II III

By K'ajji

CREAM I II III

THE STREETS WILL TALK

By Yolanda Moore

NIGHTMARES OF A HUSTLA I II III

By King Dream

CONCRETE KILLA I II III

VICIOUS LOYALTY I II

By Kingpen

HARD AND RUTHLESS I II

MOB TOWN 251

THE BILLIONAIRE BENTLEYS I II III

By Von Diesel

GHOST MOB

Stilloan Robinson

MOB TIES I II III IV V VI

SOUL OF A HUSTLER, HEART OF A KILLER

GORILLAZ IN THE TRENCHES

By SayNoMore

BODYMORE MURDERLAND I II III

THE BIRTH OF A GANGSTER I II

By Delmont Player

FOR THE LOVE OF A BOSS

By C. D. Blue

MOBBED UP I II III IV

THE BRICK MAN I II III IV

THE COCAINE PRINCESS I II III IV V

By King Rio

KILLA KOUNTY I II III

By Khufu

MONEY GAME I II

By Smoove Dolla

A GANGSTA'S KARMA I II

By FLAME

KING OF THE TRENCHES I II

by **GHOST & TRANAY ADAMS**

QUEEN OF THE ZOO I II

By **Black Migo**

GRIMEY WAYS I II

By Ray Vinci

XMAS WITH AN ATL SHOOTER

By Ca$h & Destiny Skai

KING KILLA

By Vincent "Vitto" Holloway

BETRAYAL OF A THUG

By Fre$h

THE MURDER QUEENS I II

By Michael Gallon

TREAL LOVE

By Le'Monica Jackson

FOR THE LOVE OF BLOOD

By Jamel Mitchell

HOOD CONSIGLIERE

By Keese

PROTÉGÉ OF A LEGEND

By Corey Robinson

BORN IN THE GRAVE

By Self Made Tay

MOAN IN MY MOUTH

By XTASY

BOOKS BY LDP'S CEO, CA$H

TRUST IN NO MAN
TRUST IN NO MAN 2
TRUST IN NO MAN 3
BONDED BY BLOOD
SHORTY GOT A THUG
THUGS CRY
THUGS CRY 2
THUGS CRY 3
TRUST NO BITCH
TRUST NO BITCH 2
TRUST NO BITCH 3
TIL MY CASKET DROPS
RESTRAINING ORDER
RESTRAINING ORDER 2
IN LOVE WITH A CONVICT
LIFE OF A HOOD STAR
XMAS WITH AN ATL SHOOTER

CPSIA information can be obtained
at www.ICGtesting.com
Printed in the USA
LVHW081756021222
734478LV00006B/626